"Lance, I have inherited a business out in Oregon, but I have to be married in order to claim it, so I need to know if you will marry me."

His frown deepened. "What sort of business, Marianne?"

"I don't know what kind yet, but it doesn't matter. It will be *mine*."

He gave her a long look. "And mine," he pointed out, "if we get married."

"Oh. Yes, I suppose so."

He pinned her with penetrating blue eyes. "You really want to go to Oregon? I hear it's a pretty wild frontier out there."

"Yes, I most certainly do."

He planted himself in front of her, and stuffed both hands in the back pockets of his jeans. She waited, holding her breath until she thought she might pop.

Finally, *finally*, his lips opened. "The answer is no."

"But—"

"Marianne, I guess you didn't hear me. I said no."

She stared up at him for a full minute. "Well," she said, her voice quiet, "in that case I have something to show you that may change your mind."

Author Note

I have always admired a woman who reaches for what she wants in life, takes risks and works hard to realize her dreams. And when it comes to marriage, which can be an adventure under the best of circumstances, a woman who tosses her hat in the ring—and perhaps caution out of the window—wins my respect and my prayers for her happiness ever after.

LYNNA BANNING

Marianne's Marriage of Convenience

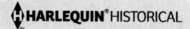
HARLEQUIN® HISTORICAL

Recycling programs
for this product may
not exist in your area.

ISBN-13: 978-1-335-05174-5

Marianne's Marriage of Convenience

Printed in U.S.A.

Lynna Banning combined a lifelong love of history and literature into a satisfying career as a writer. Born in Oregon, she graduated from Scripps College and embarked on a career as an editor and technical writer and later as a high school English teacher. She enjoys hearing from her readers. You may write to her directly at PO Box 324, Felton, CA 95018, USA, email her at carowoolston@att.net or visit Lynna's website at lynnabanning.net.

Books by Lynna Banning

Harlequin Historical

Visit the Author Profile page
at Harlequin.com for more titles.

For my daughter-in-law, Yvonne Mandarino Woolston.

Chapter One

Marianne Collingwood propped her wet mop on the back porch of the boardinghouse and staggered down the steps with the heavy bucket of dirty water. She'd been up since before dawn, cooking breakfast for the seven boarders, and she hadn't yet eaten herself; there had been no time. She could hear her stomach growling. She was headachy, hot and sticky in the humid summer air and thoroughly miserable.

She stepped into the spotless kitchen and watched Lance Burnside drop his last armload of oak logs into the now overflowing wood box. He topped up the kindling supply, then halted and closed his eyes. "Man, something sure smells good!" he murmured.

"Close the door," she ordered. "You're letting in all the hot air!"

"Uh…isn't it about time for breakfast?"

"No," she said shortly.

He sent her a long look, closed the back door and tramped back down the steps into the yard where he took refuge in the shade of a leafy maple tree, drew in a deep breath and shut his eyes. Hell's bells. In the four years Lance had worked at the boardinghouse, Marianne Collingwood had never once thanked him for anything. His momma had taught him to always say please and thank-you; he guessed Marianne's momma hadn't. Or maybe Marianne just didn't like him.

Most days he had to admit the feeling was mutual. Sure, there were other days when he had to admire the boarding-house cook and housekeeper, but when he was hot and tired they didn't come to mind. He knew Mrs. Schneiderman kept Marianne plenty busy; the stern German woman kept her housekeeper peeling pounds of potatoes and shelling dishpans full of green pea pods and baking endless pans of gingerbread and layer cakes and oatmeal cookies all day long and most of the night, too. He figured Marianne was as overworked and as tired as he was.

But she could squeeze out a few seconds for at least one please or thank-you, couldn't she?

Nah, not Marianne. She ordered him to fix the henhouse, muck out the barn, curry the horses, lug baskets of wet laundry into the backyard, wash acres of rain-splattered windows, weed the vegetable garden, tie up the sprangly red roses that covered the porch trellis…the list went on and on. But send a thank-you his way? Nothing doing. Most days, Marianne Collingwood was the wicked witch in the fairy tales his momma used to read to him at night.

He gazed around the well-kept backyard with its plum trees and neat vegetable patch and sent up a silent prayer of thanks. Even if it did come with an endless list of chores, Mrs. Schneiderman's boardinghouse here on a peaceful street in the middle of St. Louis was a safe place to hide out. Every day he gobbled down three of Marianne's delicious meals, and each night he slept in a nice quiet barn and nobody cared where he came from or what he'd done before. And he wasn't about to tell them, either. Secrets were best kept to oneself.

The back door slapped open, and Marianne leaned out to shake a crumb-covered tablecloth over the steps. At least he thought it was crumb-covered; sometimes he figured she shook out perfectly clean tablecloths just to be shaking the life out of something.

Watching her, he suppressed a groan. There were two problems with Marianne. Two *big* problems. First, she never stopped snapping out orders at him. And second, she was so darn pretty his heart stopped beating every time he looked at her. Whenever she stopped working long enough to stand still for sixty seconds, he feasted his eyes on a body that curved in and out in places that made his hands itch, hair so shiny it looked like molasses-colored satin, and eyes the color of spring grass.

He'd hate her if she wasn't so beautiful.

He levered himself off the back step and angled across to the woodpile to decide how much more wood Marianne would want in the next hour, then stood with one foot propped on the chopping block. He had just started to sharpen his axe when her voice cut into his consciousness.

"Lance!"

He jerked at the sound. Jumping Jupiter, she did nothing all day long but order him around. But, when she wasn't yelling at him, he had to admit he liked her voice, low and throaty and kinda murmury. Made him think of a breeze rustling through a dry cornfield. He heard that voice whispering in his dreams at night, and he woke up every single morning highly aroused.

"Lance! Where are you?"

"Hiding," he said under his breath. This wasn't the night-time voice he heard in his dreams. This was the voice that sent a chill up his backbone.

"Lance, I need you! Right now!"

"Coming, ma'am." He stepped around the corner of the house to see her flapping her ruffly blue apron at the red hen pecking at insects in the garden. The feisty bird fluffed up its feathers, and Marianne edged away until her back was against the fence.

"Shoo! Shoo! Lance, come and get Lucinda back in the henhouse."

Please, he muttered inside his head. He advanced on the offending chicken. "How'd she get out?"

Marianne shot him an exasperated look. "How should I know?" she retorted.

He studied the rickety chicken coop in the far corner of the yard. A section of lath had slipped sideways off the front of the structure, and the chickens were venturing through the opening. He cornered the hen, pounced on her and grabbed the scaly yellow legs. While the hen flapped and squawked he flipped her upside down, kicked the lath back in place and tossed the hen inside.

He waited for a thank-you, which didn't come. He sighed. "Anything else, ma'am?"

She propped her hands on her hips. "Yes. Repair the henhouse."

"Right now?"

"Of course right now!"

"Uh…couldn't it wait until after I've had my breakfast?"

"Don't argue. I'll save you some scrambled eggs."

"Couldn't I eat first?" he said through gritted teeth. "Lucinda won't care."

Marianne drew herself up so stiff the buttons on her blue shirtwaist threatened to pop off. "If you value your job here, Mr. Burnside, you will fix the henhouse. Now."

He gritted his teeth. "Are you sayin' you'll fire me if I don't?"

"Well, not me, exactly. But if I speak to Mrs. Schneiderman, you won't last five more minutes here."

Lance cleared his throat. "Miss Collingwood, you order me around almost twenty-four hours a day, and I do every darn thing you ask, even when it doesn't make much sense. Sometimes I wonder if you really want me around here."

"Well, yes, I do." She swallowed. "Actually, the boardinghouse couldn't function without you. I… That is, Mrs. Schneiderman and I, would be lost without your services."

"Sure am glad to hear that, ma'am. And just in time, too."

She shot him an apprehensive look. "Surely you were not thinking of leaving?"

He clenched his jaw. He would if he could. He'd thought about it often enough. But he couldn't. The boardinghouse was a safe refuge for a man on the run.

Marianne closed the back door with a sigh. She really, really hated working at the boardinghouse. But when both her parents died of cholera when she was thirteen she'd found herself alone and penniless with no other choice. An orphan girl in a city like St. Louis was lucky to be respectably employed at all.

She was frightened at first, frightened of being hungry and cold and alone. And then she realized if she didn't *want* to be hungry and cold, she would have to do something about it. She, and she alone. And so she had set out to look for work.

Mrs. Schneiderman had taken her in, and for the last eleven years she had dealt with the elderly woman's crotchets, her short temper and her constant criticism. Every morning she dragged herself out of bed to slice bacon and scramble eggs and brew gallons of coffee for the boarders, and the rest of the day she spent scrubbing floors, beating the dirt out of the parlor carpets, scouring dirty kettles and polishing the silverware.

She had felt driven by the fear of being hungry, of not making it. In all these years she'd never had time to attend a church social or read any of the books she kept in her trunk or sit on the veranda on a warm summer evening and think about her life.

She bit her lip and walked back into the kitchen. She

would be twenty-four years old on her next birthday. A spinster. On the shelf, her mother would have said. The life she saw stretching before her was totally without joy. Worse, it was without hope.

She studied the pile of dirty breakfast dishes stacked in the kitchen sink and groaned. She had no time to waste feeling sorry for herself. She had bread to bake and floors to wax and a dozen other chores to finish before she could even sit down to eat breakfast herself! She gritted her teeth and got out the mixing bowl.

She was kneading dough on the flour-dusted wooden breadboard when a messenger boy pounded up the porch steps, rapped on the front door and thrust a telegram into her hand. She stuffed it into her apron pocket until she could plop the bread dough into the greased bowl to rise, and then she sat down on the back porch step, unfolded the square of paper and smoothed it out on her lap.

> *REGRET TO INFORM YOU OF MATTHEW COLLINGWOOD'S DEATH STOP YOU ARE SOLE HEIR OF BUSINESS ESTABLISHMENT IN SMOKE RIVER OREGON STOP INQUIRE SMOKE RIVER BANK STOP WILL STIPULATES HEIR MUST BE OF GOOD CHARACTER, OVER TWENTY-ONE YEARS, AND MARRIED STOP MYERS & WALDRIP, ATTORNEYS-AT-LAW STOP*

She let out a hoarse cry. Surely she was dreaming! *Sole heir?* Oh, my stars and little chickens, she couldn't believe it! She had always dreamed of being free of Mrs. Schneiderman, of being in charge of her own life. Of even *having* a life to be in charge of!

She read the telegram again, and tears swam into her eyes. Great Uncle Matty was her grandfather's younger brother, but all she knew about the man was what Papa had told her. Uncle Matty was eccentric, and he was rich.

She read the telegram a third time. Where on earth was Smoke River, Oregon? Probably in the middle of some desert with no trees or flowers or houses or people or anything even remotely civilized. Oh, pooh, what did that matter? It was a chance to leave the endless drudgery of Mrs. Schneiderman's boardinghouse! She had dreamed of leaving for years, dreamed of striking out on her own, but no matter how carefully she hoarded her meager earnings, it was never enough.

Could this one single telegram really change my life?

She scanned the message a fourth time and clapped her hand over her mouth. Married! The heir to Matthew Collingwood's business had to be married.

"But I am *not* married," she muttered. "I have never even been engaged."

She gazed into the backyard where Lance was hammering new pickets on to the front of the henhouse. Suddenly she couldn't take her eyes off him.

She shut them and groaned. *Oh, mercy, no. Not in a million years would he consider such an idea.*

Then she popped open her lids and bit her lip.

Or would he?

Chapter Two

Marianne waited until Lance finished hammering the last picket on the henhouse, and then she slowly stood up. He pounded in one last nail and turned to go, then looked up and caught sight of her.

"It's a beautiful day, isn't it?" she called.

He gave her a startled look. "Yeah, I guess so. Been so busy I hardly noticed."

"I see that you have already repaired the henhouse."

"Yeah. Wasn't difficult."

"Thank you."

He stared at her for so long she wondered if she had carrots growing out of her ears. Finally he shifted his stance and ran one hand over his tanned face. "Is there something else you want done?"

"No. I mean, not exactly."

He frowned. "What does that mean, 'not exactly'?"

She looked everywhere but at him: the plum tree drooping with ripe fruit waiting to be preserved, the yellow rose rambling along the back fence, the clothesline strung from the corner of the house to the walnut tree ready for her to hang up the laundry.

He waited, his arms folded over his midriff. Finally she worked up her courage and drew in a long breath.

"Yes, Lance, as a matter of fact there is something I want you to do."

"Okay. What is it?"

Marianne bit her lip again and pulled in a deep breath. "I want you to marry me."

The hammer slipped out of his hand and thunked on to the grass. "Say that again? You want me to... *What'd you say?*"

"Marry me."

"Huh?" His voice was so full of disbelief she almost laughed.

She swallowed. "Yes, that is correct. I want you to marry me."

He combed his fingers through his unruly dark hair while the frown between his eyebrows grew deeper. Finally he licked his lips and opened his mouth.

"What the hell for?"

Deflated, she plopped down on the back step. "What do you mean, what for? I am making you a perfectly good offer of marriage. I should think 'what for' would be, well, obvious."

He rocked back on his heels. "You mean married as in... husband and wife?"

"Yes."

"As in...uh...living together under the same roof?"

"Yes."

He hesitated. "As in..." he cleared his throat "...sleeping in the same bed?"

"Um...well, yes, I suppose so." She hadn't thought that far ahead, but no matter. She would work out the details later.

He gave her a long, skeptical look and advanced two steps closer to where she sat. "To be honest, Marianne, I never thought you liked me very much."

Marianne blinked. "Why, whatever made you think that?"

"Maybe because you're always ordering me around. Because you never say please or thank-you. Because in all the years I've been working for you, you never once even smiled at me."

She shifted her gaze to the henhouse in the back corner of the yard. "I guess I was too busy cooking and ironing and polishing furniture to smile at anyone."

Actually, it's more than being too busy. I was too...well, unhappy to smile at anybody.

He was staring at her with the strangest expression on his face. And he hadn't spoken a single word.

"Well?" she queried.

His lips pressed into a thin line. "Well, what?"

"Lance, I have inherited a business out in Oregon," she said rapidly. "But I have to be married in order to claim it. So I need to know if you will marry me."

The frown deepened. "What kind of business?"

"I don't know what kind yet, but it doesn't matter. It will be *mine*. All mine."

He gave her a long look. "And mine," he pointed out, "if we get married."

"Oh. Yes, I suppose so."

He pinned her with penetrating blue eyes. "You really want to go to Oregon? I hear it's a pretty wild frontier out there."

"Yes, I most certainly do want to go to Oregon. And," she added quickly before she lost her nerve, "as I said, I must be married to claim my great-uncle's business."

He planted himself in front of her and stuffed both hands in the back pockets of his jeans. She waited, holding her breath until she thought she would pop.

Finally, *finally*, his lips opened. "The answer is no."

Her breath whooshed out. "But—"

He moved a step closer and gave her a look that was definitely not friendly. "Why," he asked in a strained voice, "would I want to marry a bad-tempered, bossy woman who hasn't appreciated one damn thing I've done around here for the last four years?"

"But—"

"Marianne, I guess you didn't hear me. I said no."

She stared up at him for a full minute. "Well," she said, her voice quiet. "In that case I have something to show you that may change your mind."

"Oh, yeah? What is it?"

She reached into her apron pocket and unfolded the poster she'd kept hidden in her bureau drawer. "This." She thrust it under his nose.

Lawrence Burnside Wanted For
Wells Fargo Stagecoach Robbery

There was a picture of him at the top.

He took one look at the yellowed sheet of paper, and his skin turned pasty under his tan. "Where'd you get this?"

"From the Wells Fargo office. I've kept it hidden since soon after you came to work here."

"Why?"

"Because I didn't want Mrs. Schneiderman to see it. And because I didn't really believe you were a stagecoach robber."

He frowned again. "Why not?"

She sent him a long, level look. "Because you have never shown the slightest interest in all the money the boarding-house residents leave lying around. If you were a thief, you would have taken it, but you never did. Instead, you've worked hard and kept your head down."

His eyes narrowed into hard blue slits. "Why are you showing me this Wanted poster now?"

She laughed. "I should think that is obvious. How else can I get you to marry me so I can go to Oregon and claim my inheritance?"

His mouth tightened. "That, Miss Marianne, is black-mail."

Her cheeks grew warm. "Well, yes, I suppose it is."

"Blackmail!" he repeated firmly.

After an awkward silence she glanced up at him. "Oh, all right, I admit it's blackmail," said quietly. "Is it work-ing?" She sucked in her breath and held it.

For a long, long moment he just looked at her. Then he lifted his hands out of his pockets and leaned toward her.

"Yeah," he murmured. "It sure as hell is."

Chapter Three

The train rounded a curve and picked up speed, and the passenger car began to sway from side to side. Marianne watched grassland flash by outside the window, admired the drifts of red and yellow wildflowers and studied placid-looking cows dotting the meadows. This was Oregon. It seemed the territory had no people, only cows and wild-flowers.

She caught her lower lip between her teeth and tried to tame the cadre of butterflies in her stomach. *Am I doing the right thing? Giving up my safe, secure life at Mrs. Schneiderman's and haring off into the unknown? And am I crazy to do it with Lance Burnside by my side?*

With fingers that were slick with perspiration, she folded new creases in her green bombazine travel skirt, smoothed them flat and then carefully re-creased them again. What would the Oregon frontier be like? Were there bears? Wolves? *Outlaws?*

What would it be like living in a small town after the hustle and bustle of St. Louis?

Her heart gave a little skip. An even more unnerving question was what would it be like to marry Lance Burnside, a man she didn't really know anything about other than that he was a hardworking, reliable, entirely predictable man who may or may not have been a stagecoach robber. At least he had been predictable and honest at Mrs.

Schneiderman's. How he would be in Oregon she couldn't begin to guess.

She clenched her hands together in her lap and breathed in the stale, cigar-smoky air of the coach. There was only one thing she knew for sure; for the rest of her life she would be grateful to Great Uncle Matty for naming her his heir. From what her father had said, Uncle Matty thought the Collingwood women were flighty and frivolous. That must be why his will stipulated she had to be over twenty-one and married in order to inherit.

She ran her hand over the maroon velvet upholstery she sat on and closed her fingers into a tight fist. She could scarcely believe what she was doing, traveling to a remote corner of Oregon with this man. With a twinge of guilt she thought about the blackmail she had resorted to. But when she recalled the desperation she'd felt for the last eleven years, she had to admit she wasn't that sorry. She was willing to do anything to start a new life on her own, away from Mrs. Schneiderman's boardinghouse. *Anything*, she thought with a gulp. Even join her life to Lance Burnside's.

At odd hours of the night, when she tried to get comfortable in the train seat, she wondered at her audacity. But every morning when she woke up things were once again clear; she knew exactly what she wanted. Independence. She wouldn't have done one single thing differently.

She cast a surreptitious glance at Lance in the seat next to her, calmly eating a sandwich. He was a good man. At least she hoped he was. When she took the time to look at him, really look at him, she had to admit he was quite attractive with dark, slightly wavy hair that usually flopped into his eyes. And those eyes were such a dark, smoky blue they looked like ripe blueberries. Sometimes the expression in them gave her pause.

She knew he was not really a thief, no matter what any Wanted poster said. The sheriff in St. Louis said Wells

Fargo was always printing up such posters. Every time they lost someone's luggage they claimed it was a robbery.

But what else Lance Burnside was she hadn't a clue. One thing she knew for certain; he was as anxious to leave Mrs. Schneiderman's and St. Louis as she was. "I have no future here," he admitted. "Might as well gamble that Oregon will be better."

And, Marianne thought with a stab of conscience, he was gambling that marrying her would not turn out to be a disaster. They were both gambling. They might not like Oregon. They might discover Uncle Matty's business was something awful, like laying railroad track or running a slaughterhouse. Worse, after they were married, they might find they didn't really like each other, at least not in the married sense. She already liked what she knew of Lance, she acknowledged. But maybe that wouldn't be enough.

He leaned toward her. "You want half my sandwich? It's meat loaf." He waved it beneath her nose. He had purchased it somewhere in Idaho, and while her stomach rumbled with hunger, and the smell of meat and mayonnaise was enticing, she knew she couldn't eat a bite.

"No, thank you, Lance. I'm too nervous to eat anything."

"Nervous about what?"

"About what Uncle Matty's business will turn out to be. Maybe it's a house full of shady ladies or a coal mine or a rowdy saloon."

And she was extremely apprehensive about marrying Lance, but she need not mention that.

He stretched out his long legs and bit into his sandwich. She glanced at his squashed-up-looking lunch and wrinkled her nose.

"Still not hungry?"

She sighed. "My stomach is too jumpy. Besides, we've eaten nothing but sandwiches for the past three days."

"I'm tired of sandwiches, too," he said. "Eat it anyway."

At that moment her stomach gurgled, and when he grinned at her she reluctantly accepted it. "Thank you, Lance."

His eyes widened. "You're welcome." He bit into his half and chewed quietly while she studied the gray-looking bread in her hand. "Never in all my years at Mrs. Schneiderman's have I seen a sorrier-looking sandwich."

Lance nodded and took another bite. Things sure did seem unreal. He could understand Marianne's feelings of anxiety. The last thing he ever thought he'd do in life was get married. A man on the run, a member of the notorious Sackler gang robbing stagecoaches, had no time to think about marriage, let alone court a woman. And the last woman he'd ever think of marrying would be Marianne Collingwood. Marianne acted more like a drill sergeant than a flesh and blood woman, and that was on her good days!

But the prospect of starting a new life two thousand miles away from St. Louis and an incriminating Wells Fargo poster was worth a gamble.

Maybe they didn't like each other much. He didn't want to marry her any more than she truly wanted to marry him, but she had that Wanted poster folded up in her reticule, so he figured she had him over a barrel.

After his mother died, he'd run away from Pa and joined the gang when he was just fourteen, too young to know what he was doing. But the only time he'd really done anything for them, acting as a lookout, had dictated his life from then on because his face had appeared on that poster. He'd done nothing else in his life but sweat over being found out.

Maybe the chance to get away from St. Louis and make something of himself would be worth it. And getting married looked like the price of admission. Well, so be it.

He gave her a sidelong look. "We'll be pulling into

Smoke River sometime today. What's the first thing we should do when we get there?"

She groaned. "After three days and nights on this train, all I want to do is take a long, hot bath and sleep for twenty-four hours. After that, I want to visit the mercantile and find a dressmaker."

"What for?" He gave her green traveling outfit a quick once-over. "You look okay to me."

Inexplicably, her cheeks turned pink. "Um, well, a woman only gets married once in her life. I want to have a real wedding dress."

A real wedding dress, huh? He wondered if she'd thought through all the ramifications of getting married, spending all day in each other's company. And all night. He felt his face heat up. Actually, he admitted, it was more than just his face that felt hot.

He took a long look at the woman beside him, now gazing out the train window at a herd of grazing horses. Everything in life was a gamble, he figured; but this was sure one of the biggest.

On the other hand, he pondered, finally feeling his face cool down somewhat, maybe getting married to Marianne wouldn't be so bad.

Maybe.

Chapter Four

With a puff of billowy white steam the locomotive engine chugged past the Smoke River station house, and the single passenger car gradually rolled to a stop. The uniformed conductor clunked down an iron step, and the first person to descend was Marianne Collingwood. She set one foot on the wooden platform, then two, and immediately spun in a circle to take in the view of her new home.

"Green," she murmured. "Everything is so green. And the trees are so tall." She had never seen such towers of pine and sugar maple. And the smell! She inhaled deeply and shut her eyes. The air smelled like Christmas trees!

Behind her, two elderly women in matching navy blue travel suits stepped down, followed by a tall man with a tan, weathered face wearing a wide-brimmed gray hat. A shiny silver badge was pinned to his leather vest. Only when the sheriff strode off down the street toward town did Lance step off the train, and Marianne noticed he had tipped his black felt hat down to hide his face.

"For heaven's sake," she whispered, "no sheriff out here in this wilderness will be the slightest bit interested in you."

"Yeah, how do you know that?"

"Because I've been reading the newspapers. With all the murders and barroom brawls law officers in the West have to keep up with, a five-year-old robbery back in Missouri isn't important. You are perfectly safe."

"Speak for yourself," he grumbled. "I feel like there's a big sign around my neck with *thief* printed in big black letters."

She drew in a tired breath of the hot afternoon air and turned toward him. "Lance, go inside and arrange for my trunk to be delivered."

He dropped both their travel bags at her feet, propped one hand on his hip and sent her a reproving look. "Marianne," he said firmly, "it's not too late for you to learn how to say 'please.'"

Out of habit she opened her mouth to berate him, but after a moment she gave a quick nod. "Oh, all right, 'please.'"

He flashed her a grin and disappeared into the station house. She began to pace up and down the wooden platform, studying the few one-story buildings close by. Dingy, she observed with a sniff. Badly in need of fresh paint.

It was so hot she thought her shoes would melt. And there was no shade. Even with all these trees, the sun was straight up overhead, blazing down like a big copper frying pan in the sky. Her head pounded, and she could feel perspiration soaking her camisole. She fervently hoped the worst thing about Smoke River was the heat and the run-down wooden structures with dilapidated false fronts. At the moment she felt perilously close to crying.

Lance emerged from the white-painted station house and smiled at her. "Fellow inside says he's rustled up a wagon to take us into town."

"A wagon? Not a carriage?"

"This is the frontier, Marianne. A town this small probably doesn't have carriages for hire." As he spoke a wooden wagon rattled up to the platform and the driver reined a huge gray horse to a stop. He seemed very young, olive-skinned and nice-looking, with a red bandana tied low on his forehead.

Marianne stared at him. "Is that… Is that boy an Indian?" she murmured.

"Probably." Lance hoisted her travel bag and his leather duffel in one hand and took her elbow. "Come on, Marianne. And don't stare."

The boy hopped off the driver's bench and lifted both bags out of Lance's hand. "Howdy, folks. My name's Sammy Greywolf." He swung the luggage up into the wagon bed. "Welcome to Smoke River."

"How does he know we're strangers in town?" Marianne whispered.

"Just common sense. He probably knows everybody in town by sight, and he's never laid eyes on us before."

The boy approached and offered her a hand. "Put your foot on the wheel hub right there, ma'am." He guided Marianne up onto the wooden driver's bench, then climbed up beside her. Her eyes widened. He wore moccasins that laced all the way up to his knees! He was most definitely an Indian.

The boy waited for Lance to scramble up beside her, released the brake and flapped the reins over the horse's back. The wagon jolted forward.

Marianne clapped one hand on her feather-bedecked hat and peered at the dusty street. A barbershop. A newspaper office—no, *two* newspaper offices, one across the street from the other. Ness's Mercantile, which sported a shocking-fuchsia-pink storefront. Uncle Charlie's Bakery. And, thank the Lord, right next door was a dressmaker's shop. On the opposite side of the street she spied the sheriff's office, a feed store, The Golden Partridge saloon, the Smoke River Hotel and a restaurant.

"You visitin' somebody in town?" the boy inquired. "Or maybe you want to go to the hotel?"

"Hotel," Lance said quickly. He averted his head as the wagon rolled past the sheriff's office.

The hotel was only two blocks from the train station. My goodness, Marianne had never imagined that a town could be this small! She studied the restaurant next to the hotel with unconcealed interest. Could that be Uncle Matty's business establishment? She caught her breath. Oh, Lordy, it couldn't be the saloon next door, could it? *What on earth would I do with a saloon?*

The boy pulled the wagon to a halt in front of a white two-story building with wide steps up to the glass-paned entrance door. "Here y'are, folks." He scrambled down, grabbed both bags and escorted them up the wooden steps into the hotel. "Got customers for you, Hal!" he called out. He gave Lance a grin and a two-fingered salute and disappeared.

The hotel foyer was minuscule, scarcely larger than Mrs. Schneiderman's front parlor. A red velvet settee and two matching armchairs sat opposite the scarred registration desk, which was deserted. The hot, still air smelled faintly of something cinnamony. Apple pie, maybe.

Lance stepped forward and jingled the bell beside the leather-bound sign-in register, and after a long moment a short man with a shiny bald head and a startled expression popped up from behind the counter.

"How do, folks!" He slapped the book he'd apparently been reading down beside the hotel register. Marianne craned her neck to see the title. *The Plays of William Shakespeare.* What a surprising choice way out here in this tiny Western town!

The clerk flashed her a tentative smile. "You folks new in town?"

"Yes," Lance answered. "We just got off the train from St. Louis."

"Ah, I see. What can I do for you?"

"Uh…we need hotel rooms."

"Rooms plural, as in *two* rooms? Aren't you two together?" The clerk's curious gaze shifted to Marianne. "Or not?"

"Not!" Marianne said decisively. She felt her cheeks grow warm and prayed she wasn't blushing.

"Not yet," Lance added.

Oh, dear, she was definitely blushing now.

The clerk's gray eyebrows rose. "Ah." He bent over the register. "Not together, then," he murmured, scanning the open page.

Lance cleared his throat. "We…uh…we plan to get married day after tomorrow."

"Ah!" He handed Marianne a pen. "Sign here, please, ma'am."

She scrawled her name with a hand that shook embarrassingly. "Could you send a bath up to my room? I— We have been on the train from St. Louis for the past three days and—"

"Oh, sure, ma'am, I quite understand. I'll send one up right away."

Lance nudged his elbow into her ribs. "Thank you," she said quickly.

The clerk grinned at her and turned to Lance. "And for you, sir?"

"Just a single room, thanks."

"No bath?" The man studied Lance's shadowed chin. "Maybe a visit to the barber?"

A faint flush spread over Lance's cheeks, and Marianne stared in surprise. Was it possible that Lance was a bit vain about his appearance? She had seen him dirty and disheveled, with sweat sheening his forehead and his chin all bristly after hours spent repairing a fence in the hot sun; he hadn't minded looking unshaven then. Or maybe, she thought with a twinge of guilt, she'd kept him too busy to shave.

The clerk coughed and turned to consult the wooden

rack behind him, then presented her with a shiny brass key. Number Six.

Lance accepted a second key, Number Seven, then noticed that Marianne's penetrating green eyes were glued to his face. Hot damn, she was staring at him like she'd never seen him before. Well, hell, maybe in all the years he'd worked for her she hadn't really looked at him.

He had sure looked at *her*, though. Whenever he'd been near her he'd tried hard to shut his ears so he wouldn't have to listen to the endless stream of commands coming out of her mouth. But he *had* looked at her. Couldn't help it, if he was honest. Marianne had a lot of annoying habits, but he had to admit she was one delicious-looking female.

All at once it hit him. He had a pretty good idea who Marianne was, but she didn't know diddly-squat about who *he* was. Outside of that Wanted poster she carried around with her, she didn't really know one cotton-picking thing about him. At the moment Miss Stiffer-than-Starch-Know-All-the-Answers Collingwood was actually facing something she didn't know anything about. Him!

For some reason that thought made him smile.

They lugged their bags up the staircase to the second floor and located their rooms. Lance took the key from Marianne's hand, unlocked the door to Number Six and pushed it open. The room looked dim and cool, and he caught sight of a big double bed under one window. That made him smile, too.

"Day after tomorrow we'll only need one room," he said in what he hoped was a matter-of-fact tone.

"Oh," she said. "Yes, I suppose so."

And that was all? No pre-wedding jitters? No *I'm glad we're finally here*? Nothing?

He set her travel bag inside the door and turned to go. "After you've had a bath and a chance to rest, let's meet up for supper at the restaurant, say around seven o'clock?"

She looked up, gave him an unsmiling nod and closed the door in his face.

Three hours later, after a visit to Poletti's Barbershop down the street for a bath and a shave, Lance walked into the restaurant and was shown to a table by the front window. The white-aproned waitress laid a menu in front of him and slid an order pad out of her apron pocket.

"You new in town?"

"Yeah," Lance said. "Came in on the train from St. Louis this afternoon."

"You stayin'?"

"Yeah."

"Alone?"

"Uh...not exactly. My fiancée is upstairs taking a— She'll be joining me shortly."

"Fiancée, huh?" The waitress laid another menu on the table and glanced toward the entrance. "That her?"

Lance followed her gaze and half rose from his chair at the sight of Marianne. She looked so fresh and pretty his thoughts froze for a minute. "Yeah. At least I think so."

The waitress laughed aloud. "You *think* so? How long have you two been engaged?"

"Three days," he murmured.

"Not long enough," she said. "How long have you known each other?"

He watched Marianne gliding across the dining room toward him. "Not long enough," he said.

The woman nodded. "Most men think that *after* the wedding," she said with a wink.

Marianne settled into the chair across from him and sent him a tentative smile. She wore a striped shirtwaist and a flouncy blue skirt he'd never seen before. Her hair, loosely gathered at her neck and tied with a blue ribbon, looked even shinier than molasses. And he'd never seen her wear a ribbon before. Maybe he didn't know Marianne as well as he thought.

Her skin glowed. Even after three nights with little sleep, breathing dusty air and eating nothing but stale sandwiches and cold coffee, Marianne Collingwood looked downright beautiful.

She spread out her skirt, and Lance caught a whiff of something that smelled like lilacs. He inhaled appreciatively. She'd never worn scent before, either.

"Good evening, ma'am," the waitress said.

"Yes, it is, isn't it?" Marianne replied. "I hope you have steak on your menu tonight. I am positively famished."

"This is cattle ranching country, ma'am. We have steak on the menu every night."

Marianne smiled. "Oh, of course. I'll have mine rare, please. With lots of very crispy fried potatoes."

The woman scribbled something on her order pad. "And for you, sir?"

"The same," he said. When the waitress marched off to the kitchen, Marianne leaned toward him. "Lance, I didn't know you liked your steak rare."

"Maybe that's because you never asked," he said shortly.

She gave him a long look. "I never had time to ask. I was too busy in the kitchen frying steaks for all the boarders to ask, so I fried them all the same way, even my own."

"And I always ate last," Lance reminded her. "After everyone else had finished."

Marianne pursed her lips. "You ate *next* to last," she corrected. "*I* was the one who always ate last."

"Gosh, I never realized that. Bet you were plenty hungry by the time all the boarders and then me had finished their supper."

"To be honest, I was too tired to be hungry," she said quietly. "In fact, never in the last eleven years have I eaten a meal that someone else has cooked."

Her answer stopped him in his tracks. He'd never thought about working for Mrs. Schneiderman from Marianne's point of view. Eleven years? She'd been at that boarding-house for eleven years? Lord God in heaven, no wonder she was so desperate to get away.

He fiddled with the pepper shaker, then began folding his linen napkin into smaller and smaller squares, but he wouldn't look at her. "I guess there's a whole lot of things we don't know about each other," he said at last. "Maybe we should spend time getting acquainted some before we, uh, get married."

Marianne gave him a short nod. "In a civilized world like St. Louis, an engaged couple would be expected to wait at least a year before the wedding, perhaps more, getting to know each other. But out here in the wilds of nowhere isn't exactly a civilized world."

"Maybe not," he conceded. "But *we're* civilized, aren't we?"

She leveled an appraising look at him. "Lance, we cannot afford to wait a year before marrying. When I call on Mr. Myers and Mr. Waldrip at the bank to take possession of my inheritance, I must already *be* married."

"Oh. Right."

"You're not reneging on our bargain, are you?"

"Nope. You still have that Wanted poster in your pocket, and that means I'm still gonna marry you."

She pressed her lips into a line and turned pink just as the waitress set two huge plates loaded with thick steaks and fried potatoes in front of them.

Marianne attacked her supper with a determined jab of her fork and watched the waitress march back toward the kitchen. She sent Lance an assessing look. Was it her imagination, or did he sound less than enthusiastic about the prospect of marrying her? An unfamiliar little dart of pain niggled into her heart. Was he unsure because she was forcing him into it? Or…she caught her breath. Maybe it was because she was past her prime? Was she too old and work-worn and unattractive to be of any interest to a man?

She glanced down at her bare forearm. Her skin was tan because she rolled up her sleeves and ignored the sun's rays when she worked outdoors for Mrs. Schneiderman. But her arm still looked plump, even girlish, didn't it? She hoped the rest of her did, too. At least it had the last time she'd had the chance to stop and really look at herself in the full-length mirror in her room. Except for her tanned cheeks and forearms, she still looked young.

Didn't she? A paralyzing sense of inadequacy suddenly swept through her. Over the years she had made no attempt whatsoever to look closely at her appearance, let alone enhance it as other young women did. By the time she'd crawled into bed at night she was so exhausted she'd simply unpinned her hair, gave it a cursory swipe with her worn hairbrush and closed her eyes.

All at once a crushing doubt overwhelmed her. She scarcely knew who she was, other than a boardinghouse cook and housekeeper. Worse, she had no idea who this man now sitting across from her really was. She was about to jump into a life-changing venture, and she suddenly realized she was truly frightened. She grimaced and laid down her fork.

"Lance, before we get married, perhaps we *should* become better acquainted. More than just the polite conversation we had on the train, I mean."

"Maybe," he conceded. "Sure don't have much time, though. We're getting married day after tomorrow."

"Well, perhaps we could start with our supper," she suggested.

"Yeah," he said, staring at her dinner plate. "We both like rare steaks."

"And we both like lots of fried potatoes," she said. Talking about steak and potatoes was snatching at a straw, but it was a start.

"I like lots of any kind of potatoes," he offered with a grin. "I like peas, too."

She wrinkled her nose. "I have shelled so many mountains of pea pods I am sick sick *sick* of peas!"

"Carrots?" he asked, his voice hopeful.

She shook her head. "What about cabbage?"

"Chewy," he pronounced. "Tastes like grass."

She sat up straighter. "*My* coleslaw does not taste like grass!"

His cheeks turned pink. "Nah, you're right, it doesn't. You put some kinda fancy dressing on it, so your coleslaw tastes okay, I guess. What about apples?"

She nodded. "Yes, I like apples." She picked up her knife and cut a bite of steak. "What about pears?"

"Pears are mushy."

"Really?" She laid the knife back on her plate with a sharp click. "You think my ginger-poached pears are mushy?"

"Marianne, after they've sat around for an hour or two waitin' for all the boarders to finish eatin' so I could finally sit down for supper, your pears are plenty mushy, yeah."

She frowned. She realized that neither of them had ever eaten a meal when it should be eaten, when the dishes were piping hot and bubbly from the oven and the salad greens were crisp. Even her layer cakes and cobblers tasted stale after sitting in a hot kitchen all afternoon and half the evening. Or maybe it was because she was so exhausted by the time she forked a bite past her lips she couldn't taste anything. And they had never before eaten a meal, a *real* meal, together.

"What about…houses?" he asked. "I like brown houses with white trim."

"I like *big* houses. I have never owned anything before,

certainly not a house. So I want a great big house! I know Uncle Matty was rich, so I'm quite sure my inheritance will include one. I don't care what color it is. I just hope it's the biggest house in Smoke River."

Lance studied her. "Do you think this business you've inherited is real prosperous then?"

"Of course. Uncle Matty could afford to live in New York City half the time. Out here in this little town he must have been the wealthiest man in the county."

"Maybe we should talk about—" he paused to fork a slice of fried potato into his mouth "—religion. What church should we get married in?"

"Not Lutheran," she said decisively.

"Why not?"

"Because Mrs. Schneiderman was Lutheran. She made everyone say a long fancy grace before every single meal, even breakfast."

"Okay, not Lutheran."

"And not Catholic," she added. "The priest at St. Timothy's in St. Louis refused to let one of the boarder's daughters attend Sunday school just because they were Russian. Lance, you're not Catholic, are you?"

"Don't know. But I've got nothing against them. I don't think I'm Catholic, anyway. My folks never said."

"Oh? Where were you brought up? In St. Louis?"

"Nah. Little tiny town in Indiana called Tulip Flat."

She put down her knife. "How did you—?"

"Come to rob a stagecoach?"

"Well…not exactly." She could tell her cheeks were flushing. She hadn't wanted to embarrass him; the question just slipped out. "I mean, how did your picture get on that Wanted poster? I told you before I don't really think you're an actual thief."

"Yeah, well, you're wrong there. I am a thief."

Her fork clattered on to her plate. "What? Good heavens, Lance, I can't go into business with someone who's dishonest! And I certainly can't marry someone who is really a thief. Why didn't you tell me this before?"

"You didn't ask," he said drily. "You just said all the reasons why I *couldn't* be a thief."

"You mean you really did rob a stagecoach?"

He looked up and held her gaze. "Yeah, I really did. I stole a piggy bank from a snotty ten-year-old kid because he was acting like an ass, braggin' about how smart he was. Been sorry about it ever since."

She stared at him. "But why did they think—?"

"Because his momma complained to the sheriff and said I was the only other passenger so it had to be me."

"So it wasn't a Wells Fargo gold shipment?"

"Yeah, it was. But it wasn't me that stole it. I got off at the next stop, in Valdez. The robbery happened somewhere between Valdez and St. Louis."

"But they blamed you? Why?"

He sighed. "Because nobody would believe that a proper-looking momma with a ten-year-old kid would rob a stagecoach. I'd left the Sackler gang by then because they'd shot a stage driver, but it kept me on the run until I landed at Mrs. Schneiderman's."

Marianne bit her lip. That meant the Wanted poster in her reticule was not only outdated, it was based on a false assumption. She felt her hold over Lance Burnside slipping away.

"Marianne, listen." Lance leaned across the table toward her and lowered his voice. "There's two reasons why you could pressure me into marrying you. One is that it'd take me a lot of time and money to prove I'm innocent of that Well Fargo robbery, and I've never had a lot of time or money."

"Oh," she said with a nod. "I can understand that."

"The second reason is that by marrying you I get to own

half of some kind of business. It's my chance to make a different life for myself, and I'd have to be soft in the head not to see the advantage in that."

Again she nodded.

And the third reason is that, even with all your starchy manners, I've lusted after you for years.

Chapter Five

Marianne found the dressmaker, Verena Forester, next to Uncle Charlie's Bakery. The shop was a small establishment whose display window had seven outlandish ribbon-bedecked summer hats and an elegant green crepe gown with ruffles around the hem. Too fancy for a working girl, she thought.

She walked through the shop entrance with trepidation. Never in her entire life had she ordered anything from a dressmaker. Ever since she was a girl, all her clothes had been hand-me-downs; even her camisoles and under-drawers had been given to her by Mrs. Schneiderman's boarders or donated by the St. Timothy's church ladies. Now here she was entering a dressmaking establishment for the very first time in her life, and her hands felt sweaty.

Verena Forester turned out to be a tall, fortyish woman with gray streaks in her once dark hair and a sour expression on her narrow face. Marianne introduced herself and explained what she needed.

"A wedding dress," the dressmaker said, her tone disapproving. "By tomorrow." She sniffed and cast an accusing look at Marianne's waistline. "Some reason you're in such a hurry?"

"Well, yes, there is a reason, but it is a legal matter, not a physical one."

"Hmm." The dressmaker sounded unconvinced. "What

kind of wedding dress did you have in mind for a hurry-up ceremony that's going to happen just twenty-four hours from now?"

Marianne bit her lip. "A very simple one. No fancy flounces or bustles or—"

"You mean plain," Verena inserted.

"Oh, not too plain," Marianne said. "I'd like it to be attractive, but I would also like it to be useful later on, something I can wear after the wedding. I am a businesswoman, you see, and—"

"Come with me," Verena snapped. She led the way to the tall shelves along the wall where bolts of fabric were stacked up as high as the ceiling. "Pale green lawn, perhaps?" She pointed to a bolt halfway up the stack. "That'd go nice with your dark hair, Miss."

Marianne shook her head. Lawn was so light and summery. It wouldn't do for year-round wear.

"Then there's that pale green *peau de soie* up there next to it. Bring out your eyes. You havin' a reception?"

Marianne blinked. "Why, no, we're not. My fiancé and I are new in Smoke River. We don't know anyone in town."

The dressmaker pinned her with beady eyes. "That's too bad, Miss. This here's a real friendly town."

"I'm sure it is, Miss Forester. But you see, as I explained before, we are in somewhat of a hurry. Arranging for a wedding reception takes time, and—"

"So?" Verena's thick eyebrows went up.

She gulped. Were people in small towns like this always so nosy? She didn't want to confide everything about Lance and herself to a perfect stranger, at least not within her first twenty-four hours in Smoke River. Especially since she was beginning to feel just a tad frightened at the prospect now staring her in the face, getting married to a man she didn't know all that well and then taking on her inherited business establishment, which was still a mystery.

At the moment, Marianne admitted, she was most nervous about the getting married part. Somehow when she was back in St. Louis it had all seemed like a perfectly straightforward matter; she would get married and then she could claim her inheritance. But now that it was actually right around the corner, she was...well, terrified.

The dressmaker poked a bony forefinger at a fat bolt of fabric at eye level. "How about a nice practical—"

"Yellow gingham," Marianne finished. "Yes, that one." She pointed at the bolt. "Gingham will get lots more wear than a fancy silk or a sheer lawn."

Verena sniffed again, manhandled the bolt of yellow gingham onto the counter and flipped out her tape measure. "Twenty-four hours, you say?"

"Y-yes. Can you do that?"

The dressmaker's thin face broke into a grin. "You just watch me, Miss, I am the best dressmaker in the county. I have accomplished miracles before, and I can certainly do so again."

"Oh, I have no doubt—"

"Now," Verena ordered, "raise your arms so I can take your measurements."

Lance paced up and down in front of Ness's Mercantile, past bushel baskets of ripe peaches and apricots, crates of apples and burlap sacks bulging with potatoes. Inside, the air smelled enticingly of lavender. Lavender? This must be the only mercantile in the world that didn't smell of pickles or coffee beans or aged cheese. Then he noticed beribboned bundles of the fragrant herb hanging from a rafter.

The store had neatly arranged aisles with displays of garden rakes and boys' leather boots, even a rack of flower seeds. Fat glass jars of caramels and lemon drops and jelly beans lined one shelf.

The proprietor looked up from the newspaper spread on the wooden counter and surveyed him with a scowl.

"Good morning," Lance said. "My name is Lawrence Burnside, I just arrived in town yesterday from St. Louis, and I'm looking for a new shirt and a church."

The man, owner Carl Ness, jerked his head to the left. "Gents' shirts are down that aisle," he said shortly. "And we only got one church in town."

Lance stared at the mercantile owner's face. "Smoke River has just one church? What denomination is it?"

Ness frowned. "Look, mister...Burnside, is it? This ain't a big city like St. Louis. Here we got the Smoke River Community Church and that's it. Suited Smoke River folks for the last forty years. Doesn't really have a 'denomination' so to speak."

"Do they marry people, Mr. Ness?"

"Well, whaddya think, son? How else are people out here gonna get hitched?"

Lance grunted. "Yeah, I see what you mean."

"You gettin' yourself married, are ya?"

"Yes, Mr. Ness, I am. Tomorrow, in fact."

The mercantile owner gave him an assessing look. "You know this girl for a long time?"

"About four years," Lance said.

"How long you been engaged?"

Lance blinked. "Um...four days."

Carl Ness slapped his palm down on the counter. "Four days? Son, are you crazy? That's not even long enough to learn a gal's middle name."

Lance took a step back and nervously ran his fingers through the hair flopping into his eyes. Well, that much was true. He had no idea what Marianne's middle name might be. Adelaide? Nah, too old-maidish. Samantha? Too fussy. What about Euphemia? Nope. Too fancy.

"Look, Mr. Ness, all I need is a shirt so I can get married tomorrow."

The proprietor rolled his eyes, but the frown went away and his eyes lit up. "Second aisle, next to the fly swatters."

Lance chose a long-sleeved blue chambray shirt with white pearl buttons on the cuffs and added a tan leather vest with two pockets and a secret one on the inside. When Lance reached the counter, Mr. Ness had another question for him.

"You got a wedding ring?"

He stared at the paunchy man behind the cash register. A wedding ring? Heck, no, he didn't have a wedding ring. Until four days ago he'd never had a single thought about a wedding, or a wedding ring. Ever since the prospect of marrying Marianne had presented itself, he'd been on a train chugging its way across the prairie toward Smoke River. But… He gulped. No doubt about it, he was getting married tomorrow, so maybe a wedding ring was a good idea.

"Uh, I don't suppose you have a jewelry store in town, do you?"

"Nope. Got a tray of gold rings, though. You want to see 'em?"

Lance hesitated. He had exactly seven dollars in his pocket, and that had to cover their hotel room and all their meals until Marianne took over her business and they would have a steady income. "Um…"

Before he could come up with a coherent answer, the proprietor slid a velvet case of shiny gold rings on to the counter. Lance studied them and frowned. What kind of ring would Marianne like? A plain band or one with curlicues engraved all over it? She had never struck him as being a curlicue type of woman, so he moved his gaze over to the plain gold rings on the tray.

"Take yer time, son," Ness said. "A man only gets married once. If he's lucky, that is."

"You married, Mr. Ness?"

The proprietor rolled his eyes. "Huh! You see the front of my store? That's the most god-awful pink I've ever laid eyes on. Last week it was apple-green, and the week before that it was purple."

"Does your wife paint your storefront?"

"Nope. My daughter does. For years my wife's been tellin' my Edith that she's artistic and that her father's a mean old fuddy-duddy with no sense of adventure. I'm so married I can't look my wife in the face and tell her she's crazy."

"Yeah, I see your problem, Mr. Ness. I couldn't tell my fiancée she's crazy, either."

"I'm tellin' ya, a man's gotta think real careful about gettin' himself tied down to a woman. It's kinda like Russian roulette, if you know what I mean."

Lance bit back a chuckle. "Seems to me if you're married you could say that to your wife, couldn't you? You know, just be honest with her?"

"Oh, well, maybe I could. And maybe I'd sleep in the barn for the next twenty years. You got a lot to learn about women, son."

Lance sighed. What did he know about Marianne, apart from her tendency to give orders and never say thank-you? But he liked what he *did* know about her. She was sensible and hardworking and generally fair-minded. *And darn good-looking.*

He continued to mull carefully over the tray of rings until his eye fell on a medium-wide gold band with some design carved on the surface, some kind of flowers, roses, maybe. He bent to look at it close up. "How much is that one?"

"Four dollars."

He hesitated.

"I got cheaper rings, son."

Still he hesitated. But for some reason he wanted the one with the roses engraved on it. Something about it just felt like Marianne. He spilled four silver dollars on to the counter and slipped the ring into his pocket. No matter what her middle name was, he liked Marianne, and he wanted her to have a pretty wedding ring.

Marianne was late to supper, so Lance took a seat in the dining room and gave the waitress a grin.

"Where's your girl tonight?" the woman asked.

"Still over at the dressmaker's, I guess."

The woman laughed softly. "Is she ordering a dress to be made up?"

"Yeah. A wedding dress."

She snorted. "If I know Verena Forester, that could take most of the night. You probably won't see your girl 'til morning, so you might as well have some supper." She slapped down a menu.

But before he could study it, Marianne appeared. She was out of breath, and her face looked kinda shiny, like she was lit up from the inside. His heart gave a horse-sized kick.

Before he could stand up even halfway, she plopped on to the chair across from him. "I have had the most trying afternoon!"

"Me, too," he admitted.

"I've just spent three hours at the dressmaker's." She leaned across the table and lowered her voice. "Lance, I've never even been *inside* a dressmaker's shop before. I had no idea about… Anyway, Verena Forester, she's the dressmaker, helped me choose a dress pattern and took my measurements and everything. I felt like Cinderella."

Lance chuckled. "Well, Cinderella, I found out there's only one church in town. Not Lutheran and not Catholic, just a plain old church. Smoke River Community Church."

He didn't mention the two hours he'd spent at Ness's Mercantile, poring over the tray of wedding rings.

The waitress tapped her pencil on her order pad. "We have chicken tonight. Fried, baked or stewed."

"Fried," they said together.

"Potatoes?"

"Fried," they chorused again.

The waitress laughed. "Is there anything you two disagree about?"

"Not so far," Lance said.

"Wait," Marianne countered. "We do disagree on something, Lance. My ginger-poached pears, remember?"

"Got peach pie tonight," the waitress said. "You agree on that?"

"Sure," Lance said.

"With ice cream," Marianne added.

"Yeah. Chocolate ice cream," he said.

"Chocolate!" Marianne blurted out. "Ick!"

The waitress grinned and headed for the kitchen. When she had disappeared, Marianne reached over and caught his sleeve.

"Lance, I... I have a confession to make."

His belly flip-flopped. "What about? You don't like chocolate ice cream?"

"It's not about ice cream. It's about...well, I'm getting nervous."

Another flip-flop. "What are you nervous about, Marianne?"

"About tomorrow. Getting married. I've never been married before."

He released the breath he'd been holding. Bridal jitters. What made her think a man didn't get the jitters, too?

"Marianne, I've never been married before, either. What exactly are you nervous about?"

"The next forty years," she said in a subdued voice.

"Oh." Relief made his voice sound strained. He'd thought maybe it was *him* she was nervous about. Or maybe their— he swallowed hard—wedding night. Oh, God, she had to be a virgin. Funny, he'd never thought about it before. He'd just assumed…

"Could you be more specific?" he ventured. "What *about* the next forty years makes you nervous?"

She dropped her forehead on to her palm. "The forty years part. Marriage is such a, well, a permanent thing. Do you think we will like each other for the next forty years?"

"There's no way to know that now," he said with a smile. "Ask me again in forty years."

She lifted her head and tried to smile at him. Her mouth wasn't working quite right because it looked like something halfway between a lopsided grimace and a shaky *O*.

"I'm also worried about my wedding dress," she said.

"Huh? You mean whether it'll be ready in time?"

She shook her head. "No. I mean whether you will like it."

All at once he felt warm all over. *She cares about whether I will like her wedding dress?* He started to smile, and then another thought popped into his brain. Maybe that meant she was worried about how she would *look* in her wedding dress? Maybe she really cared about how she would look *to him*?

Or maybe he wasn't the least bit important in this business. She needed him only because she needed to marry somebody, and he was the handiest somebody around.

The waitress reappeared. "Two fried chicken dinners and two coffees, right?" She plopped down both plates and the coffee cups. "Gonna have to wait on the peach pie. It's not out of the oven yet."

An uneasy silence fell. Marianne picked up her fork to stab a slice of fried potato, then set it back down on the table. She'd lost her appetite. An entire afternoon spent answering dressmaker Verena Forester's questions and trying to calm the butterflies careening around her stomach was taking its toll. The last thing she needed to do was add a fried potato to the battle going on inside of her.

"Marianne? You look like a ghost just up and poked you in the chest. What's wrong?"

"N-nothing." She hadn't the foggiest notion what was wrong.

His blue eyes held hers in an extra-penetrating look. "Yeah? Nothing is wrong?"

"Of course not," she said shakily.

Of course something is wrong! In exactly twenty-four hours I am going to promise to spend the rest of my life with someone I scarcely know. Anyone with an ounce of intelligence and a lick of good sense would be frightened half to death.

He reached over and lifted the salt shaker out of her hand. "Then how come you just salted your coffee?"

She bit her lip. "Oh. Well, perhaps I am a bit unnerved. Actually—" she lowered her voice "—I am, um, well, I am getting downright scared."

"Thank God," he muttered. "I was beginning to think getting married didn't matter enough to you to ruffle even one feather."

A choked laugh burst out of her mouth. "Oh, I have a feather ruffled, all right," she said in a shaky voice. "It isn't every day a woman gets married."

Lance quickly switched their coffee cups and signaled the waitress. "Could you bring me another cup of coffee?"

The woman studied the full cup of coffee at his elbow. "Something wrong with this one?"

"I…um…I accidentally added too much…sugar," he said. "Wedding jitters, I guess."

The waitress grinned at him and whisked the cup away.

"Thank you," Marianne murmured.

Lance blinked. An unprompted thank you from the queen of orders that must be obeyed? He found himself staring at her, and his heart gave a little jump. Did he really know this woman at all?

"Marianne?"

"Yes, Lance?"

"I have something to ask you."

Her face changed. "Yes? What is it?"

"Marianne, what is your middle name?"

Her eyes widened. "My middle name? It's Jane," she said. "I was christened Marianne Jane. Why on earth is that important?"

Jane! It was a simple name. Unaffected, straightforward and honest. "It's not important, really. I was just curious."

He addressed his fried chicken, but all during their supper he could think of nothing else but Marianne's middle name. Jane. He liked it. He liked it a lot.

Then she startled him with a question of her own. "Lance, what is *your* middle name?"

Oh, God, he'd do anything to avoid telling her that. The waitress saved him by bringing a fresh cup of coffee and setting it down in front of him. He stared at it.

"Lance?" Marianne persisted. "I asked you a question."

"Yeah, I heard you."

Her hand hovered over her cup. "Well, what is it? Your middle name?"

He grimaced. "Rockefeller."

"What?" she cried.

Every diner in the crowded restaurant stopped talking and stared at them. After a long, awkward pause, she leaned toward him. "What?" she repeated in a whisper.

"Not the rich Rockefeller," he whispered back. "The poor one."

"I didn't know there *was* a poor one," she murmured.

"Oh, yeah. Your Great-Uncle Matty was rich. *My* great-uncle was poor. Ignatius M. Rockefeller. Ever heard of him?"

"No, I haven't."

"Neither has anyone else. Great-Uncle Iggy died in a gold mining accident in Montana thirty years ago. He didn't have a dime."

She started to laugh and the buzz of conversation in the dining room resumed.

"Marianne, what's so funny?"

"You," she sputtered. "Me. Us. We're getting married tomorrow and here we are, asking each other about our middle names."

"Yeah. Maybe it's because we're both a little bit nervous about tomorrow."

"Oh, Lance," she whispered. "I am more than just a 'little bit' nervous. I have to confess I am a *lot* nervous!"

He reached across the table and covered her hand with his. He was apprehensive, too. But never in a million years would he admit that to Marianne.

Chapter Six

After supper they climbed the stairs to the second floor and stopped before the door to Marianne's room. Lance cleared his throat.

"Tomorrow…"

"Yes?" Marianne looked up expectantly.

"Well, uh, tomorrow I guess we're getting married."

"Yes. Are you getting cold feet?"

He slid his gaze to the closed door. "Nope. Just thinking ahead. Tomorrow we'll only need one room, and I was wondering, um, well, whether you wanted to move into my room or…"

"Oh."

He pressed on through a dry mouth. "My room just has a single bed, and I noticed that yours has a…"

"Oh," she said again. "Yes, I see."

"See what?" he ventured. Suddenly he wondered if Marianne knew the first thing about being married, that after tomorrow they would only need one bed. At least he assumed they would need only one bed. Or did she have some kind of funny idea about marriage that she hadn't told him?

"I realize that when we're married we will need only one hotel room," she acknowledged. "That is obvious."

"Oh, yeah. Obvious." It was also obvious that one bed and two people meant… He frowned. Did she really understand the implications of only one hotel room and only one bed? Marianne was a lot of things, but she was not dumb.

But it did make him wonder.

"Occupying one room instead of two will save us some money," she said. She dug in her reticule for her room key, stuffed it into the lock and turned the knob. The door swung open, and once again he glimpsed the double bed in the center of the room.

He stopped dead. Jumping jennies, it was the *bride* who was supposed to be nervous about getting married, not the groom!

She looked up at him. "Lance, are you… Well, I mean, are you absolutely sure you want to marry me?"

Sure? Hell, no, he wasn't sure. And neither was she if she had any smarts. But a promise was a promise.

"Yeah, I'm sure. I'll meet you at the church tomorrow, Marianne. Three o'clock, right?"

"Yes, three o'clock. Good night, Lance."

Before he could reply, she disappeared inside and closed the door. He stood stock still for a long minute, shaking his head. Was he imagining it, or did Marianne now not seem anxious or scared or even the least bit ruffled, as if getting married was something she did every day, like washing up the dishes? Well it sure wasn't something *he* did every day! His nerves were strung up tight as a new barbed wire fence.

Still shaking his head he moved down the hall to Number Seven and unlocked the door to his room.

At half past two the next afternoon Lance slowly made his way toward the small white-painted church that sat on top of the hill at the far end of town. Puffs of frothy white mayweed and swaths of golden buttercups carpeted the ground, and three large maple trees shaded the building. It looked like a picture in a storybook. His pulse sped up.

Tall, gray-haired Reverend Pollock stood on the church steps, a black leather-bound Bible in his hands, and surveyed Lance with sympathetic brown eyes. Lance's already tight chest got tighter. Why would the minister be feeling sorry for a man on his wedding day? There must be a whole lot of things about marriage that nobody was telling him.

The warm summer air was sweet with the scent of honeysuckle. As he reached the bottom step of the sanctuary, he tried to breathe normally, but for some reason he felt like he was drowning.

The minister stepped forward and extended his hand. "Mr. Burnside, welcome. This is an important day."

Lance returned the reverend's firm grip, then found he couldn't utter a word.

"Nervous?" the reverend asked.

"Yeah. Didn't expect to be, either."

The minister grinned. "Most men are terrified when they get married. Or they should be."

Lance stared at the man. "Dammit, Reverend, you tryin' to scare me off?"

Pollock shook his head. "Certainly not, son. You look like a man who doesn't scare easy."

Lance groaned quietly. "Up until this morning I'd have agreed with you. Right now I'm not so sure."

"Come on inside, Mr. Burnside. Your two witnesses are already here."

He stopped short. "What two witnesses?"

"The waitress at the Smoke River Restaurant, Rita Sheltonburg. And Verena Forester, the town dressmaker."

He had forgotten that they would need witnesses. Marianne must have organized them. Actually he was so tightly strung all he could remember was the gold wedding band he'd slipped into his inside pocket.

He hadn't seen Marianne yet today. Maybe that was just as well. He hadn't been able to eat a single forkful of his scrambled eggs, and his breakfast toast had tasted like a buttered pot holder. At the moment he figured he wasn't the best of company.

He followed the minister into the small church, and the two middle-aged women sitting in the first pew twisted their heads to stare at him. He nodded at the waitress, Rita, and she sent him an encouraging smile. The other woman pinned him with hard blue eyes and a sour look.

Reverend Pollock guided him to the front of the church and turned to him. "Your bride seems to be a little late," he intoned.

Lance groaned inwardly. Had Marianne chickened out at the last minute? Maybe she'd decided she didn't want to stay in a pokey little town like Smoke River. Maybe she'd decided she didn't want to marry him after all. Maybe…

He closed his fists convulsively, then concentrated on slowly opening his fingers one by one. Before he was aware of it he'd tightened his hands into fists again.

The two women bent their heads together and began talking in low tones. Their voices sounded like a hive full of honeybees. Lance closed his eyes involuntarily, then opened them when Reverend Pollock jostled his arm. He pointed to the pew across the aisle from the witnesses. "Sit."

"Can't," he murmured. "I'm scared I won't be able to stand up again." To his credit the minister nodded, then took up a position beside him. It seemed like hours crept by while Lance sweated and tried not to think.

"Want to change your mind about this, son?"

He jerked. No, he didn't. That thought had never occurred to him. He shook his head, and the minister smiled and ran his pale hands over the Bible.

Lance watched him for a few minutes, then began to pace back and forth in front of the wooden altar. The two witnesses followed him with their eyes, moving their heads from left to right and back again. At one point he thought he saw the waitress, Rita, smile, but when she caught him looking at her, her face went carefully blank.

He established a route from Reverend Pollock on one side to Rita and the dressmaker on the other, and every time he made a turn he glanced toward the back of the church. *Where is Marianne?*

He thought only brides got left standing at the altar, not grooms. Well, here he was, standing at the altar feeling like a lost puppy.

Where is she?

He made one more circuit and had just started another when suddenly he saw a movement. *Marianne.*

At the sight of her his eyes widened. She wore a simple yellow dress, the hem just brushing the tops of her shoes, and the late afternoon light bathed her in a warm golden glow. She looked like a shaft of summer sunshine.

His mouth went dry. Both witnesses stood up, and Reverend Pollock drew him into position in front of the altar. Marianne started down the aisle toward him, hesitated and then resolutely stepped forward. All at once Verena Forester moved into her path and held out a bouquet of yellow roses.

Marianne paused to accept the flowers, then watched Verena's gaze run over the yellow gingham wedding dress she had cobbled together in such a hurry. The woman's narrow face beamed.

At the altar, Lance was staring at her as if he'd never laid eyes on her before. She gripped her bouquet of roses and continued on down the aisle toward him. Dear God, was she really doing this? Marrying a man she had blackmailed into taking her as his wife? She should feel a huge measure of guilty shame, but for some strange reason she didn't. Instead she felt as if she had just swallowed a bolt of lightning.

She caught Lance's gaze and her heart stopped. Goodness, he looked so serious! Not a hint of a smile touched his mouth. His usually unruly dark hair was neatly combed, and as she watched, his smoky blue eyes went wide.

Was he as scared as she was? Worse, did he regret agreeing to marry her?

Her heart thumped erratically. Why was she so frightened? This man, Lance Burnside, meant nothing to her, wasn't that true? She was simply using him for her own ends, wasn't she? Why should *she* be frightened?

The answer brought her to an abrupt halt halfway down the aisle. *I am frightened because this really* does *matter!*

She took another step toward the man waiting at the altar, and he moved toward her and held out his hand. He had the strangest look on his face, as if he'd just seen a ghost. He enfolded her hand in his, and she noticed that his eyes looked shiny and they never left hers.

Verena Forester came to stand on her left; Rita positioned herself beside Lance. Then the minister stepped forward and opened his Bible.

"Dearly beloved…"

She could feel Lance trembling. Even so, his grip on her hand remained steady and his eyes continued to look into hers. All at once the reverend's words leaped into her consciousness.

"Lawrence Burnside, do you take this woman…?"

Lance gave her hand a little squeeze. "I do." His voice was steady, but she noticed that his shirtfront was fluttering.

Then the minister's question was directed to her.

"Marianne Jane Collingwood, do you take this man…?"

Merciful God in heaven, can I really promise to love a man I scarcely know? She closed her eyes.

Lance waited. Did he understand her hesitation?

The gentle pressure of his fingers told her that he did understand, but he was waiting for her answer anyway.

Her mind cleared and she opened her eyes. No, she did

not really know this man. But she had worked side by side with him for four years. She had watched him. For some reason she trusted him. And, she had to admit, she liked him.

"I—I do," she breathed.

Reverend Pollock looked from Lance to Marianne and smiled. "I now pronounce you husband and wife." Then his smile broadened into a grin. "Mr. Burnside, you may kiss your bride."

Lance gulped. He released the hand he held in his own and reached to curve his fingers about Marianne's shoulders. Damn, she was shaking like an aspen leaf in a summer breeze. He tried to smile at her, but his mouth wasn't working right.

She was still staring up at him, a dazed expression on her face. Maybe she was waiting for him to kiss her, like the reverend said. She didn't look scared or apprehensive; she was just waiting.

Outside the open sanctuary door he could hear some crazy bird singing its heart out. He became aware of his breath pulling in and out of his lungs, and then all at once he was aware of everything, the long silence, Reverend Pollock drumming his fingers on the Bible, even the occasional sniffing of Rita and the dressmaker. Good God, those two ladies were actually crying!

He felt like crying, too.

Marianne was still staring at him, waiting for him to kiss her, he guessed. Okay, he'd better do it and get it over with. He tightened his hands on her shoulders and drew her toward him.

She lifted her face to his, and in that instant he saw that her eyes were wet. His heart soared up and then thunked into his stomach. He pulled her close enough that the ruffle around the neck of her yellow dress touched his shirtfront, bent his head and brushed his lips against hers.

She closed her eyes, but she didn't move. Her lips were soft, and she smelled faintly of roses, and unexpectedly his heart gave another thump as he moved slightly away from her. She felt sweet and unguarded in his arms, and suddenly he wanted to *really* kiss her.

And then she did something he would remember for the rest of his life. She opened her eyes, smiled at him and rose up on her tiptoes and pressed her mouth to his.

A locomotive ploughed into his chest and starbursts of hot light exploded in his brain. Some part of him felt the earth stop spinning on its axis, and then he lost himself in a big bubble of a fine new place he'd never been before. He tightened his arms around her and just held on.

After a long moment, a *very* long moment, he heard the minister cough politely, and he opened his eyes. What had just happened? Why were his eyelids stinging?

The two witnesses descended on them, mopping at their faces with lacy handkerchiefs and saying something. He couldn't hear the words because of the roaring noise inside his head, but Rita's face was one big grin and even the sobersides dressmaker was all smiles.

Reverend Pollock shook his hand. "Congratulations, Mr. Burnside," he said loudly. He released his hand and then shook it again, pecked Marianne's cheek and shook her hand, too.

Rita advanced and threw her arms around him, then turned to Marianne and smacked a kiss on her cheek. "Now, my dear, we have a little surprise for you. Sarah and Rooney Cloudman are giving you a wedding reception at Rose Cottage. That's Sarah's boardinghouse over on Maple Street."

"Wedding reception!" Marianne gasped. "But we don't know anyone in town."

"Well," Verena Forester announced, "pretty quick you're gonna know everybody."

Suddenly Lance stiffened. "Wait! I forgot the ring!"

Marianne blinked. "What ring?"

"The wedding ring I bought for you at the mercantile yesterday."

Reverend Pollock laughed aloud. "Well, now," he said with a twinkle in his eyes, "maybe you'd better get this ring on her finger before your wedding reception."

Lance fumbled inside his vest and drew out an engraved gold band. "Give me your hand, Marianne."

Shyly, she held out her hand. He lifted it in his and slipped the gold wedding band on to her fourth finger.

Marianne looked down at her hand and the lovely gold ring Lance had placed there. She couldn't stop staring at it. Tiny roses were engraved all over it, like the roses she still carried in one hand. "Oh, it's beautiful! It's p-perfectly beauti—" She burst into tears.

Lance folded her into his arms. "Thank you," she said against his chest. "Oh, Lance, thank you!"

"You're welcome, Marianne. I wanted you to have a wedding ring."

They stood in each other's arms until he felt a gentle touch at his back.

"Come on, you two," Rita said. "We'll walk you over to Rose Cottage."

Rose Cottage turned out to be the prettiest house Marianne had yet seen in Smoke River, a three-story structure with a wide front porch and a trellis covered with yellow rambling roses. Townspeople were spilling out the open front door and down the porch steps, calling out their congratulations. Marianne felt Lance check his stride.

"Whoa," he said under his breath. "This is kinda scary."

Marianne nodded. "I feel like I used to when Mrs. Schneiderman had a bad day."

"Well, we lived through that," he murmured. "I guess we'll live through this, too."

The first person to reach them was a plump, attractive older woman in a full-skirted green dress. "Welcome!" she called. "I'm Sarah Cloudman." She grasped Marianne's hands in hers and pulled her up the porch steps onto the veranda. "And congratulations."

"Thank you, Mrs. Cloudman. And thank you for inviting us to your home."

"You're welcome, my dear. It isn't every day a girl gets married, and we all know you're both new in Smoke River, so we thought you should celebrate with friends."

A lean, grizzled-looking man with a salt-and-pepper beard slapped out the screen door and shook Lance's hand. "Every man deserves a good woman," he boomed. He turned to Marianne and kissed both her cheeks. "Don't know if I've ever seen a prettier bride 'less it was my Sarah, but you sure do come close."

People swirled onto the front porch, and in no time she and Lance were surrounded by townspeople. Sarah Cloudman took her arm. "Come inside, both of you. We have wedding cake and lemonade waiting."

"And some whiskey for the gentlemen," Rooney Cloudman added.

Marianne knew she would never forget this afternoon, even if she lived to be a hundred. She and Lance must have received the good wishes of everyone in town from Carl Ness's wife, Linda-Lou, and their twin daughters, Edith and Noralee, to tall, tanned sheriff Hawk Rivera, who looked straight into Lance's face without a flicker of recognition. The two newspaper editors, Cole and Jessamine Sanders, welcomed them and asked all kinds of questions, and then there were the rotund barber Whitey Poletti, the old doctor, Samuel Graham, who lived at Rose Cottage, and the new doctor, Zane Dougherty and his wife Winifred, who lived in the big house at the top of the steepest hill in town. So many townspeople came to offer congratulations, Marianne was sure she would never remember all their names.

She recognized the young Indian boy Sammy Greywolf and met his handsome mother, Rosie Greywolf. Cattle ranchers, wheat farmers, the pretty young schoolteacher, Mrs. Panovsky, even a crusty old sheepherder who camped in the hills all stopped by Rose Cottage to wish them well.

But the highlight of the afternoon for Marianne was her introduction to a grinning Chinese man everyone called Uncle Charlie, the baker who had made the elegant four-tier wedding cake resting on Sarah's walnut dining table. His wife, Iris, confided that his Chinese name was actually Ming Cha.

Marianne also met Uncle Charlie's niece, Leah Mac-Allister, her husband Thad, and their nine-year-old son, Teddy, along with Judge Jericho Silver and his wife, Maddie, and their twin boys. Of all things, Maddie turned out to be a Pinkerton agent! My, the population of Smoke River was certainly interesting. And, Marianne noted with relief, the Pinkerton agent also didn't give Lance a second look.

All afternoon Marianne couldn't help wondering which business establishment it was that Uncle Matty had willed to her. It wouldn't be Sarah Cloudman's boardinghouse. Or the barbershop. Or the Smoke River Hotel or the restaurant. And she prayed again that it wasn't the Golden Partridge saloon next to the hotel.

Lance shook so many hands and downed so many shots of Rooney Cloudman's whiskey that by suppertime he was struggling to focus his thoughts. Marianne had long since disappeared into a chattering circle of women well-wishers. He wondered if she felt half as dizzy as he did. Probably not, unless she was lacing her lemonade with shots of Rooney Cloudman's whiskey.

What a day! He couldn't wait for it to be over so he could enjoy a quiet supper with Marianne at the restaurant. He caught her eye across the dining room where she was cutting more slices of Uncle Charlie's applesauce spice wedding cake, but as he watched she was quickly drawn into another conversation with more chattering ladies.

He escaped to the veranda and sank on to the porch swing to rest a while. After some minutes, Rooney Cloudman joined him.

"Had enough?"

"Of what?" Lance said tiredly.

"Enough of all this fuss and folderol," the older man said with a grin. "All a man really wants is to get the I-do over with and start the honeymoon."

Lance suddenly jerked upright. Honeymoon! Oh, God, there was that double bed in Marianne's hotel room, but he hadn't really thought about it until this moment. Now he had to seriously consider what a honeymoon would mean.

For the first time he wondered if Marianne was planning to have a marriage of convenience.

Was she?

Well, he sure as hell wasn't!

"What's the matter, son? You look like you just swallowed a fishhook the size of a pick-ax."

"Rooney, how long have you been married?"

The older man laughed. "Not near long enough."

"You recall how you, uh, ended up gettin' married in the first place?"

Rooney leaned back and pushed the swing into motion with his foot. "Yeah, I sure do. I was married before, see. 'Cept it wasn't in a church or anything 'cuz I'm half Cherokee. My wife, she was full-blooded Cherokee. Anyway, she died before I came to Smoke River, and when I met my Sarah I was mighty leery about gettin' hitched up again."

"What changed your mind?"

"Well, hell, I went and fell in love. Sarah, now, she didn't feel that way about me fer a lotta years. So...I waited."

Lance nodded. "What do you think changed her mind?"

Rooney slapped a gnarled hand on his knee. "Son, if I knew the answer to that, I'd be a rich man."

Lance could think of nothing to say to that.

Rooney stuck an elbow into his ribs. "Chances are you're not gonna understand a whole lotta things about yer wife, even if you both live to a ripe old age. But that's not what's important, see? Understandin' her, I mean. What's important is real simple. Just keep on lovin' her."

"That's it? That's all?"

"Yep, that's pretty much it. And," Rooney added with a chuckle, "don't ask too many questions."

Lance nodded his head. "Thanks, Rooney. I'll remember that."

"And remember them real smart words 'for better or worse.'"

At that moment Lance made himself a solemn promise. For better or worse, no matter what came, he would do everything in his power to be a good husband to Marianne.

Chapter Seven

By the time Lance and Marianne made their way back to the hotel, the entire day seemed like a dream. A good dream, Lance thought. Unexpectedly satisfying, even sweet, a word he never thought he'd use in regard to Marianne.

"You hungry?" Lance asked when they reached the foyer.

Marianne looked up at him. "After all that wedding cake and lemonade?"

"And whiskey," he reminded her.

"Actually," she said with a soft laugh, "I am starving. I hope Rita hasn't taken steak off the menu tonight."

They walked to the restaurant, and the beaming waitress headed across the dining room toward them, waving her order pad. "Coffee?" she inquired. She sent a surreptitious look at Lance.

"Oh, yes, please," Marianne murmured. "I need lots of—"

"Sure," Rita quipped. "Comin' right up."

"You, too?" Lance whispered.

"My temples feel like squashed biscuits," she confessed as they sat down.

"I'd laugh," he said, "but it would make my head hurt too much."

"Oh, Lance, this entire day seems unreal."

"Yeah, that's what it feels like to me, too. Guess it's because neither one of us has gotten married before."

"Imagine," she said with a giggle, "getting pie-eyed on your wedding day!"

"Your wedding day, too," he reminded her.

"Are we really married?" she whispered. "It feels like I'm having a dream."

"Yeah, we're really married. Since three o'clock this afternoon. Unless we're still dreaming," he added.

Rita brought two steaming cups of coffee and discreetly melted away. Marianne raised her cup to him. "Happy Anniversary."

"It's too soon for that, don't you think?"

"Not at all," she murmured. "We're old married folks now. We've been married for a whole three hours."

"Four hours," Lance corrected.

Rita popped up again. "Steak?"

They both nodded.

"Fried potatoes?"

Another nod.

"Peach pie?"

"Oh, yes," Marianne murmured.

"My stars," Rita blurted out, "you two are predictable as blackberries in the summertime. Oughtta have a long and happy life together." Humming, she headed toward the kitchen.

Marianne downed a gulp of her coffee. "Lance, I—"

"You don't need to say anything, Marianne. I understand."

"Say anything about what?"

Lance wished his head would stop spinning. "About… well, about tonight."

Marianne looked blank. "Tonight? I wasn't going to say anything about tonight, Lance. I was going to thank you again for my wedding ring. It truly is lovely."

Now his heart was pounding right along with his head. That ring really meant something to her. Not in a month of Sundays would he have thought Marianne Collingwood would be sentimental about anything except an oven full of baking apple pies and a full wood box. Women were sure surprising.

Correction, *Marianne* was surprising.

They ate in almost total silence because Lance couldn't think of a single sensible thing to say to his bride. Once, she requested that he pass the salt, and later he asked if she wanted chocolate ice cream on her peach pie. Then they lingered over coffee until her eyelids began to droop, and by the time she had drained her cup down to the shiny bottom, he was about ready to jump out of his skin.

He kept remembering Rooney's question about a honeymoon, and whether he and Marianne would be having one. Now the big fat question that kept bumbling around in his brain was different. Would he and Marianne be having a *wedding night*? In the same hotel room? In the same—he gulped—bed?

He'd bet a stack of shiny gold bars she didn't remember that tonight he would be moving into her hotel room. The more he thought about it, the more convinced he became she wasn't thinking about tonight. The next problem was how to get from here, in the dining room, to there, her hotel room.

Just ask her, I guess.

"Marianne, if you've finished your coffee, shall we, um, go back to the hotel?"

She glanced across the table at him. "Yes, let's," she said, her voice drowsy.

All the way across the hotel foyer to retrieve the key from the desk clerk his nerves felt jumpy as a roomful of grasshoppers.

"We moved your luggage from your old room to Miss Collingwood's room, Mr. Burnside," the clerk said.

"It's Mrs. Burnside now," he corrected. "We were married this afternoon."

"Oh, I know, sir. Everybody in town's been talking about the big doings over at Rose Cottage. Congratulations!"

"Thanks, Hal. And thanks for moving my luggage to her room."

Now Marianne was wide awake. "What did you say?"

"Excuse me, ma'am. I understand you two got married this afternoon."

"Yes," she said, her voice unsteady. "We did."

The clerk reached over and dropped the room key into Lance's open palm. "Mr. Burnside, Mrs. Burnside. Congratulations again. And sleep well," he added with a smile.

Marianne looked up. *Oh, my Lord, we are married*, she thought. *And tonight we will be sleeping in the same room together.*

Of course "together," you goose.

She stared into Lance's oddly tense face. For some reason it was hard to adjust to being married. She glanced down at her left hand. *With a wedding ring and everything.*

Lance took her elbow and guided her up the stairs to the second floor. When they reached the landing he laid a hand on her arm and brought her to a stop. "Marianne?"

"Y-yes, Lance?"

"You didn't really think about…this part of being married, did you?"

She pivoted to face him. "N-no, I didn't."

"You wanted me to marry you, remember?"

"Yes."

"So I did."

"Yes," she said in a small voice. "You did."

He drew in a careful breath. "Well, you didn't think

much beyond the wedding, I guess. About what would happen afterward, did you?"

She bit her lip. "I—I thought I would go to the bank and claim my inheritance."

He studied her for a long minute and then bent toward her. "I mean what did you think would happen *tonight*?"

Right before his eyes Marianne Jane Collingwood changed from an efficient, hardworking boardinghouse taskmaster into a shy, unsure-of-herself girl.

"I didn't think about tonight," she said slowly. "I suppose I just thought it would be a marriage of convenience until…"

"Until what?"

She looked everywhere but at him, at the patterned carpet runner on the floor, the blue-flowered wallpaper on the ceiling overhead, at the hotel room key in his hand. Finally she looked up into his eyes.

"Until…until you kissed me." Her eyes darkened to an unforgettable shade of green, like a dew-misted meadow.

"Yeah?"

"Something changed when you kissed me," she confessed.

A zing of recognition buzzed into his brain. "Something changed for me, too, Marianne." He took her hand, turned her toward the door of Number Six and, without a word, unlocked it and pushed it open.

Her room was larger than his, with two big windows overlooking the street and a tall, double-width wardrobe against one wall. And, he remembered with a catch in his throat, the big double bed.

He lit the kerosene lamp on the nightstand, and all at once he didn't know what to do next. He hesitated for a moment, then paced to the window and stood looking out on to the street below to think things over while his pulse did a crazy dance and he tried to get some moisture into his mouth.

It was plain as pancakes Marianne hadn't thought through what actually marrying him would mean. Well, neither had he. He hadn't expected to like her as much as he did. And she was obviously feeling off balance at finding herself sharing her room with him.

She had surprised him today. All these years he'd known her as the stern-faced single-minded housekeeper who kept him hopping every hour of the day, a woman who rarely smiled and never thanked him for anything. He would never have guessed that beneath her businesslike exterior lurked a girl who felt joy and fear and uncertainty just like other people did.

With a jolt he realized again that Marianne was as much a stranger to him as he was to her.

He turned away from the window to find her perched stiff as a department store mannequin on the bed's blue-patterned quilt. "Marianne, can I sit down beside you?"

Without a word she edged over to make room, and he lowered himself onto the bed. A full minute passed in complete silence.

"I don't know what to do next," she said softly.

"Yeah, I figured that."

"It isn't that I don't like you, Lance. I do like you. I just feel...overwhelmed, I guess. And a little, well, uncertain."

"I figured that, too. So here's what we're gonna do. This bed is plenty big enough for both of us. We'll each take half of it and get some sleep tonight. And tomorrow we'll go to the bank and find this Mr. Waldrip and move into the house your uncle left for you. It's probably got more than one bedroom, so we won't be...crowded."

He almost said "sleeping together," but he thought that might scare her. She looked real lost sitting there so straight and stiff with her backbone all rigid. His chest tightened into an ache.

He shot a quick look at her face. Her cheeks were pink, but her shoulders were drawn up tight so he knew she'd heard him. The honest truth was he wouldn't mind at all making love with Marianne, but it sure wasn't going to be tonight. He leaned over and puffed out the kerosene lamp, leaving the room illuminated only by the faint light from the street below.

"I'm gonna get my duds off now," he said in as matter-of-fact a voice as he could manage. "Then I'm gonna lie down on my side of the bed. I'll stay on top of the quilt, so you could just…uh…take off your dress and crawl between the sheets. All right?"

She said nothing, but after a moment he felt her weight shift off the bed. He stood up in the dark, quickly stripped down to his drawers and stretched out on top of the quilt. He heard her skirt rustle as she moved about the room, but after a while the rustling stopped and he heard nothing at all. A minute later the space beside him dipped as she lay down next to him.

He realized with surprise that she hadn't bothered to peel back the quilt on her side of the bed and slip between the sheets as he'd suggested. She was lying right next to him, so close he could reach out and touch her.

But he didn't. He closed his eyes and tried not to smell the lemony scent of her hair or listen to her soft breathing. Then all at once her breathing wasn't soft anymore; it was jerky and uneven, and he knew she was crying.

"Marianne?"

"Yes?" she said in an unsteady voice.

"What's wrong?"

She snuffled, and then she gave a small kind of broken laugh. "*Everything* is wrong, Lance. I scarcely know where to begin."

"Well, just…you know, give it a try."

"I—I am just now realizing that I have been very, very selfish. And…and…"

"Manipulative?" he suggested, his voice quiet.

"Yes. And worse. In a very real way I am getting exactly what I deserve for being so…"

"Dishonest?"

"Yes." She snuffled again. "Well, I wasn't dishonest about everything."

"Yeah?" His voice came out louder than he'd intended. "What haven't you been dishonest about?"

She was quiet for a long minute. "I wasn't being dishonest when I thanked you for my wedding ring. And I wasn't being dishonest when…when I kissed you at the wedding."

His heartbeat kicked back into a gallop. He didn't know what to say. He didn't know what to think, either. He knew what *he* had felt when their lips met, like Fourth of July fireworks were shooting off in his brain. He had no cotton-pickin' idea what *she* felt.

The snuffling sounds started again.

"Look, Marianne, it's been a real long day. We're both tired and maybe we've done enough confessing for one night. I'm gonna get some sleep now, and I think you should do the same. We can talk more in the morning."

He closed his eyes. If she'd just stop crying he might be able to get his heart to calm down. He waited, then waited some more. After a while he didn't hear anything from her side of the bed, so he steepled his hands over his stomach and said the only prayer he could think of.

Dear Lord, I guess Marianne and I are stuck together now, for better or worse. But if You have any sense of humor, Lord, don't let it be too hard on her.

Chapter Eight

The Smoke River Bank sat on the corner of Main and Maple Street, across from Stockett's Feed & Seed and five blocks from the Rose Cottage boardinghouse. The brick-and-wrought-iron entrance looked inviting enough, Marianne thought. It was what awaited her inside that had her stomach doing somersaults.

Her eyes felt grainy from lack of sleep, and she knew they must look red and swollen from crying. Nevertheless, she had wakened before Lance and slipped quietly off the bed, donned her green bombazine travel dress and her feathered hat and forced down some toast and a cup of coffee diluted with half the pitcher of cream. Now she stood with Lance in front of the Smoke River Bank, ready to finally lay claim to Uncle Matty's bequest. The butterflies dancing in her stomach at this moment were almost worse than the ones she felt yesterday when she had married Lance.

The interior of the bank was cool and respectable-looking, with polished wood floors and large oil paintings of grim-faced gentlemen on the walls. She made her way to the teller's window and waited while a large woman ahead of her wearing a flowered calico skirt chattered on and on with the sandy-haired clerk about the unseasonably hot weather. Finally Lance purposefully cleared his throat, and the woman glared at him, snapped her shopping bag shut and stepped aside.

The young teller looked up with a smile. "Good morning, folks. What can I do for you today?"

Marianne cleared her throat. "I would like to speak to Mr. Waldrip, please. Or Mr. Myers."

The clerk frowned. "I'm afraid Mr. Waldrip took the train to Philadelphia this morning. But Mr. Myers is here. He's the president of the bank. I'll see if he's in his office. Who shall I say wants to see him?"

"Marianne Collingwood."

"Wait here, please." The clerk disappeared into a doorway, returned in a few moments and motioned them through a low swinging gate and into a cramped office. The gray-haired man behind the desk rose with a smile. "Miss Collingwood, welcome to Smoke River."

Lance sent her a look.

"It's actually Mrs. Burnside," Marianne corrected. "This is my…my husband, Lawrence Burnside."

He shook Lance's hand and turned to her. "Your great uncle, Matthew Collingwood, ran a fine business establishment here in town, one of the oldest businesses in Smoke River. I expect you will want to take possession of it as soon as possible."

"And the house," Marianne reminded him.

The bank president looked blank. "House?"

"I presume Uncle Matty owned a house in town?"

"Well, no, not exactly. Mr. Collingwood maintained living quarters here in town, yes. But I wouldn't exactly call it a house."

An uneasy flutter settled into Marianne's stomach. If it wasn't a house, what exactly was it? She should ask what Uncle Matty's business was, but she was so rattled about the house she couldn't think. It took a minute to recover her tongue.

"Where is Uncle Matty's business located?"

Mr. Myers tramped over to a large street map pinned on

the wall and jabbed his forefinger at a spot. "The shop is right here, between the blacksmith's and the livery stable. Collingwood Boots."

Marianne's reticule slipped out of her fingers and tumbled to the floor. "Boots!"

"Oh, yes, ma'am. Collingwood Boots has a very fine reputation."

"You mean the business establishment I have inherited is one that...that sells boots?"

"It most certainly is," he assured her. "Custom-made right here in Smoke River. People come from miles around—"

"Boots?" she repeated in a weak voice.

"Yes, Mrs. Burnside. Boots. I'm sure you've heard of Collingwood Boots. As I said, it has a very fine reputation."

"No," she said weakly. "I have never heard of Collingwood Boots."

"Well now, you folks will want to inspect the premises, so I won't keep you. Here's the key." He dropped a large brass key into her hand. "Good luck to you, Mrs. Burnside!"

"Thank you," she said.

Mr. Myers beamed at her. "And don't mind Abe!"

"Abe?" she said. "Who's Abe?"

Mr. Myers just grinned at her and ushered them out of his office.

The minute they were back on the sidewalk Marianne drew Lance to a stop. "Did we meet anyone called Abe at the reception yesterday?"

He shook his head. "Nope. Come on, Marianne. It's time we found out some things." He took her hand and turned her toward the livery stable at the edge of town.

Collingwood Boots sat next to the blacksmith's shop and had a big red hand-lettered sign across the front. Lance bent over the lock, but just as he inserted the key the door

drifted open and a hoarse voice yelled, "Mistah Collingwood ain't here."

Marianne started forward, but Lance laid his hand on her
arm. "Who are you?" he called into the shadowy interior.

"Better question might be who're you?" the voice shouted.

"My name is Lance Burnside. With me is Marianne
Collingwood, the new owner."

"New owner!" came the raspy voice. "Nobody told me
'bout any new owner." In the next moment a diminutive
man with a face so black it looked like a lump of polished
coal ambled forward, his hand outstretched.

Lance stepped forward to meet him and shook it. "Didn't
anyone tell you about Matthew Collingwood's death?" Marianne asked.

"Yep. A telegram came 'bout two weeks back, but I
didn't pay it no mind. Figured ol' man Collingwood was
never gonna die, so I didn't believe it and jes' went back
to work."

"I am Mr. Collingwood's great-niece. May we come
in, Mr.—?"

"Why, shore ya can. My name's Garland. Abraham Garland. Warn't expectin' a lady."

Lance peered into the interior and then moved on into
the shop. Marianne followed. "Mr. Garland, this is my wife,
Marianne Coll—uh...Burnside."

Abe executed an awkward curtsey, and Marianne's eyes
widened.

"Miz Burnside, huh? Thought yer name was Collingwood."

"It was until yesterday, when we were married."

Abe nodded. A grin split his face, revealing two dim-
ples. "I reckon that musta been what all that fuss 'n folderol was about yesterday afternoon. Ever'body in town was
goin' someplace. I figured it was a barn-raisin'." His grin
widened. "My, you folks are shore a fine-lookin' couple!"

Lance peered into the gloom behind the man. "Mr. Garland, are you the caretaker here?"

"Caretaker! I ain't caretook nothing since the army, and that was plenty 'nuff fer me. I'm the only employee Mr. Collingwood ever had."

"But who makes the boots?"

"I do, natcherly. There ain't nuthin' anybody can teach ol' Abe here 'bout working leather, so I's *it*!"

"'It'," Marianne echoed.

"Yes'm, that's what I done said. *It*."

"Don't you have any helpers?" Lance ventured.

"Nope. Never had no helpers. But I reckon now with you two here, I got helpers. Ah shore am glad for that. 'Bout worked my fingers off this past month."

"Oh?" Lance said. "How come?"

"Big order, ya see. Gent comes up all the way from Texas and bought pret' much ever'thing in stock and ordered some more."

"You made all the boots by yourself?" Marianne asked.

Abe nodded. "Seven pairs. All in a rush, like. Said he was a Texas Ranger."

"You have any boots left?" Lance asked.

"Yeah, one pair. You lookin' fer a pair?"

"Maybe. Why don't you show me one?"

Abe trotted away to the back of the shop and emerged a moment later holding up the best-looking pair of boots Lance had ever laid eyes on.

"G'wan, feel 'em. That's the best leather north of the Rio Grande."

Lance inspected them inch by inch, then ran his palm over the butter-soft leather. "Marianne," he said under his breath, "this is the finest pair of boots I've ever seen."

She looked at him and nodded.

"Abe, where did you learn to make boots like these?" Lance asked.

"Mexico. They got leather workers down there you wouldn't believe. Taught me ever'thing they knew, and the rest I picked up from Californios along the way. Ya know, them Mexicans really understand leather saddles and riatas and real fine boots. Ladies' boots, too, if yer interested, Miz Collingwood. I mean Miz Burnside." His glance took in her trim green travel dress. "Or mebbe not, seein' as your getup tells me you're a real fine lady. You prob'ly don't wear boots."

Marianne laughed at that. "I might start wearing them, now that I'm out here in Oregon. Abe, I understand my uncle had living quarters somewhere?"

"Oh, yes'm. Right up those stairs at the back. He never stayed there much, though. Said he didn't like the smell of glue and boot polish. Leather smell didn't bother him so much. Guess that's why this here business got so famous."

Lance handed back the boot he'd been inspecting. "Where do you live, Abe?"

"Oh, I got me a dandy cubbyhole out back. Right cozy it is, too."

"You mean you live here at the shop?"

"Well, sure, mister. Ya don't think I'd leave all these fancy boots unguarded, do ya? Some lowlife rides in and fancies somethin' he can't pay for, I'm not about to let him steal it, no, sirree."

"Very commendable," Marianne murmured.

"Lookee here, folks, you go on up those stairs yonder and take a gander at yer quarters, and I'll be gettin' back to work. Gotta cut out some leather pieces."

Lance studied the man for a moment, then started up the rickety wooden stairs Abe indicated, with Marianne at his heels. Dust puffed up at each step. Marianne sneezed, and he stopped to press his handkerchief into her hand. She covered her mouth and nose and doggedly followed him to the doorway at the top where he twisted the knob and pushed open the oak door.

She stepped inside and gasped. The place looked like it hadn't been occupied in years. Cobwebs hung from the ceiling, and a thick layer of dust covered the few pieces of furniture. A narrow cot sat against one wall, flanked by a many-drawered walnut desk and a fancy carved armoire with chipped paint. A bank of cobwebby, dust-smeared windows ran along one dirt-streaked wall. In the second small room stood a round kitchen table and two straight-backed chairs, a china cabinet with a stack of dusty blue plates and a row of cups dangling from hooks, a dry sink and a tiny potbellied wood stove. The air smelled like a mildewed carpet.

"Bet this mess makes your fingers itch," Lance said with a laugh. "This is ten times worse than Mrs. Schneiderman's boardinghouse."

"Oh, my dear Lord," Marianne wailed. "Uncle Matty must have lived at the hotel, not here. Somehow I always pictured him in a big brick house. With servants," she added in a small voice. Her shoulders sagged. "Just the thought of scrubbing these floors and everything that's sitting on them makes my knees hurt."

Lance squeezed her shoulder. "We'll have to carry up firewood," he said. "At least I won't have to chop it three times a day. Stove isn't big enough."

Her stomach turned over. "Boots," she murmured. "Just imagine, I have inherited a boot-making shop." She gave a shaky sigh.

Lance said nothing, just studied the potbellied stove.

"What about Abe?" she asked.

"What about him? Looks to me like Abe is the pot of gold at the end of the rainbow, Marianne. He's probably what made your uncle's boot business the success it is. I think we'd be nuts not to keep him right where he is, doing what he's been doing all along."

Marianne nodded. "I guess you're right."

Lance blinked. In the past four years he could count the times Marianne had accepted his advice on the fingers of one hand. Maybe… He racked his brain. Maybe once, and that was just two nights ago, when she'd asked his opinion about chocolate ice cream on top of peach pie.

She groaned and turned away to study the filthy room they stood in. "This is what I always imagined a witch's cave in a bad fairy tale would look like," she said with another sigh. "Are we really going to live here?"

"I don't think we have a choice, Marianne. At least not right now."

She worried her lower lip between her teeth. Lance sent her a look. "You okay?"

"I… I think so. I am trying really hard not to be disappointed."

"Yeah, me, too."

She closed her eyes briefly. "How much money do you have?"

"I have three dollars left."

She frowned. "Left? Left after what?"

"Left over after buying shirts—and your wedding ring."

"Oh. That was a lovely thing for you to do, Lance. Really it was."

"Yeah, well, like I said, I wanted you to have a nice wedding ring."

She gazed at him for a long moment and then straightened her shoulders and looked around the dreary space. "I guess we should go over to the mercantile and buy some soap, scrub brushes and buckets."

"On the way, I'll have a talk with Abe," Lance said. "God only knows whether your uncle paid him for his work, but I think we need to keep him on. A man that skilled at making boots could work anywhere."

She looked up at him and blinked hard. "This is ironic, don't you think? Who would ever have guessed that I would leave the drudgery of mopping and sweeping for Mrs. Schneiderman's in St. Louis for the drudgery of mopping and sweeping in Smoke River? Maybe I'll wake up in a moment and find this is all a nightmare."

"Could be worse, I guess."

She gritted her teeth. "How could it possibly be worse?"

"It'd be worse if it was just you tackling all this by yourself instead of it being the two of us. And," he added, "if we didn't have Abe."

She tried to smile. "And if we didn't have lots of soap and water available."

He reached over and squeezed her shoulder. "Come on, Marianne. Let's go get some of that soap and water."

An hour later they staggered out of Ness's Mercantile loaded down with buckets and mops and brushes, plus four bars of hard yellow soap. Just looking at what faced them made Marianne more tired than she'd ever felt at Mrs. Schneiderman's. But Lance was right; there *were* two of them. And neither of them was a stranger to hard work.

Chapter Nine

They ate a quick lunch at the restaurant, so disheartened at what they faced they barely spoke three words to each other all during the meal.

"Is the honeymoon over already?" Rita quipped. "You two look like you just lost your favorite puppy."

Marianne groaned, and the waitress instantly wiped the smile off her face and bent toward her. "Golly, I didn't mean anything by that, honest. It's just that you two look plumb discouraged, and you've only been married for twenty-four hours."

"We are discouraged," Lance said. "Collingwood Boots might be a successful business, but—"

"It came as a shock," Marianne offered. "Neither one of us knows anything about making boots. Uncle Matty had put Abe Garland in charge, and he seems very capable, but he's only one person."

Rita chewed the end of her pencil. "Folks all over the West send orders to Collingwood's, and Abe fulfills 'em. Every week for years, rain or shine, that man took a big leather bag of cash over to Mr. Myers at the bank, so I'd guess the Collingwood account is overflowing."

"Maybe," Marianne said wearily. "But from the state of the living quarters over the store I'd say the business was just scraping by."

Rita pursed her lips. "Pretty bad, huh?"

"Worse than bad," Lance said. "It's gonna take a week of elbow grease to make the place even halfway livable."

"No wonder you two look so glum. And Miss Marianne, you sure aren't dressed for house-cleanin' this afternoon."

Marianne sighed and dropped her gaze to the hot chicken sandwich getting cold on her plate. She wasn't hungry, but she knew she couldn't work all afternoon on an empty stomach. She picked up her fork. "I wonder how Abe gets his meals," she murmured.

"I wonder where the man sleeps," Lance said. "Didn't look to me like there's much room at the back of the shop."

"Let's take him a chicken sandwich," Marianne suggested.

Lance stared at her. It was nice that she was concerned about Abe's lunch; at the boardinghouse she had never worried about whether *he* had eaten lunch or not.

Marianne continued to surprise him. Was this the same woman who never did anything but give orders to fill her wood box and fix the loose slats on the chicken house and a hundred other things? Part of him didn't believe a leopard could change its spots. But twenty-four hours ago he would never have believed that a kiss could flip his heart upside down.

After lunch Marianne went up to their hotel room to change into her blue denim work skirt and a worn blue shirtwaist, and then they once again visited Ness's Mercantile where they bought two sturdy brooms, a hammer and two pounds of nails, and a gallon of bleach. The mercantile proprietor offered to send everything over to the shop in Sammy Greywolf's wagon. And he added a flour sack full of clean rags.

Fifteen minutes later, the wagon rattled to a stop in front of the mercantile and Sammy leaped down from the bench. "I hear you're moving into old man Collingwood's boot shop," he quipped as he loaded their purchases into the wagon bed.

Marianne twitched her work skirt in annoyance. "'Old man Collingwood' was my great-uncle," she said sharply. "I inherited that shop from him."

"Lotsa luck," the boy said. They climbed aboard, and Sammy flapped the reins, guided the wagon down the main street and careened around the corner.

"I've always wanted to learn how to make real boots, not like these moccasins," the boy announced. He extended one leg. "Real boots, like the ones Abe makes."

"You have?" Marianne poked her elbow into Lance's side. "Lance," she murmured, "did you hear that?"

"Yeah, I heard, but don't get too excited. We should ask Abe first if he wants a helper."

"We don't need to ask him, do we? I own the business now, and I think Abe should have a helper."

He laid a restraining hand on her arm. "Marianne, you're acting like bossy old Mrs. Schneiderman. You only took over the shop an hour before lunch. Maybe you should also remember that now it's half mine, as well."

"Oh." She sounded so chastened he instantly regretted his words. He guessed it would be hard for Marianne to give up her old ordering-everybody-about ways, and he didn't expect it would happen overnight. But it was his business, too. His chance to make something of himself. Since he was now an equal partner in her new venture, he'd be darned if he was going to let her mess it up.

Sammy helped them unload the cleaning supplies, and then hung around the shop watching Abe cut leather pieces out of a big sheet of cowhide while Marianne and Lance filled the mop buckets with soapy water and lugged them upstairs.

All afternoon they scrubbed floors, washed walls and windows, scraped dirt off the counters, swept cobwebs down from the ceiling, and dusted every single piece of furniture. Twice. Downstairs, the metallic tap-tap of Abe's boot-maker's hammer was punctuated by Sammy's questions and the old man's raspy answers.

By suppertime Marianne was so exhausted she could scarcely hold herself upright. Her head throbbed as if iron bolts were pounding into both her temples. Her legs trembled. Her back and shoulders ached, and her knees… She lifted her skirt to peer at them. Merciful heavens, her knees looked swollen and red and ugly as an old woman's!

She closed her eyes. Yesterday she'd been a bride in a beautiful yellow dress, with her hair all shiny and her knees looking like…knees. Today she was a wreck.

She looked over at Lance, brushing a last cobweb off the roof beam. He must be even more tired than she was. He had worked alongside her all afternoon, lifting the heavy buckets of wash water and swatting at the ceiling cobwebs she couldn't reach. He hadn't said much, and neither had she. There was no need to give him orders; it was painfully obvious what needed doing in the musty, unused apartment, so they just buckled down and did it without talking.

Finally Lance tossed his scrub brush into the pail of dirty water at his elbow. "We've done enough for one day, so let's go get some supper before the cook goes home for the night."

Too tired to respond, she simply nodded. Sammy had long since driven the wagon off down the street, and Abe had stopped banging on whatever he was doing and was nowhere to be found.

Marianne staggered up the stairs one last time, propped her hands on her hips, and gave the two small rooms one final inspection. Surprisingly, from beneath the grime had emerged walls papered with tiny blue-and-yellow flowers. The floors were so clean they squeaked when she walked across them, the china cabinet and the armoire and the

kitchen table shone with polish, and Lance had filled the
wood box next to the potbellied stove chock full.

"Place looks halfway decent," Lance muttered. "But *we*
sure don't. Come on, Marianne."

They limped back to the restaurant and stumbled into
the now deserted dining room to find Rita busy filling the
saltshakers.

"My stars, you two look like you've just come off a
battlefield!"

Lance managed a grin. "Yeah. It was a battle, all right.
We won, I think, but it sure took the starch out of us."

"I never saw a couple more tuckered," Rita said sym-
pathetically. "Don't know as you two are going to survive
another day of married life."

"Even my teeth feel dusty," Marianne confessed. "But
tonight I want another big steak, and after that I want a
bath. Tomorrow we can move our things over, and Sammy
said he'd bring my trunk from the railroad station so I can
unpack it."

Lance caught Rita's eye. "Two steak dinners," he ordered. "Rare. With lots of fried potatoes."

"And peach pie," Marianne added.

"Ice cream?" Rita asked.

"Chocolate," they said in unison.

Lance's eyebrows went up, and Marianne had to laugh.
She had to admit she liked surprising him. He thought she
was nothing but a bossy, know-it-all woman who liked
nothing better than giving him orders. And, she thought
with a stab of remorse, that had certainly been true at Mrs.
Schneiderman's.

She must have made his life miserable. Maybe that's
why only a few days ago he'd said that they didn't like each
other very much. At the time that was probably true. Now
she was beginning to wonder.

Now, she thought with a start, they were husband and

wife! When she had blackmailed Lance into marrying her, they had agreed to share everything, starting with her inherited business, Collingwood Boots. And, she realized, they now shared the same hotel room. And the same bed!

Lance was looking at her oddly. Maybe he was wondering what sort of woman he had married. Or maybe he was regretting marrying her in the first place. In a way she couldn't blame him.

"You have never seen me this tired and bedraggled, have you?" she remarked.

He shook his head.

"Or this dirty. I washed my face and hands before supper, but my skirt is splattered with muddy water and my shirtwaist smells like…well, never mind what. And my elbows and knees could use a good scrubbing with lots of soap and…"

She broke off at the expression on his face. "Lance, what is the matter? Are you…are you *laughing* at me?"

At that moment Rita set down two dinner plates loaded with thick steaks and so many fried potatoes they spilled over the edge. Lance didn't even look down at his supper, he just kept staring at her with that odd grin on his face.

She started to feel hot all over. "Would you mind," she said in the iciest tone she could manage, "telling me what is so funny?"

"You are," he said.

"Lance Burnside, I may be many things, but 'funny' is not one of them."

"Marianne," he pronounced carefully, "you don't know anything at all about what amuses a man who's been railroaded into marriage, traveled two thousand miles on a train to God-knows-where, gotten himself through a wedding and a fancy reception and then slaved for hours cleaning up an apartment that's not big enough for one person, let alone two."

She stared at him. "None of those things is particularly amusing," she said. "But right now you are sitting there grinning at me so strangely I thought… Oh, good heavens, I'm so tired I no longer know what I think."

He reached over and laid his hand on hers. "Eat your steak, Marianne. You can decide what you think later."

She dropped her gaze. His green-striped shirt was as dirt-streaked and sweat-stained as her garments were, she noted. They were both dead tired and they both needed a bath.

But first they needed food. Without another word she picked up her fork and stabbed it into a slice of fried potato. Lance did the same.

In silence they devoured their steaks, two slices of peach pie topped with generous scoops of chocolate ice cream, and gulped down so many brimming cups of coffee she lost count.

Finally, Lance leaned across the table toward her. "Feeling better?"

She nodded, but she couldn't speak. All at once she didn't trust her voice because she felt like crying. Fatigue, she guessed. Or discouragement at the daunting prospect before her. She had inherited a business she knew nothing about. Not only that, she had to admit she knew absolutely nothing about running *any* business. And on top of that, they had inherited a too-small living space upstairs in which she and Lance, two people who scarcely knew each other, were going to try to coexist.

Tears finally welled up in her eyes, and she blinked hard.

Lance reached across the table and took her hand. "Come on, Marianne," he announced in a no-nonsense tone. "I know things seem pretty grim right now, but let's go arrange with the desk clerk for a bathtub to be sent up to our room."

Chapter Ten

A young Mexican couple hauled buckets of hot water up to their hotel room and poured them into the tub. It took so long for the tin bathtub to be filled that Lance finally stretched out on the bed and closed his eyes while Marianne paced back and forth in front of the window.

What would she do when the bathtub was full? Undress? The picture that brought to mind made him smile. Or would she step into the water with all her clothes on?

That picture made him chuckle.

But as he waited, his exhaustion caught up with him, and by the time the bath was ready, he was sound asleep.

Poised beside the brimming tub, Marianne studied him. One arm rested over his eyes, and his chest rose and fell in a regular rhythm, but she hesitated. Her longed-for bath beckoned, but she would have to take off all her clothes to climb into the tub, and something in her held back. Not only that, but if she splashed any water, wouldn't he hear her and wake up? She caught her breath. *Would he watch her?*

She watched him for another few minutes, but he didn't move a muscle, so very quietly, she shed her sturdy work shoes and then the blue skirt. She unbuttoned her shirt-waist, dropped it to the carpet, and stood motionless in her thin chemise and petticoat and her lacy drawers. A cake of lavender soap lay on the folded washcloth and towel beside the tub, and her fingers itched to strip off the last of her garments and sink into the soothing water.

But did she dare? Her skin felt dirt-smudged and sticky, and she longed to sponge away the perspiration from hours of scrubbing during the long day, but still she hesitated. She stood quietly and watched Lance's steady breathing until she couldn't stand it one more minute.

She began to pin her hair up on top of her head, then paused, studying him. He slept on. She tossed caution to the wind and shed her petticoat and finally her chemise and lacy underdrawers. Naked, she clasped her arms over her bare breasts and lifted one leg to dip her toe in the warm water; then she took a deep breath, splashed in and shot another look at the bed.

Lance's chest continued to rise and fall. She let out a sigh of relief, reached for the fragrant bar of soap and sank up to her neck in the warm water. Oh, what bliss! She slid down until she could rest her neck against the edge of the tub and closed her eyes.

Lance heard the splash, but he had sense enough not to open his eyes and let Marianne know he was awake. Instead, he watched her through half-closed eyelids. He had to admit he felt a bit guilty for spying on her, even though all he could see was her face and the top of her shoulders.

Hold on a minute, Burnside. Marianne is your wife! You have a right to look at her, don't you?

Well, maybe. And maybe not. He shut his eyes.

A soft splash started his imagination working, and an intriguing picture began to etch itself on his brain. Another splash and the image got clearer. In his mind's eye he saw her reaching one arm toward the cake of soap on the floor beside the tub. Next he heard a soft ripple that suggested she was now smoothing the soap all over her skin, all over her…

He clenched his jaw and tried desperately to keep his eyes closed until he heard the sound of trickling water. Slow trickles. Leisurely trickles. God help him. Against his will he cracked open one eyelid.

Marianne had stretched one slim arm up toward the ceiling while the other smoothed the cake of soap over her skin. Water sheened her bare shoulders and trickled between her breasts. He couldn't help the groan that escaped him.

Marianne froze. Instantly she let out a little squeak and sank below the surface of the bathwater until only her eyes and the top of her head were showing.

Lance laughed out loud, rolled off the bed and strode toward the tub. He hesitated for a split second, then reached out both hands, grasped her bare shoulders and pulled her up. She emerged spluttering and spitting, her eyes shut tight.

"You're not asleep!" she accused.

"I tried to be, Marianne. Honest." And he was trying hard not to stare at her wet, glistening body, her perfectly formed breasts. He sucked in air. Marianne was an attractive woman on the outside, with her shiny dark hair and those mossy green eyes. But he had no idea that underneath all those clothes she was so beautiful it made his mouth go dry.

Marianne opened her eyes and looked up at him. He was standing stock still, trying not to stare at her, and his cheeks were slowly turning crimson. He looked exactly like Mrs. Schneiderman's eight-year-old grandson when she'd caught him with his hand in the cookie jar. She wanted to laugh. More than that, some imp inside her wanted to shock him!

She caught her breath. Never in her entire life had she had such a wayward thought. *What* was wrong with her?

She must be a great deal more tired than she'd realized; either that or getting married had unleashed something inside her that was decidedly unlike the Marianne Collingwood she had always been before this.

Then again, maybe she was only dreaming.

She clasped her arms over her chest and slowly stood

all the way up. Water sluiced off her body, dampening the carpet and splashing on to Lance's feet. He stood transfixed for a moment, then bent to grab the folded towel on the floor, shook it out and offered it to her.

She snatched it out of his hand and turned her back. "The bathwater is still warm," she said over her shoulder. "You shouldn't let it go to waste." Then she wrapped the towel around her body and turned to face him.

"What?" he said stupidly. "Oh, yeah, I guess I shouldn't."

She waited, but he made no move toward the tub, just stood staring at her. She didn't know what to do next. Should she dry herself off? Or stand quietly until the water beading on her skin evaporated? She decided she would wait until Lance decided what *he* would do next.

They stood in silence, gazing at each other.

Lance suddenly realized how dirty he was. He couldn't lie next to Marianne smelling like he'd been mucking out a barn! He hesitated for a long, long moment, then reached one hand to his belt buckle.

She let out a faint hiccup and spun away, so he shed his jeans and stripped off everything else and waited. Still wrapped in the towel, she moved across the room to the armoire, keeping her back to him. He couldn't help watching her. She hastily pulled on a sheer-looking white nightgown, and then she streaked past him, dove on to the bed and yanked the quilt up to her chin.

He decided he'd better stop watching her and instead stepped into the tub and concentrated on soaping himself all over and splashing off the bubbles. He even dunked his head and washed his hair, then stepped out of the tub and toweled off with the discarded towel Marianne had dropped.

Was *she* watching *him*? He shook the thought out of his head and continued to dry himself. Jupiter, instead of smelling like a sweaty working man who'd washed off layers of dirt, now he smelled like lavender! He hoped Marianne would appreciate it. The thought made him smile.

When someone tapped on the door, he pulled on a pair of clean trousers and opened it to find the young Mexican couple standing outside. "*Senor*, my wife and me, we empty bath now?"

Lance waited while they carted away the buckets of now cold bathwater and dragged the tub out into the hallway, and then he closed the door behind them and walked over to the bed where Marianne was curled up under the quilt. She lay on her side, her cheek snuggled against a fluffy pillow.

Sound asleep.

With a sigh of disappointment he carefully lay down beside her, folded his hands over his belly and studied the ceiling. For the next hour he thought about himself and his new wife. They had both worked themselves to the bone today, doing what was necessary without talking about it. Probably because of all those years working together at Mrs. Schneiderman's boardinghouse.

They made a good team, he thought with an inward smile. They had even taken a bath practically in front of each other. Finally he sighed, closed his eyes and drifted into an exhausted sleep.

Chapter Eleven

Lance woke to bright sunlight warming his closed eyelids. He groaned and rolled toward Marianne's side of the bed.

Empty. *Empty?* He jerked fully awake to find she was gone. Also gone were her blue denim work skirt and the striped shirtwaist she had been wearing yesterday.

He dressed hurriedly and pounded down the stairs and headed to the restaurant, where he expected to find Marianne drinking coffee and buttering a stack of toast. But when he entered, Rita just frowned at him.

"Sorry, Lance. I haven't seen Miss Marianne this morning. You want some coffee?"

"No, thanks, Rita. I need to find my wife." He strode out onto the board sidewalk and headed for the boot shop.

She wasn't there. "Golly, no, Mr. Burnside," Abe said with a puzzled look on his dark face. "She ain't been here this morning. But Sammy Greywolf came by a while back. Wants to help me cut out some leather pieces, and I could sure use the help. That be okay with you?"

"What? Oh, sure, Abe. Sure."

He checked upstairs in case Marianne had slipped past him while he was talking to Abe. Cautiously he opened the door to the apartment, expecting to find her busy polishing something, but…no Marianne. After all the scrubbing they'd done yesterday, the apartment gleamed, and it still smelled like bleach and furniture polish. But Marianne wasn't there.

He walked down to the mercantile, but Carl Ness raised his eyebrows and shook his head. "Lost yer wife, huh? Try the dressmaker's, just down the street. That's where my wife has usually been when she disappears."

On the way to the dressmaker's shop he stepped into Uncle Charlie's Bakery. The rich scent of fresh-baked bread made his stomach growl, and he suddenly remembered he hadn't eaten any breakfast. Still, he didn't stop but went next door to the dressmaker.

Narrow-faced Verena Forester shook her head. "Lord-a-mercy, Mr. Burnside, a body would think a new husband could keep track of his own wife!"

He studied the shops across the street. Stockett's Feed & Seed didn't seem likely; Marianne had no animals to feed and no garden to plant any seeds in. Next to the feed store was the sheriff's office, and his heart gave an unexpected thump. He'd shaken the man's hand at the wedding reception without a second thought. But this morning an unwelcome idea halted him in his tracks.

Marianne wouldn't turn me in, would she?

With a jolt he realized he hadn't the faintest idea what Marianne would do. Yeah, she'd said she didn't really believe he was a Wells Fargo stage robber, but when it came right down to it, he didn't have a clue what actually went on in Marianne's head. Would she change her mind about him just because he'd scooped her up out of her bath when she hadn't a stitch of clothing on?

He had to admit that in many ways Marianne was an unknown quantity. His widowed father always said a woman was a mystery to a man until the day he died. "Your momma could make me laugh and cry and beat my head against the wall, but so help me, she never explained herself. She puzzled me all to hell."

Until this moment Lance had never understood how a woman could do that to a man, puzzle him to the point where he would beat his head against the wall. After his mother died, Papa had worked himself to death in his law office.

Then a devastating thought struck him. *Had Marianne left him?* His stomach dropped to his toes.

He about-faced and paced up and down the boardwalk to calm his nerves. Finally he found himself in front of Uncle Charlie's bakery again, gazing through the window at the shiny glass display case inside. He must have looked hungry, because the Chinese proprietor saw him and waved him inside.

"Look like need cookie," the proprietor announced with a grin.

Uncertain how to answer, Lance stared into the man's twinkling eyes.

"Here." Charlie thrust a dark, crinkle-topped cookie at him. "Molasses," he said. "Good for troubles."

"Thanks," Lance managed. "I didn't realize my troubles were so obvious."

Charlie grinned. "Plenty plain. My guess woman trouble."

Lance nodded. "Yeah. Sure is hard to understand them sometimes."

"Hard to understand *all* time," the bakery owner quipped. He handed another molasses cookie over the display case.

Lance groaned, popped the cookie in his mouth and stepped out onto the sidewalk. Suddenly a flash of blue denim caught his attention. Marianne!

He choked on the cookie and started forward. He caught up with her just as she turned the corner onto Maple Street, grabbed her arm and pulled her to a stop.

"Marianne, where have you been?"

She blinked. "At the bank," she said, her voice matter of fact. "Why?"

"Well, I—I woke up and you were gone. Rita said you'd skipped breakfast, and I couldn't figure—"

"I did skip breakfast," she acknowledged. "I couldn't sleep one more minute without checking the Collingwood bank account. I needed to know how much money we have."

Lance offered her the other molasses cookie. "I skipped breakfast, too," he explained. "Uncle Charlie took pity on me."

She nodded, her mouth full.

"So how much money does the Collingwood account have?"

She sighed. "Not enough. Less than two hundred dollars, in fact. That must be pretty close to the bottom of the barrel for a viable business."

"Well, that's sure more money than *I've* seen in a lot of years," he offered.

She bit her lip. "But maybe it's not enough to run Collingwood Boots. Abe told me he hasn't taken any salary for his work in over six months, and I'm sure he will need to order supplies. And we still have to pay Carl Ness for all those purchases we made at the mercantile yesterday."

"Marianne, I can't think on an empty stomach. Let's go back to the restaurant and get some breakfast."

"Couldn't we eat these cookies instead?"

"Don't you want some coffee?"

"Well…if I could have six more of those cookies I could do without coffee."

Lance was so relieved at finding his wife and having a perfectly normal conversation with her, that he took Marianne's arm and piloted her back to the bakery. When they entered, Charlie popped up from behind the display case. "Want more cookie?"

"Six more," Lance said. "And…" He surveyed the shelves of delectable-looking offerings.

"Cupcakes," Marianne announced. "Chocolate ones."

"One for each?" Charlie asked.

"Three," Marianne said decisively. "We can take one to Abe. And one for Sammy, that makes four."

"You think Sammy might work for Abe?"

"Yes, don't you?"

Lance nodded. Uncle Charlie wrapped up the cupcakes and half a dozen molasses cookies, handed them over the counter to Lance and pocketed the coins.

"If Sammy works with Abe I think we should pay him," Lance pointed out when they were outside. "That will cut into the money left in the bank."

"Maybe it can't be helped," she said. "It's clear to me that we need to sell more boots than Abe can make by himself. Otherwise, the business will go under."

"Yeah, but—"

"Lance, I am responsible for the success of this business now." She spun away and quick-marched on down the sidewalk.

He felt as if a big bucket of ice water had been dumped over his head. He caught up with her and yanked her around to face him. "Hold on a damn minute, Marianne! Don't you mean *we* are responsible for the business? *Both* of us own Collingwood Boots. Or had you forgotten our bargain?"

Her face changed. "Oh. Yes, of course I remember our bargain, Lance."

He gritted his teeth. "Yeah? Well, you reacted like you would have back in St. Louis when you were running Mrs. Schneiderman's boardinghouse. But you're not back at Mrs. Schneiderman's, Marianne. You're here in Smoke River. With me."

"Oh, yes, of course," she said. Her voice sounded subdued.

"And we are running this business together, like we agreed. Aren't we?"

She nodded, and they walked on in tense silence for a

dozen steps until Sammy Greywolf drove past them with Marianne's trunk loaded in the back of his wagon. The boy grinned and saluted, then rattled on past, kicking up dust in the road, and turned the corner.

Marianne picked up her pace. "Lance, let's hurry. I packed a coffeepot in my trunk, and I suddenly have the wildest desire to eat my cupcake in my very own kitchen. Now, I want you to—"

"Marianne, you're doing it again," Lance said. "You're giving me orders!"

Marianne clamped her mouth shut. He was right. Would she ever conquer the impulse to just snap out orders without thinking? For most of her life, that was how she had survived, by being decisive. By taking charge. But now... she had to get used to having a partner. Now that she and Lance were married, she had to remind herself she was only half of a team.

She swallowed. She had more than a partner; she had a *husband*. She wondered not only whether she...they... could ever in a million years learn to run a boot-making business, but... She swallowed again. She was too used to being on her own. Independent. She wondered if she would ever learn the secrets of a successful marriage.

They walked on without talking, and by the time they arrived at the shop, Abe and Sammy had manhandled her trunk up the stairs and into their tiny living quarters. Marianne stuffed down her eagerness to start unpacking and went looking for Abe.

"Abe? We've brought you a chocolate cupcake from Uncle Charlie's."

A raspy voice sounded from the shadowy interior of the shop. "C'mon back, Miss Marianne. See where ol' Abe hangs his hat."

With Lance close behind her she picked her way through the shelves of tools and leather scraps, pulled aside a canvas curtain and ducked into a room no bigger than a closet. She stared around her in surprise.

The space was a marvel of organization, the walls covered with Abe's possessions hanging on nails—a skillet, an iron griddle, a pair of boots, two worn Stetsons and a red flannel shirt. A blue speckleware coffeepot sat on the tiny stove in the center of the room. Sunlight from a small window fell across a narrow cot with a painted bookshelf nailed in place at the head. It held a small kerosene lamp and a jumble of dime novels.

"Ain't never allowed nobody back here," Abe said. "'Cept I reckon you two are okay, so make yerselves at home."

It was like a dollhouse, Marianne thought. So neat and tidy it looked unreal. The plank floor gleamed, and the stove looked so shiny she surmised Abe rubbed it with boot polish.

"How do you manage in such a tiny space?" she asked.

"I cook small," Abe explained. "And I heat up a teakettle of water for doin' my dishes and washin' out my duds and takin' a wash." He gestured at the speckleware coffeepot. "Care for some coffee?"

Marianne handed over the bag of cupcakes, and Abe unhooked three china mugs from the wall. "Ain't got much sit-down room, but…" He gestured for Marianne to seat herself on the cot, which was neatly made up with a thick fur coverlet.

Abe grinned at them and took a big bite of his cupcake.

"Now, Miss Marianne, what's on yer mind this morning? I kin tell yer thinkin', 'cuz yer face looks all consternated."

Lance chuckled. "That's the best description of Marianne's face I've ever heard."

"And yers," Abe continued with a sly grin, "looks purely constipated."

At that, a laugh bubbled out of Marianne's mouth.

"So," Abe went on, wolfing down another bite of his cupcake, "what's up?"

"Abe, I checked the bank account this morning. It's running very low."

"Figured as much. I ain't been spendin' any money lately, jest fer food and essentials like soap and boot polish, but, as I told you, pretty soon I gotta send away to Mexico for more cowhides and then there's tacks and silk thread and a bunch of other stuff, and that's gonna cost pretty near ever'thing we got saved at the bank. You two got some idee what we outta do?"

Marianne blinked. Do? She had absolutely no idea what to do. She hadn't the faintest idea how to bring more money into a business she knew nothing about. She had to admit what she and Lance knew about making boots they could put in a thimble. A very small thimble.

Nevertheless, she couldn't let the business fail—it was her inheritance! Well, she amended quickly, hers and Lance's. It was what she had dreamed of for years, being independent.

"Abe, what did my uncle do when funds ran low?"

"Oh, he— Heck, Miss Marianne. Ev'ry time Mr. Collingwood went back to New York, orders started pouring in like maple syrup on a flapjack." He handed them each a mug of coffee and filled one for himself. "Sorry I don't got milk. Miz MacAllister's cow's goin' dry. Care for sugar?"

Marianne shook her head and watched the man dump three heaping spoonfuls of sugar into his cup. It tickled her that Abe had a sweet tooth; she wished they'd brought him more cupcakes.

"Is Sammy coming back today?" Lance asked suddenly.

"Dunno. Might do, if his momma don't need him. Rosie Greywolf works at the restaurant, washin' dishes. The two of 'em together barely make enough to feed a sparrow."

"You think Sammy would be interested in learning the boot-making trade?" Lance asked.

Abe's lined face lit up. "Ah shore do think so. Kid could hardly keep his hands off my leather workin' tools, and he shot questions at me faster'n I could think up answers."

Lance caught Marianne's eye. "Abe, would you like to take him on as an apprentice?"

"Have to pay 'im," Abe said slowly. "Ain't right to work somebody as hard as I'd work 'em for no pay."

"If Sammy was helping you, we could make more boots," Marianne said.

Lance straightened suddenly. "Could you use me, too? Since I'm part owner—" he sent Marianne a significant glance "—I would work without any wages."

Marianne stared at him. "Lance, do you know anything about making boots?"

"Nope. But a man can learn, can't he?"

She had no answer to that. She herself had to learn about the boot-making business.

"What about it, Abe?" Lance persisted. "Could you train me, too?"

"Well, I reckon I could, providin' you're not too dumb. Making boots ain't for sissies."

"Oh, Lance is certainly not dumb," Marianne blurted out. "He is very intelligent. And he works hard."

"Marianne can vouch for that," Lance said drily. He raised one eyebrow and sent her a bland smile.

After a moment she straightened her spine. "And I will come up with a new business plan."

"Huh?" Abe snorted. "All by yerself yer gonna think up how to increase orders? Heck, Miss Marianne, you jest got married day before yesterday. Ain't even unpacked yer fancy trunk yet."

"There is nothing fancy in my trunk, Abe. I was a working woman before I ever heard of Smoke River and Uncle

Matty's boot shop, and I didn't pack fancy things. I packed like a girl who knows about work."

"You two sure you don't want to take some time before you leap into this? Maybe have yerselves a honeymoon?"

Marianne and Lance locked gazes. "I'm sure," she said. Lance sent her a long, intense look, and then he nodded.

Abe rolled his eyes and poured more coffee.

While Lance and Abe discussed leather and boot-making, Marianne climbed the stairs to the apartment and spent the rest of the day unpacking her trunk, stowing the pots and pans and dishes and towels she had shipped from St. Louis on the shiny scrubbed shelves and in the cabinets in the kitchen and shaking the wrinkles out of her work skirts.

When she came to the bed linens, the sheets and embroidered pillowcases she had saved in her hope chest all these years, her hands fell to her sides. There was only one bed, the narrow cot under the front window. She propped both hands on her hips and stared at it. Why on earth had she not noticed how small it was? She shook out one muslin sheet, spread it over the cot and tucked in the corners. Now what?

At the hotel she and Lance had managed to sleep next to each other without touching, but here? On this tiny cot? It would never be big enough.

She stood for a moment in the open door, listening to the voices of Abe and Lance floating from the shop below. Then, with a final look at the narrow cot, she slipped down the stairs and headed for the mercantile.

Carl Ness tore his gaze from the newspaper spread on the counter and gave her a thin-lipped smile. "Miss—uh… Miz Burnside, what can I do for you?"

"Good morning, Mr. Ness. Have you a Montgomery Ward catalog?"

"Yep." He bent, fished a thick volume from a shelf under the counter and slapped it down next to his newspaper. "You want something I don't carry here at the mercantile?"

"I—" Oh, this was embarrassing! "That is, we... Mr. Burnside and myself, are in need of a—" she drew in a fortifying breath "—a bed."

The graying eyebrows rose. "Your living quarters over the boot shop don't have a bed?"

"Well, yes, there is a bed of sorts, but—" she sucked in another gulp of air "—it is very narrow. More like a cot, in fact."

Mr. Ness pursed his lips, but Marianne saw the telltale smile he tried to hide. "Not, um, big enough, huh?"

"N-no."

He riffled through the catalog and flipped it open at the section featuring home furnishings, then turned it around to face her. Marianne bent over the page and read the extremely small type. "Heavy iron bedstead with brass rod and knobs, finished in white enamel."

But it was only four feet wide! In fact, the largest bed in the catalog was only four feet wide. That would allow scarcely two feet of sleeping space for each of them. The bed in their hotel room was larger than that, and all at once she realized why. That bed was wider because it was two single beds shoved together. So if they butted the cot up to a regular-sized double bed, it would be as wide as the one in their hotel room.

"Mr. Ness, if I ordered a bed today, how long will it take for it to reach Smoke River?"

Before the proprietor could answer, a bell jangled and the mercantile door banged open. In swept a large, bosomy woman wearing a bright yellow calico print dress and a red hat so swathed in bird feathers Marianne half expected it to burst into song.

Mr. Ness groaned under his breath. "Be right with you, Miz Ridley."

The woman bustled up to the counter and craned her neck to see the open catalog page Marianne had spread before her. "Ordering something, dearie?"

Carl Ness earned Marianne's everlasting gratitude by reaching over and snapping the volume shut.

"It could take a few weeks from today depending on what other orders they have to fill," he said, practically whispering. "Furniture comes from Chicago by rail, but in Omaha they unload it and freight it over the mountains by wagon."

Mrs. Ridley tilted her head, all the better to hear what was being said.

"You wanna order the bed?" the proprietor murmured.

"A bed!" Mrs. Ridley chirped. "How nice."

"It's for Abe, over at Collingwood's shop," Mr. Ness said quickly. He sent Marianne a surreptitious wink and patted the closed catalog. "I'll add a mattress," he whispered. "Need any pillows?"

Marianne nodded and held up two fingers.

Mrs. Ridley stepped closer, inspected the closed catalog and gave a loud huff before heading down the garden tool aisle.

Carl Ness leaned over the counter toward Marianne. "Watch out for that woman, Miz Burnside. Eugenia Ridley's the biggest busybody in town."

"Thank you, Mr. Ness. I will be back tomorrow to buy our food supplies for the week."

"You can send your husband or Abe over with a list, ma'am. I'll load everything up and Sammy Greywolf can drive it over in his wagon."

Before she left the mercantile, she bought five yards of blue gingham to make curtains for the windows, a thick pad of notepaper and seven pencils. On impulse she added a small folding screen. Mr. Ness said he would deliver the screen himself after he closed up the shop.

On her way out the door Marianne watched Eugenia Ridley sweep up to the counter and thumb through the Montgomery Ward catalog on the counter. The town busy-body, was she? Thanks to Mr. Ness, the woman would never know about her separate bed sleeping arrangements with Lance. In a small town like this, that would make rich fodder for gossip.

She headed back to the shop and had just turned on to Maple Street when a thought stopped her in her tracks. A few weeks! Whatever would they do while they waited a few weeks for the other half of their bed to arrive? *And what of the nights?* Sleeping next to Lance on the large bed in their hotel room had been awkward, to say the least. But now they weren't in the hotel.

Now... She closed her eyes. Now their bed was one single narrow cot. A *very* narrow cot.

All at once she gave a guilty start. She had *liked* sleeping next to Lance. And she had to acknowledge something else, something that had happened at their wedding. When the minister had invited Lance to kiss the bride, she had anticipated a light peck on the cheek. She certainly hadn't expected him to really kiss her. That was for two people who loved each other, not for two people who were embarking on a business arrangement and a marriage of convenience.

But he *had* kissed her, really kissed her, and at that moment something unexpected had happened. His lips were firm and warm, and their gentle pressure on her mouth sent a sweet, insistent heat flowing through her entire body. She had stopped breathing, and her heart had slammed hard against her rib cage. And then...

She shivered at the memory of what happened next. Then she had kissed him back! *Whatever had she been thinking to do something so bold?*

The truth was she had *not* been thinking. She had simply been reacting. And that was so unlike her ordinarily dry-as-day-old-bread self it gave her pause. She caught her breath. And, oh, my goodness, had she really stood up from the bathtub in front of him without a stitch on?

Her footsteps slowed and then stopped altogether as another thought struck her. Now that she and Lance were married, were husband and wife and living together in the same tiny apartment, would he kiss her again?

She stumbled blindly on toward Collingwood Boots. Abe met her at the door of the shop. "Mr. Lance, he's upstairs," he said, punching his forefinger toward the ceiling. "And, Miss Marianne, Ah shore do hope you like what we went and done."

Chapter Twelve

Lance watched Marianne's face as she came through the apartment door. She stared at the cot arrangement he and Abe had devised, and her eyes widened. Then she got the oddest look on her face. She glanced up at him for a split second, then instantly turned her gaze back to the cots. "I don't understand, Lance. When I left, that was just a single cot. Now it's…"

"Abe thought we needed a bigger bed," he explained. "You're looking at both the old cot and Abe's cot. We carried it upstairs just before you came in."

She surveyed the two cots now sitting side by side to make a double bed of sorts. "But what is Abe sleeping on?"

"He made up a pallet on his floor. Wouldn't take no for an answer, either. He said a man only gets married once and that we, um, we shouldn't waste it."

Marianne's cheeks turned the prettiest shade of pink. She turned toward the kitchen where he had cobbled together a simple supper of cheese sandwiches and slabs of apple pie he had brought from the restaurant.

"Oh." Her voice shook the slightest bit. "That was thoughtful of him."

Her face was a study, the pink in her cheeks darkening to rose, her green eyes pensive. He'd give anything to know what she was thinking.

"Where did you go when you slipped out of here this afternoon?" he asked.

"The mercantile."

"Yeah? What for? Thought we already bought out Ness's supply of soap and bleach."

She bit her lower lip. "I… Well, I bought some yard goods and a notepad and some pencils to work on our business plan."

"You were gone over an hour. That's all you bought, pencils and paper?"

"I… I also looked at the Montgomery Ward catalog."

"What for?"

She studied the floor, then focused on the bare windows over the sink. Finally her gaze moved to the two cots he and Abe had shoved together. "I ordered a bed. When it's delivered, we can arrange a cot next to it to make one, um, big bed."

Lance stared at her while a bubble of something fizzy swirled around in his brain. "One big bed," he repeated. Hot damn! *One big bed!* All at once he wanted to shout hallelujah.

Right before his eyes she blushed an even deeper shade of pink. "Of course," she said in that no-nonsense tone he knew so well.

He knew better than to press her, so he just nodded. "Are you hungry? I made a couple of cheese sandwiches."

"Yes, I'm starving. I worked up quite an appetite at the mercantile." She didn't explain why. Seated across from each other at the round walnut table, they devoured the sandwiches without further conversation. Every so often he glanced at her face, but she'd gone back to her stonewall expression, which told him absolutely nothing about what she might be thinking.

Then without a word of explanation she set the plates in the sink, re-seated herself at the table and bent over a notepad. Every so often she tapped her pencil against her teeth and gazed off into space. She looked like she was turning something over and over in her mind, but she didn't explain what it was, and he was too smart to ask. It never paid to push Marianne when she was preoccupied.

Lance watched her chew on her pencil and scribble sporadically in the notepad until he couldn't stand it any longer. "Marianne, what in blazes are you doing?"

She sent him an exasperated look. "I'm doing what I said I would do this morning. Working out a business plan for the shop."

"It must be really complicated," he said. "You've crumpled up at least twenty of those note pages so far."

She ripped off another sheet, squashed that up as well, and tossed it down to join the field of white paper snowballs littering the floor.

"Making any progress?" he asked cautiously.

She didn't even glance up. "Some."

"Need any help?" He was going to say "advice," but he thought better of it. But the instant the word "help" left his mouth he realized that, too, was a mistake. "Help" was something he had never once seen Marianne seek. She was always so convinced she knew better than everyone else that nobody ever bothered to risk an opinion.

To be fair, that was because she was usually right. Mrs. Schneiderman's boardinghouse ran like an efficient clock on a strict no-nonsense schedule, and he knew without a doubt that old Mrs. Schneiderman had little to do with the success of her establishment.

But nobody could be perfect all the time, even Marianne. No matter what anyone at the boardinghouse had thought, Marianne was only human. And she knew nothing about the business of making boots.

Squish-squash went another sheet of notepaper. With a groan she bent over the table, twiddling her tooth-marked pencil between her thumb and first finger. Lance pulled out his pocketknife, gathered up a fistful of the dull pencils scattered over the kitchen table and whittled on them until their points were sharp once more.

He stared at the empty coffeepot she'd unpacked and set on the stove. Marianne was so preoccupied he knew if he wanted a cup of coffee he'd have to make it himself. He rummaged around in the cabinet under the sink, found the coffee beans in a tin canister, located the coffee mill and filled the pot with water. Then he realized the stove was stone cold.

He grabbed the coffeepot and clattered down the stairs. "Abe, can I set this to boil on your stove?"

The man nodded and lifted it out of his hand. "Might not be polite to ask, but what's Miss Marianne doin'?"

"She's...thinking."

Abe pursed his lips. "That right?"

"Yeah. She's been doing that a lot lately. Usually she's pretty good at thinking, so I can't guess what's got her so stumped tonight."

Abe studied him for a moment. "Mebbe it's the Collingwood Boots business," he suggested.

Lance nodded, and the two men's eyes met. "Listen," Abe said after a moment. "You go on back upstairs an' keep Miss Marianne company, all right? I'll bring up the coffee when it's ready."

Upstairs, Lance found Marianne pacing back and forth in front of the china cabinet, a sharpened pencil clenched between her teeth. He took one look at her, scooped four more pencils with the lead worn down off the table and whittled them to a point, too.

"Thank you," she murmured.

He smiled at her, but she wasn't looking at him. He watched her for a few moments, then decided he needed to do something else besides stare at her, wondering what she was up to. He wrenched his gaze away from her and turned his attention to their living quarters.

She had spent all afternoon unpacking the heavy trunk he and Sammy had lugged upstairs, and he had to admit the place looked far more homey now than it did yesterday. Plates and cups were neatly stacked in the china cabinet. In the armoire he found his shirts and two pairs of jeans hanging next to her yellow wedding dress and the green travel suit she'd worn on the train. One drawer in the bureau in the corner held his socks and clean drawers.

When he slid open the other drawer he almost choked. Marianne's lacy-looking camisoles and underdrawers were arranged in neat, soft-looking rows. Staring down at them made his groin swell. He resisted an impulse to run his fingers over them and wrenched his gaze away.

In the far corner stood a folding screen he'd not noticed before, but before he could peek behind it, Abe rapped at the door and handed him the coffeepot. "Made it real strong," the older man confided. "Figured ya might need it."

Lance filled a cup for Marianne and set it on the table near her elbow, then poured one for himself and settled in the straight-backed chair across from her with one of Abe's dime novels titled *Riders of Red River*. Marianne went on scribbling away on her notepad and ignored the coffee.

He took a sip of the brew and winced. Abe wasn't kidding about making it strong! He downed two big gulps and opened the book. The only sound was the ticking of the alarm clock on the top shelf of the china cabinet and the occasional rustle of Marianne crumpling up notepaper.

He'd give a silver dollar to know what she was doing, but he'd learned at Mrs. Schneiderman's not to interrupt Marianne when she was figuring something out. Once when he'd forgotten this unspoken rule and asked what she was doing, he hadn't got any dessert that night.

The outside light faded to gray-blue twilight, and after a while he got up to light the kerosene lamp and set it down on the table between them. Marianne worked on, scratching notes all over fresh sheets of paper and muttering to herself while Lance read about gun-toting rustlers and impossibly brave cowboys. Every once in a while he looked up to find her head still bent over her notepad. Sitting across from each other without talking, they probably looked like an old married couple, he thought wryly.

Except that...

He shot a glance at the double cot arrangement he and Abe had come up with this afternoon. The longer he looked at it, the warmer he felt. A single blue-flowered quilt covered both cots, but he knew the bed was divided down the middle, and that would keep Marianne plenty separate from him. Still, they would be close together. All night.

He wondered if thinking about their sleeping arrangement made her as nervous as it was making him. Maybe not. She'd flabbergasted him last night in their hotel room when she'd stood before him buck naked and dripping wet. It didn't seem to unnerve her, but it had sure unnerved him!

He went back to his novel and tried to concentrate on the rustlers and the posse chasing them.

Around midnight she suddenly flapped her notebook shut and stood up with a sigh. "I am completely exhausted," she announced. "I can't put one more idea into my brain tonight, so I'm going to bed to get some sleep."

Lance's belly flip-flopped. He was right in the middle of a fistfight between the hero and the outlaw, and he didn't really want to close the book, but the thought of going to bed with Marianne was pretty tempting.

She leaned across the table and studied him. "What are you reading?"

"One of Abe's dime novels. Pretty exciting stuff."

"Is it a good story?"

Lance nodded without losing his place. "Gotta see how this fight ends."

He heard nothing more until she sat down on one of the cots and it squeaked. He looked up and lost his place.

She was wearing her long white nightgown, and she'd let her hair down. It hung past her shoulders in dark, shiny waves, and Lance clenched his jaw and dropped his gaze to the floor. God, her bare toes were peeking out from under the hem of her gown! His groin started to ache.

With a tired sigh she sank on to one side of the bed and curled up under the quilt. As much as he wanted to find out how the fight between Slim and Injun Joe ended, the prospect of lying anywhere near Marianne tonight drove all other thoughts from his mind. He puffed out the lamp, stripped down to his drawers, and crawled on to the cot next to her.

She was asleep before he could even say good-night.

Disappointment warred with frustration. He folded his arms under his head and lay staring up at the exposed timber beams. *Guess we really do have a marriage of convenience, like she says.*

Finally he couldn't keep his eyes open and drifted off to sleep, only to be awakened hours later by a hoarse scream.

"That's it!" Marianne bolted straight up in bed. "That's it!"

Half asleep, Lance rolled toward her and sat up. "What's 'it'?"

"I just figured out the perfect business plan!" She flopped back down on her side of the bed, and with a little satisfied humming sound she was instantly asleep again.

Lance had a sudden suspicion that he wasn't going to like her "perfect business plan" any more than he liked his marriage of convenience. The way things were going he figured he'd never have the chance to even kiss her again.

An hour later it was his turn to jerk upright with an idea. Marianne had a business plan, did she? Well maybe he had come up with a plan, too. A seduction plan.

He lay back down with a wide smile on his face.

Chapter Thirteen

The next morning when Lance went downstairs Abe took one look at him, handed him a tack hammer and sent him a knowing grin. "Didn't get much sleep last night, huh? Guess them double cots are workin' out all right."

"You're right, Abe. I didn't get much sleep last night, but not for the reason you're thinking."

Abe's grin widened. "Oh, sure. An' chickens on a hot day lay fried eggs. No need to shilly-shay around the bush, son. Not with me, anyway, 'cuz I know all about it."

Sammy Greywolf set aside the piece of calfskin he was cutting and looked up. "All about what?"

"All about women," Abe answered. He sent the boy a speculative look. "You know about women, do ya, Sammy?"

Sammy's blush turned his skin a darker shade. "I know about girls, if that's what you mean. Don't know much about women, I guess."

Lance caught Abe's twinkly dark eyes. "How old are you, Sammy?"

"I'll be fourteen in November, Mr. Burnside."

"Tha's plenty old enough," Abe said. "I know ya ain't got a pa, Sammy. Did yer momma ever talk to you 'bout them things?"

The boy's black eyebrows pulled into a frown. "What

things? You mean about moving your cot upstairs so Lance and Miss Marianne can—?"

"Yeah," Abe said quickly. "Them things."

Lance set down the tack hammer with a decisive snick. "Look here, Abe. I didn't get much sleep last night because I was reading that damn novel you lent me, *Riders of Red River*."

"Oh, sure, son," the older man said in a skeptical tone. "I believe ya."

"Well, it's the truth."

"Them double cots aren't doin' much fer your marriage, seein' as how you stay up all night readin' 'stead of doin'… other things. You might want to borry a few more of my dime novels. I got dozens of 'em. The mercantile sells them books by the crate."

"Can I read some?" Sammy asked. "All Ma's got at home is the Bible and the newspapers she saves from Miss Jessamine at the *Sentinel*."

"Sammy, kin you read?" Abe asked.

The boy looked startled. "Read! Sure I can read. I was top of my class in reading, tied with Annamarie Panovsky. You got some books I can read, Abe?"

Abe shot a look at Lance. "Well, I dunno. Might be too much S-E-X in 'em for a boy who's only thirteen."

"I can spell, too!" Sammy said indignantly. "And I know about sex because Ma explained all about it."

Lance chuckled. "Just 'knowing all about it' isn't enough," he said very quietly.

"I got sharp ears, too, Mr. Burnside," Sammy shot back. "How come knowing about it isn't enough?"

"Yeah, Mr. Burnside," Abe echoed with a sly smile. "How come knowin' all about it ain't enough?"

Lance caught the old man's gaze. "Mind your own business, Abe."

"Hell's half acre, son," Abe snorted. "It *is* my business! That's my cot you say you're not gettin' any sleep on."

Lance sent a significant glance toward Sammy, but it did no good. Once Abe got something between his teeth he was like a hungry terrier with a steak bone. "Abe," he said patiently, knowing Sammy was curious about what was going on in the S-E-X department, "Marianne spent most of the night working on her new business plan, and I was reading *Riders of Red River*. Didn't leave much time for...other things."

A puzzled expression crossed Sammy's face, but Abe sent him a sharp look, and the boy resumed his leather cutting. Abe stepped closer to Lance. "Ya mean no time a t'all fer 'other things'?" he murmured. "None?"

Lance hesitated. "That's right. None."

"Somethin' ain't right about that." He raised an eyebrow at Lance and beckoned him out the back door, beyond Sammy's hearing. "Son, ya been married three days an' you're not yet—?"

Lance let out a long sigh. "Look, Abe, Marianne and I have, uh, a special arrangement. It's what you'd call a marriage of convenience. That means we don't—"

"Marriage of convenience? Horse feathers!"

Lance grimaced. "Well, you may be right there, Abe, but we—"

"Nuh-uh," Abe interrupted. "I seen the way you look at Miss Marianne. An' I seen the way she looks at you when you're not watchin'. Ya better wise up, son, 'cuz your eyesight ain't too good."

Lance blew out an exasperated breath. "You ever been married, Abe?"

"Heck, yes. Four times. So I know somethin' about it, see?"

Lance frowned. "You've been married four times?"

Abe dug the toe of his boot into the ground. "Yep, that's

what I said. My first wife died of the cholera down in Texas. Second wife divorced me for smokin' in her prissy clean kitchen. Third wife died havin' my baby. An' my fourth wife, she jest run off somewhere after a couple of years and I never heard from her again."

Lance studied the man more closely. The grin was gone now, and in its place was a steady, tight-lipped look and a bruised expression in his dark eyes.

"Why d'ya think I work so hard makin' all them fancy boots?" Abe said in a subdued tone. "Keeps my mind off wives and things."

Lance knew enough to keep quiet at that point. Instead he reached out and gripped Abe's bony shoulder in a wordless gesture of sympathy.

"'Nuff said, I reckon," Abe muttered. "Guess both you'n me got the woman mis'ry, huh?"

Late that morning Marianne flew down the stairs waving her notepad. "Gentlemen," she announced. "I am calling a business meeting."

Lance and Sammy looked up from the table of calfskin pieces in front of them. Abe gaped at her, his hammer poised over a three-penny nail.

"Provided, of course," she quickly added, "that this is a convenient time to discuss a business plan?"

Abe's tack hammer thunked on to the table and he straightened. "What kinda busyness plan, Miss Marianne?"

"One that's going to make lots of money for Collingwood Boots." *I hope*, she added silently.

"Okey-dokey, let's hear it."

Lance and Sammy moved closer to the bottom step where she stood. Lance had an odd, patient look on his face, the kind of look he used to give her at Mrs. Schneiderman's when she asked him to fill the wood box for the third time in a single afternoon.

"Yeah," he said quietly, "let's hear it, Marianne."

She unfolded a sheet of paper from her notepad and scanned the numbered items. "First, we need to increase production. Of course—" she directed a smile at Sammy "—I see that task is already well under way."

Sammy grinned.

"Second, Abe and Sammy will draw wages in proportion to our profits. And third…" She paused for effect. "The third part of my plan is word-of-mouth advertising."

She waited. Lance and Abe stared at her as if she had a watermelon balanced on her head. Sammy's eyes just looked puzzled. "You mean," the boy ventured, "we're just going to *talk* about what we're doing?"

"That is it exactly, Sammy."

"I dunno, Miss Marianne," he said. "I already talk plenty when I drive people around or deliver stuff. None of them ever orders a pair of boots."

"First things first, Sammy. You start by noticing things about your customers."

"Oh. I notice lots of things when I'm carrying freight around the county. Thad MacAllister is planting twice as much wheat as last year, and Wash Halliday is getting his daughter a pony for her birthday, and Mrs. Panovsky, the schoolteacher, orders a box of books every week and…" His voice trailed off.

"Sammy, your observations are very valuable," Marianne said. She turned to Abe and Lance. "You do see the opportunities here, don't you?"

Abe snorted. "What opportunities, Miss Marianne? Miz Panovsky don't own a horse and she don't wear riding boots."

"But *Mr.* Panovsky does."

"No, he don't, ma'am. Ivan Panovsky works at the sawmill and—"

"The sawmill!" Marianne clapped her hands in delight.

"A perfect place for another way to advertise. And then there's—"

Lance suddenly came to life. "The newspapers! The *Smoke River Sentinel* and the *Lake County Lark* publish newspapers twice a week on different days."

"But the best thing of all," Marianne announced with a smile, "are Abe's dime novels!"

Abe jerked. "Huh? What's my novels got to do with sellin' boots?"

"Advertisements," Marianne answered. "This morning I looked through that book Lance is reading, and I learned something important."

"Yeah? What'd you learn about rustlers and sheriffs, Miss Marianne?"

"I learned that every single book has at least one advertisement for something, horse liniment, saddle soap, boot polish, even horseshoe nails. We should definitely advertise Collingwood Boots in those novels."

"How much does it cost to advertise in one of those books?" Lance asked.

"I don't know yet," she admitted. "But we can find out. Those novels are published by Brooks and Cassidy in Philadelphia. Tomorrow morning I will send the publisher a telegram."

The men looked at each other and then studied her with doubt written all over their faces. "And," she continued, "we could also put advertising posters in all the businesses in town, including Ness's mercantile, the barber shop, even the sheriff's office and the dressmaker's."

"Beggin' yer pardon, Miss Marianne," Abe interjected, "but ever'body here in Smoke River already knows about Collingwood Boots."

"Yes, they do, Abe. But the information in an advertisement at the barber shop will reach not only all the customers who come in for haircuts, but their wives, and their friends, and their relatives in Montana or back in Missouri or down in Arkansas or wherever. I think word of mouth might be a powerful advertising force. Don't you, Lance?"

"Well, sure, Marianne. Advertising for a business is always a good idea."

"Could be Miss Jessamine at the *Sentinel* would print up some of them posters for us," Abe suggested.

Sammy's eyes snapped with excitement. "I could spread them around everywhere I go in the wagon."

"And," Marianne said, directing a special smile at Lance, "we could start composing these ads right after supper tonight. We will work all night if we have to."

Abe and Lance exchanged a pointed look. "All night, huh?" Lance said under his breath. "Like hell."

"Damn right," Abe muttered.

Sammy looked from the older man to the younger and a perplexed expression crossed his face. "What's wrong with working all night?"

Abe coughed. And Lance couldn't suppress a groan.

Chapter Fourteen

That night Marianne cooked Lance's second favorite supper, fried chicken and mashed potatoes, and topped it off with a lemon cake with burnt sugar icing. It was a lucky man who ate at Marianne's table, he reflected. Nothing beat her cooking, unless maybe it was the steak at the restaurant.

Nothing beat her sense of duty, either, he thought with a groan. The instant supper was over, she whisked all the dishes off the table and had them washed up in a trice. Lance picked up a dish towel and was leisurely drying a plate when Marianne jarred his sense of well-being.

"Hurry up, Lance. We have to start composing our advertisements."

He dropped the towel on the counter and turned to face her. "We don't *have* to do anything, Marianne."

She blinked at him and opened her mouth to protest, but he reached out, placed his hand on her cheek and nudged her jaw closed.

"Marianne, do you know what I'd like?"

"No," she said suspiciously. "What?"

He curved his hands around her shoulders. "I'd like you to stop giving me orders like I was some damn soldier in your own private army."

"Oh," she said quietly. "I did it again, didn't I?"

"You sure as hell did."

"Oh," she said again. "I guess I'm so used to… I didn't realize what I was doing."

"Well, maybe it's time you did realize it. You and I are not master and slave. We are equal partners. For better or worse, if you remember."

She didn't reply for so long he thought she hadn't heard him. Then, in a very small voice, she said, "I do remember, Lance."

"Old habits die hard, I guess," he said with a wry smile.

She nodded and then suddenly looked up at him. Hell and damn, he could see tears shimmering in her eyes. He cleared his throat. "How about I give *you* an order for a change?"

"All—all right. What is it?"

He reached out and pulled her toward him. "Kiss me."

Her eyes opened wide, but he drew her so close the ruffles on her gingham apron brushed his chest. She hesitated, then closed her eyes and tipped her face up to his.

Yes! he sang inside. He bent his head and covered her mouth with his. She didn't flinch or jerk away as he feared she might. Instead her hand crept up to his shirt collar and she opened her lips under his. *Double yes!*

His brain spun. Maybe Marianne actually *liked* kissing him? Not only liked it but wanted more?

He deepened the kiss and felt something catch fire deep inside. After a long minute he lifted his head. "You are a lot of things, Marianne. And not all of them are admirable." He felt her head dip in a nod. "Some of them," he added, "aren't even likable."

Her head moved in another slow nod.

"But," he continued, his voice growing hoarse, "you are the most enticing female I've ever known." Her breath jerked in, but he didn't stop. "Touching you, kissing you, blows the top of my head to kingdom come."

They stood in silence for another long minute, both of

them short of oxygen. "Abe has been married four times," he whispered at last. "That's three wives too many."

"Lance, what are you trying to say?"

"I'm saying that getting married once is plenty for me, and I plan to make it stick." He pressed his lips to her forehead. "And I'm saying that I damn well plan to have it mean something."

Again he felt her head dip in a nod. "Do you remember when you kissed me at the wedding?" she asked.

"Yeah. I'll never forget it."

"I was scared. Could you tell?"

"Nope. You didn't seem scared to me, Marianne. You seemed sweet and soft and you were so beautiful my throat got all tight."

"Oh," she murmured. "Do you remember when you told me that we didn't like each other very much? Before we came out to Oregon."

He closed his eyes and bit back a groan. "Yeah, I remember."

"I think maybe you were wrong, Lance."

His heart stuttered. "Yeah? How much wrong?"

She gave a soft laugh. "Just a little bit wrong."

Suddenly he knew for certain that he wanted more out of this marriage of convenience arrangement. A lot more. God help him, he wanted everything. All of her!

"Dammit, Marianne, how much 'wrong' is 'a little bit wrong'?"

She looked up at him. "Lance, what exactly are you asking?"

"Marianne..." He closed his mouth, then opened it again. "Marianne, I'm asking if we could not just sleep *next* to each other. Maybe—" he gave her a hopeful look "—maybe we could sleep *with* each other? You know, maybe we could touch each other, just a little bit?"

"Maybe." Her voice had a smile in it, but he didn't know what to make of it.

"What do you mean 'maybe'?"

A long silence fell. "I don't know," she breathed. Her cheeks turned pink. "I have never…been with a man before."

"Yeah, I guessed that. Tonight, after we do all this advertisement thing, I'm going to reach over to your side of the bed and touch you, okay?"

She dipped her head again, but she didn't say a word.

"And," he continued, wondering why his throat was feeling so tight, "if you…um…like it, you could—"

"Reach over to your side and touch *you*," she finished.

He chuckled. "You're a quick study, Marianne. There isn't a day that goes by when you don't surprise me all to hell."

She laughed softly. "Is that good?"

"Yes, it's good. No man wants a boring wife."

Slowly they pulled away from each other, and Lance purposefully laid the notepad and all seven sharpened pencils on the kitchen table so they could get down to the business of composing ads. He had to work extremely hard to keep his gaze from straying to the bed.

They worked until long past midnight, suggesting one wording and then another, moving phrases around, trying out different verbs and richer adjectives. After the first hour Lance felt his body start to ache with wanting her. It got so bad he had to recite multiplication problems in his head to keep from slapping down his pencil and dragging her into his arms.

Finally, *finally*, Marianne reached across the table and laid her hand on his. "Lance," she said quietly. "We have done enough for one night. I think it's time we got some sleep."

Lance pushed back his chair and stood up, then held

out his hand. When she came to stand next to him he laid his forefinger under her chin and tipped her face up to his.

"I've been thinking about this all evening," he murmured.

"You were supposed to be thinking about our advertising posters," she said. But she smiled when she said it, and he thought maybe she wasn't being her usual work-until-you-drop self. She was at least *thinking* about something else besides business.

A spark of hope warmed his chest. Very slowly he folded his hands about her shoulders and pulled her into his arms. When he lowered his mouth to hers she didn't pull away; instead, she brought her hands to his chest, so he went on kissing her.

A buzzing began in the back of his brain. Excitement, he guessed.

But she didn't move away, and somewhere deep inside of him a hot bubble of joy began to swell into an aching need. Some instinct told him he needed to slow down or he'd scare her off, so he tried the multiplication table again.

Didn't work.

Chapter Fifteen

Marianne just about melted when Lance kissed her. His lips were gentle and a little hesitant, and then his kiss turned into something else, and a sweet hunger bloomed in her body.

His tongue touched hers, withdrew to trace her lips, then explored her mouth with slow, insistent strokes, asking her something, inviting. The feelings he incited were exquisite. Dangerous, even. It was frightening, and at the same time it was also thrilling. A rush of sensation swept through her, and after a while she could no longer think.

He lifted his mouth from hers. His breathing was uneven. "Is this telling you something?" he murmured.

"Yes." She whispered the word into his ear causing a sweet frisson to shiver down his neck. "It tells me you like kissing me."

"Yeah, I do like it, Marianne."

"Lance," she whispered. "We're both tired. I think maybe we should…get some sleep."

A chuckle escaped him. Guess she didn't want to come right out and say "go to bed."

She stepped away from him and disappeared behind the screen in the corner. After a moment he heard the soft thud of her shoes dropping on to the floor, and then she draped her blue skirt over the top of the screen, followed by her striped shirtwaist and then a white petticoat and an embroidered camisole.

Lance tore his gaze away, quickly stripped down to his drawers and stretched out on the bed. After a few moments Marianne appeared wearing her white nightgown; she floated across the room and crawled under the quilt.

He rose up on one elbow and leaned over her. "When I kiss you does it feel nice?"

She didn't answer for so long he thought maybe she'd fallen asleep.

"Marianne?" he pressed.

"Yes, Lance, when you kiss me it does feel nice. It feels frightening and sunshiny at the same time." She gave a quiet laugh. "That doesn't make much sense, does it?"

"It makes sense to me," Lance said softly. "Would you, um, like me to kiss you again?"

"Yes," she said softly. "N-no. Well, I do want you to kiss me again, Lance. But what I really want is for you to stop asking me all these questions and continue on with it."

Her answer sent a hot arrow into his chest. He would bet a thousand dollars Marianne had never in her life uttered words like that, words that were so bold. Arousing.

So he kissed her again.

And then he found himself at a crossroads. If he kept on kissing her maybe he could seduce her completely. But if it pulled her into something maybe she wasn't quite ready for, it would be a mistake they might both regret.

Suddenly *he* was the one who was hesitant. He wanted to taste her, swirl his tongue over her breasts, but something held him back. He didn't want to just physically seduce Marianne. He wanted to be close to her in a way that wasn't purely physical.

With a groan he rolled sideways and pulled her against

him. Her hair smelled like violets and something lemony, and he closed his eyes and inhaled deeply. She nestled her head under his chin and he felt something flutter underneath his breastbone.

He worked to steady his heartbeat, which was hammering away in his chest, and when she fell asleep, he just went on holding her. Lying in bed with Marianne in his arms made him happier than he could ever remember.

The next morning when they came downstairs Abe was bent over his leather-cutting table. He glanced up and stared at them for a long moment, and then his face cracked into a smile. "Glory be," he murmured, trying to hide his grin. "You two look plumb wore out, like you've been up all night." He set down his leather shears and waited.

Marianne suddenly felt tongue-tied. It was Lance who finally broke the silence. "We spent most of the night working on the Collingwood Boots advertisements."

"Ya did, huh?" Abe's amused eyes held his. "I sure do want to hear all about it. Yessir, that shows real…dedication. Real…" He coughed politely. "Uh…hard work."

Marianne thought Abe's grin spread so wide his face might split.

"Well," the older man said, "let's hear about yer plan."

She stepped forward and cleared her throat. "This morning I am going to send a telegram to the publisher, Brooks and Cassidy, in Philadelphia and inquire about their advertising rates. Then I…" She shot a quick look at Lance. "That is, I mean *we* will take the advertising copy we composed last night over to the editor of the *Sentinel* and have some posters printed up."

"And on Tuesday," Lance added, "I will personally deliver a stack of posters to every business establishment in Smoke River."

Abe nodded encouragingly. "Might take some to Gillette Springs, too," he suggested.

Marianne agreed. "And then, we will just stand back and watch the orders pour in."

Abe propped his hands on his hips. "Miss Marianne, I'm real sorry to say this, but we ain't hardly ready for a lot of orders to pour in. It'll take some time to teach Lance and Sammy here what they gotta know about this boot-makin' business. It ain't simple, like bakin' cookies. Ain't quick and easy 'til ya know what yer doin'."

Unperturbed, Marianne nodded. This morning she felt so filled with sunshine she would agree to anything and she would worry about how they would fulfill the orders once they came in. She gathered up the pages of advertising copy she and Lance had written, flashed him a smile, and set off for the newspaper offices.

The town's two rival newspapers, the *Smoke River Sentinel* and the *Lake County Lark*, sat directly across the street from each other. Jessamine Sanders was the editor of the *Sentinel*; her husband, Cole, ran the *Lark*. Marianne decided that separate advertisements for Collingwood Boots should appear in each newspaper, but she chose the *Sentinel* for printing up the posters. First, though, she would visit the *Lark*.

She stepped into the office to find a young girl seated before a rack of lead type. "I'm the typesetter," she explained. "Noralee Ness."

"Well, good morning, Noralee. Is your father the owner of Ness's Mercantile?"

"Yes, ma'am, he is."

"And are you the one who paints the storefront such pretty colors?"

"Oh, no. That's my sister, Edith. Papa hates it, but Edith wants to be an artist and Mama, um, makes him let Edith do whatever she wants."

Marianne laughed. "It certainly makes the mercantile appear unusual, doesn't it? Now," she explained, "I am the owner of Collingwood Boots, and I would like to run an advertisement in the *Lark*."

"Oh, yes, ma'am," the girl said instantly. "I can type-set it today, and it will come out in the Saturday edition."

Marianne thanked her, arranged for payment, and walked across the street to the *Sentinel* office. Eli, an older man with graying hair and a salt-and-pepper beard, greeted her at the counter.

"I would like to put an advertisement in your next edition. Could that be arranged?"

"Why, shore. Jes' lemme have them words you want printed and I'll see to it." He promised he would personally typeset the ad "soon as Miss Jessamine gets back from breakfast down at the restaurant with the editor of the *Lark*. They do that every morning," he confided. "Comparin' notes, you might say. Miss Jessamine says it keeps 'em both on their toes, newspaper-wise. Makes no sense to me, but them two seem to like doin' it."

Marianne understood perfectly. The two had a partner-ship, like she and Lance did. She left the *Sentinel* office and headed straight for the railroad station and the telegraph operator.

"A telegram? Sure thing, Miss," the man behind the desk said. "Whaddya want to say in this wire?"

She slowly recited the words of the telegram while he jotted them down, and when he finished she read over the completed message.

WISH TO PLACE ADVERTISEMENTS IN YOUR PUBLISHED BOOKS STOP PLEASE SEND RATES TO BURNSIDE, CARE OF COLLINGWOOD BOOTS STOP MARIANNE COLLINGWOOD BURNSIDE.

When she left the telegraph office she was so buoyed up at the prospect of hundreds of boot orders flooding in she made a beeline for the restaurant and ordered a big slice of Rita's peach pie.

"My stars," the waitress exclaimed. "You just missed your husband by sixty seconds. Don't you two eat together anymore?"

"Lance was here? What did he—?"

"Gosh, he talked so fast I could hardly tell what was on his mind. Something about leather-punching awls and ten-penny nails. But he sure smiled a lot."

Marianne studied the snowy tablecloth, feeling her cheeks grow warm. Was Lance happy because he was learning to make boots? Or was it because they were married?

Or was it because he had kissed her and held her in his arms last night?

"Rita, could I also have a big cup of coffee?"

"Sure. Funny, that's what Lance wanted, too. Your stove workin' okay?"

"Why, yes. I made a pot of coffee just this morning."

"Maybe somebody stopped by your shop and drank it all up," Rita joked.

"But who would do such a thing?"

The waitress bent toward her. "You know that woman, Eugenia Ridley? She came into the restaurant early this morning and was asking all about you and Collingwood Boots. Then she sailed out of here and headed straight for the livery stable."

"I fail to see—"

"Eugenia Ridley doesn't see to her own horse. She doesn't drive a buggy, either. And," Rita said in a confidential tone, "Collingwood Boots is right next door to the livery stable. I figure she just wants to snoop around."

"Oh." Marianne gulped down the mug of coffee Rita

set in front of her, waved away the pie, and set off for the shop. On the boardwalk outside the shop entrance she met Lance, and to her embarrassment he greeted her with a very public hug.

"Thank God you're back!"

"Why? What has happened?"

"Some busybody woman barged into the shop and pushed her way up the stairs into our living quarters. She asked about five hundred questions and drank up every last drop of our coffee!"

"Questions about what?"

Lance groaned. "Where did we come from? Who were 'our people'? What happened to Matthew Collingwood? And while she was guzzling down our coffee she kept eyeing everything in the place, especially our bed."

A giggle bubbled out of Marianne's mouth, and Lance's dark eyebrows went up. "That woman was Eugenia Ridley," she explained. "She turned up at Ness's mercantile when I was ordering our new bed, and she was over-interested in the Montgomery Ward catalog page I was consulting."

"If I'd known that, I'd have asked her to sit down. On the bed," he added.

Marianne laughed aloud, and then suddenly sobered. "I wonder how Mrs. Ridley got past Abe?"

"Abe's been bent over a hunk of cowhide all morning, swearing like a sailor. He hardly even looked up when Sammy arrived this morning. And that's another thing on Mrs. Ridley's sniff list. Sammy. And Abe."

"What about Sammy and Abe? Did Abe say anything insulting to her?"

"No. But she seemed awful interested in the fact that Sammy's an Indian and Abe is Negro."

Marianne frowned. "Why would that be any of Eugenia Ridley's business?"

"It isn't," Lance growled. "I think she just doesn't like Indians or Negroes."

Marianne felt a whisper of uneasiness crawl up her backbone. "Let's try to forget about Eugenia Ridley," she said. "We have more important things to discuss."

When they walked inside the shop, Abe looked up from the cutting table and grinned. "Glad yer back, Miss Marianne. Any luck with the newspapers?"

"Our advertisements will be published in tomorrow's issue of the *Sentinel* and the Saturday morning *Lark*. I can hardly wait to see them."

"Guess we better get us ready for a real rush of orders, huh?" Abe blurted out.

"I'm ready!" Sammy called from the back.

"Me, too," Lance added.

Abe snorted. "Not yet yer not. You two fellas got no idee how much work's involved in makin' a high-quality pair of ridin' boots. No cotton-pickin' idee."

His statement was met with silence.

"And," Marianne said after a moment, "I wired Brooks and Cassidy in Philadelphia about their advertising rates."

"Oh, lordy," Abe groaned. "We're gonna be flooded with more work than we kin handle in a month of Sundays. I think I need a shot of whiskey. Lance, you wanna join me?"

"Sure."

"I'll join you, too," Marianne murmured.

Abe's eyes widened. "Aw, you're a lady, Miss Marianne. Ladies don't—"

"This lady does," she said firmly.

"What about me?" Sammy yelled.

"You're too young!" three voices answered in unison.

Late that afternoon Sammy brought over a telegram from the telegraph office. Lance ripped it open while Marianne peered over his shoulder.

"Three hundred dollars!" she cried. "They want three hundred dollars to advertise in one of their books? Why, that's outrageous!"

"We only got two hundred dollars in the bank," Abe pointed out. "We cain't afford this Bricks and Corsets publishing place in Philadelphia."

"No, we can't," Marianne admitted. "Lance, what are we going to do? Think of something!"

Lance took her hand in his. "I would if I could, Marianne. My brain's been kinda blank ever since last night."

She turned the most delicious shade of rose-pink. Then she bit her lip until it turned a shade darker than a ripe strawberry, and he had to turn away.

She spun toward Sammy and Abe, who was still gripping his hammer in one hand and holding a handful of long nails in the other. "Think!" she ordered.

"When an Indian needs something they hold a potlatch," Sammy offered.

"A what? Spell it," Lance directed.

Sammy grinned. "P-O-T-L-A-T-C-H."

"Sort of a trade fair, right?"

"Yeah, sort of," the boy said.

"I seen one once," Abe said. "Got me a fancy huntin' knife and a year's supply of pemmican. Stuff tasted awful, like ground-up skunks."

"A trade fair…" Marianne murmured. "Maybe…"

Abe frowned. "Miss Marianne, I kin see them wheels turnin' in yer head. Kinda scares me, to tell the truth."

"Me, too," Lance admitted with a grin. "Marianne with an idea in her head is like a tornado looking for a place to touch down. Anybody in the way had better stand back and watch out."

"What if…" Marianne continued, tapping her forefinger on her chin. "What if we held a…a contest of some kind?"

Lance frowned. "What kind of contest?"

"I don't know. Maybe a contest of skill. Women hold cake bake-offs... What do men do?"

"Play mumblety-peg?" Sammy suggested.

"Or poker," Lance offered.

Abe thought for a minute and then his face lit up. "How 'bout marksmanship? Fellers always like to show off how good they can shoot."

"What about...a horse race?" Marianne murmured. "What if Collingwood Boots sponsored a horse race?"

Lance stared at her and then closed his mouth with a snap. "That's a smart idea, Marianne. Every man with a competitive bone in his body likes to show off his riding skill."

"Boys, too," Sammy insisted. "There could be a junior race. You know, for boys under sixteen."

"And maybe one for girls," Marianne said with a smile.

Sammy looked horrified. "Girls! You mean boys and girls in the same race?"

"Nah," Abe countered. "No self-respectin' male would race against a female."

Marianne looked thoughtful. "All right, we could hold three races, one for boys, and one for women, including girls, and one for all the competitive horseback-riding males in the county."

"We could charge an entry fee," Lance said. "Say, five dollars."

Abe scratched his chin. "Whaddya figure on offerin' as a prize, Miss Marianne?"

"Well, let me see..." She gazed around the shop with a calculating look on her face. "The first place winner in each race could win a pair of fine custom-made Collingwood riding boots. You can make junior-sized boots, can't you, Abe?"

Abe nodded. "Sure I can. As long as they're not too itty-bitty."

"Any rider with really small feet would be too young to enter a horse race, much less win a prize," Lance said.

They stared at one another until Lance broke the silence. "It's a good idea, Marianne. I bet Sammy knows all the trails in the valley. He could lay out the course."

"And Miss Marianne could line up the judges," Abe said with a chortle. "All she'd have to do is smile at 'em nice to get 'em to volunteer."

Marianne brought the chatter to a halt with a single question. "When?"

Abe scratched his graying head. "What about Fourth of July? There's always a big celebration on the Fourth, lotsa picnics and horseshoe games and such. And that'd mean lotsa spectators."

"And most people in the county come into town for the fireworks," Sammy volunteered. "There'll be plenty of horses."

"Which means," Marianne said with a slow smile, "plenty of people who will be needing riding boots."

Chapter Sixteen

News of the Fourth of July horse race sponsored by Collingwood Boots went through the county like wildfire. Both the *Smoke River Sentinel* and the *Lake County Lark* ran feature stories about it, and the men who gathered at Whitey Poletti's barbershop spent long hours discussing horseflesh and riding skill. After the first week, they also started placing bets.

Young boys suddenly began finishing up all their chores in record time and sneaking off to saddle up their ponies and practice careening around the hay bales in farmers' fields.

And people began pouring into Collingwood Boots to sign up for the race and pay the five dollar entry fee. One morning when Marianne was checking over the list of potential competitors for the women's race she discovered it even included one young girl, thirteen-year-old Annamarie Panovsky. Sammy confided that Annamarie could ride like the prairie wind, and that very day he signed himself up to ride in the junior boys' race.

To the delight of Carl Ness, the mercantile's stock of leather gloves and bandanas and fancy Stetsons sold out, and Stockett's Feed & Seed saw a huge increase in high-quality oat sales. And there were many nights when dressmaker Verena Forester stayed up past midnight stitching fancy new shirts in boys' and men's sizes.

While making deliveries with his wagon, Sammy made sure everyone in the county knew which ranchers and townspeople were entering the race, and betting at the barbershop ratcheted up. The Golden Partridge saloon sloshed more whiskey into more shot glasses and settled more arguments than bartender Tom Jameson could ever remember.

Every morning Abe marched off to the bank with a leather satchel bulging with entry fees. So far, forty riders had signed up, and the Fourth of July was less than three weeks away.

"Forty!" Marianne marveled. "That's two hundred dollars!"

"Who'd a thought folks in Smoke River was so competitive," Abe mused.

"Or so willing to fork over five bucks to see whether their horse could run faster than anybody else's," Lance added.

"Well, that's people fer ya," Abe scoffed. "Allus willin' to lay out their, uh…beggin yer pardon, Miss Marianne… lay out their, um, well, you know…to see whose is longest."

Marianne turned scarlet, and Lance laughed so hard he had to turn away.

"Even my mother will ride in the women's race," Sammy confessed one afternoon.

"Huh?" Abe exclaimed. "Didn't know Rosie even owned a horse."

"Yes," the boy confirmed. "My mother owns three horses. She taught me to ride on a fine black mare, and now I have my own horse."

The next afternoon in the utensil aisle at the mercantile Marianne overheard Eugenia Ridley's voice complaining loudly about Sammy's mother, Rosie Greywolf. "It's indecent, that's what it is! Positively indecent. Why, that woman is…well, everyone knows she's an Indian, for heaven's sake!"

"So what?" Marianne heard Carl Ness inquire. "Miz Ridley, is there somethin' about an Indian woman that makes her unable to ride a horse? Are they nearsighted, maybe? Or deaf?"

Marianne instantly decided to bake Carl a three-layer chocolate cake that very afternoon.

As the Fourth of July drew closer, Marianne began staying up past midnight every night, writing advertising copy for the newspapers. Lance worked on the planning details for the coming horse races, but he usually gave up long before Marianne did, puffed out the kerosene lamp and lay in the dark listening to the *scritch-scratch* of her pencil as she made notes on her notepad.

For the past week he'd been studying his wife, noticing how short-tempered she grew when she was tired or hungry and how she smiled at him a lot more when she was rested and her stomach was full. Tonight they had splurged on a supper of steak and fried potatoes at the restaurant, and while they lingered over their apple pie and coffee he noticed that Marianne was smiling warmly at him.

He guessed maybe it was time to advance his seduction plan one step forward. He thought it over during a second cup of coffee and then rolled his courage up into a ball and leaned across the table.

"Marianne?"

"Yes, Lance?"

"Marianne, I have a question for you."

She looked up and narrowed her eyes. "Oh? What is it?"

He opened his mouth, closed it, then opened it again, while she looked on in bemusement. "You, uh, you do like me, don't you?"

She waited such a long time before answering he began to sweat.

"Yes, of course I like you," she murmured. "People don't get married if they don't like each other."

"Some do," he said slowly. "Then there are people who, uh, resort to blackmail." He raised a pointed eyebrow.

She stared across the table at him. "Lance," she said in a hushed tone. "Are you saying you regret marrying me?"

"Oh, heck, no."

"Regret" was the furthest thing from his mind. In fact, there were days when he felt like dropping to his knees and thanking God he was the man Marianne had chosen to blackmail!

"I don't regret marrying you one bit," he assured her. "But…"

"But? But what?"

"Well, right now we have what some folks might call only half a marriage. You know, a marriage of convenience."

She said nothing, so he screwed up his courage and plunged ahead. "So I was just wondering if that's what we're gonna always have?"

Her eyes began to look troubled. "Well, maybe. I had not thought too far ahead."

Maybe? He ran that around in his brain for a good two minutes while Rita refilled their coffee cups and swished off into the kitchen.

"Lance, I don't really know how to describe our marriage."

He sighed. "Yeah. You didn't think about what being married really meant, did you? You just needed a husband so you could inherit your uncle's business, and I was it."

"Oh, no, it was more than that, Lance. Now I wish I hadn't blackmailed you into marrying me. It was dishonest."

"Yeah, it was dishonest all right." He let that sink in a moment. "But, Marianne, you know what? I'm not sorry."

Her knife clattered on to her plate. "You're not? Did you just say you're not sorry we got married?"

"No, I'm not sorry."

"W-well, why aren't you?"

That made him laugh. "Well, I guess it's because when it comes right down to it, I like you. Sure, you can be bossy and demanding and sometimes you think you know everything, but…I still like you."

She blinked hard and her eyes got all shiny. "Are you sure?"

He chuckled. "Sure I'm sure."

Then she asked him a single question that made him wish he'd never brought up the subject of marriage in the first place.

"Why do you like me?"

"Hell if I know," he muttered.

What he really wanted to know was whether Marianne wanted him the way he wanted her. But a man didn't just come right out and ask a woman that. She said she liked kissing him, but he wondered if that was all there would ever be to their marriage, just kissing?

She'd gotten what she wanted, a husband and her inheritance. And according to the bargain they'd made, he got what he'd wanted. He now owned half of Collingwood Boots.

But that wasn't all he wanted.

He didn't know whether he could stand lying beside Marianne every night and just kissing her. He wanted to touch her, all over. He wanted her to touch *him*. Some nights while she slept beside him he lay awake for hours, physically aching for her.

The truth settled in his chest like a rock. He was falling in love with Marianne, his marriage of convenience wife. And what he really wanted now was for her to love him back.

They finished their coffee and walked back to the shop in a silence so thick it was like wading through melted cheese. He wasn't about to give up on his Seduce Marianne campaign, but when she settled herself at the kitchen table with her notepad and a handful of pencils she'd worn down to a nub, he saw that, once again, nothing was going to happen between them tonight, and his heart sank into his boots. It looked like she'd retreated into herself the way she had back in St. Louis when something was on her mind. Guess he'd have to think some more about his seduction plan.

He took one of Abe's dime novels to bed, and for the next two hours he tried his best to concentrate on *Chasing the Dakota Kid*. He kept losing the plot, forgetting which character was the bad guy and not caring all that much about the outcome. After another hour Marianne gathered the pencils into a bunch, puffed out the lamp on the kitchen table and disappeared behind the folding screen in the corner to undress.

Lance snapped his book shut, doused the lamp and shed his clothes. Then he stretched out full-length on the bed to wait for her.

The rustles he heard coming from behind the screen were enough to inflame his imagination in ways a dime novel never could. What was she taking off? Her petticoat? Her chemise? He closed his eyes. Was there a lot of lace on whatever it was?

He was so tense his muscles quivered. Why were women's garments so complicated? They must be designed to drive men crazy by leaving them in a permanent state of arousal.

He heard something soft plop on to the floor, and the little sigh after that made him smother a groan. Water-splashing noises followed. Oh, for God's sake, she was standing there without a stitch on, taking a spit bath. The vision of her smoothing a wet cloth over her bare skin made his teeth clench.

Then she stepped from behind the screen. Moonlight illuminated the thin nightgown she wore, and Lance feasted
his gaze on the lush body he could glimpse through the
gauzy fabric. She moved to the china cabinet, where she
picked up a glass, pumped it full at the sink and drank it
while staring out the window.

After what felt like an interminable minute she set the
glass in the sink and slowly turned toward him. "Are you
awake?" she whispered.

Lance bit the inside of his cheek. If he admitted he had
been awake, watching her, she might put off coming to
bed. But if she thought he was asleep, maybe she'd just
walk across the room and get into bed next to him. So he
said nothing.

She slipped on to the double cot and with a sigh lay
down beside him. Before he could second-guess himself,
he twisted toward her and slid his arm across her waist.

With a squeak she jolted upright, and he stuffed down
a laugh.

"Oh! You're not asleep!" she accused.

"Nope."

"I—I thought you were. You should have said something."

"Why should I?"

"Oh." She said nothing for a full minute, and Lance
held his breath. Did she notice that his arm was still resting across her waist?

"Did you want to, um, talk about something?" she asked.

Talk! Hell, no, he didn't want to talk. He wanted to kiss
her silly!

"Nope."

"Lance, are you aware you are speaking only words of
one syllable?"

He almost choked. "No, I didn't realize that."

She lay without moving for so long he wondered if she'd

drifted off to sleep. Could she do that, with his arm draped across her? For the hundredth time in the last month he began to wonder just who Marianne Collingwood really was underneath the surface.

"Marianne?" he whispered.

"Y-yes?"

"There's something I've been meaning to ask you."

"What is it? About the shop?"

"Not about the shop, no. It's about…us."

He felt her body tense. "Oh," she breathed. "The 'us' of our business partnership? Or the 'us' of…well, *us*?"

"The 'us' of us."

She lay without moving, and that puzzled him. Was she staring up at the ceiling? Or were her eyes closed?

He rolled on to his side to face her and tightened his arm over her waist. "It's like this," he began. "I know we decided to be equal partners in the business."

"You don't want to change that, do you?" she said quickly. "Lance, you're needed at Collingwood Boots. Abe needs you. And…" She hesitated. "I need you."

"You do?"

"Yes, I do."

He found he couldn't stop smiling. "No, I don't want to change our partnership, Marianne. I want it to be… I want it to be more."

"You mean more than fifty-fifty, as we agreed?"

Lance expelled the air in his lungs. "I want to change the arrangement about our marriage."

Her body jerked. "You can't possibly want a divorce already? We've been married less than a month!"

"Hell, no, I don't want a—Marianne, I don't want a divorce. But I also don't want a marriage of convenience."

Her breathing changed, but she didn't say a word. Had she heard him? Did she understand what he was driving at?

"You don't want a marriage of convenience," she acknowledged, her voice quiet. "What…what *do* you want, then?"

"Remember back in St. Louis when you railroaded me into marrying you? I didn't fight against it too much because, to be honest, I kinda liked you all along."

She sat halfway up. "You did? Really?"

"Yeah, really."

"But I was so hard on you," she blurted out. "I ordered you around and complained about everything and—"

"Yeah," he said with a chuckle. "You were hard to get along with, all right. There are still times when that's true."

Marianne bit her lip. Was she really hard to get along with? Oh, of course she was, she admitted. Sometimes she heard herself snapping out orders just as she had back at Mrs. Schneiderman's.

"Lance, why are you bringing this up again now?" She glanced at him, trying to see his expression, but shadows obscured his face.

"Because I enjoyed getting married to you. I didn't think I would, but I did."

"Yes," she admitted. "That was very pleasant. The townspeople were nice to us, giving us that wedding reception."

"Marianne, that's not what I'm talking about here, and you know it."

Marianne let out a long breath. Yes, she did know it. The truth was she didn't know what to say. An even bigger truth was that she didn't have the first clue what to *do*. She had liked getting married to him, too. She had liked it so much she suspected she had been afflicted with "first man flush," something the older women boarders talked about.

She had never cared for a man before. Of course, she'd been so busy working for Mrs. Schneiderman she had never even walked out with a man. She had never attended an ice

cream social or a church service or a dance with a man.
She hadn't had time to set foot outside the boardinghouse!
Her girlhood had gotten gobbled up by endless batches of
pancake batter and afternoons communing with furniture
polish.

But now…

"I am failing at our bargain, aren't I?" she said in a
small voice.

He squeezed his eyes shut. "Part of it, maybe," he said.
"But it's not the business part I'm talking about. It's the
other part, the marriage part. And you're not 'failing' at it,
Marianne. I just want to change it."

For a moment she again couldn't think of what to say.
She'd never felt so unsure of herself. Underneath she felt
she was unattractive as a woman. Past her prime.

"Marianne, tell me what you're thinking." Then he
laughed quietly. "Actually, I don't figure I'm ever going
to know what you're *really* thinking. But, yeah, please tell
me what you're thinking."

She kept him waiting for a minute while she considered
what to share with him. "I am thinking that I don't know
what to do when I'm not in control of things. It makes me
uneasy."

"Yeah, I understand that. Being in control of pies and
roast chickens and a lot of dusty furniture is what you've
been used to, but maybe that isn't very satisfying."

"But it's what I know. That's all I'd been doing for years
and years before Uncle Matty's telegram came."

He said nothing.

"There's something else, too," she said. "I—I hate feeling that you're not happy with me."

He chuckled at that, and all at once she was afraid she'd
said the wrong thing. When he raised his head and pressed
a kiss on to her cheek, a warm glow of relief swept over her.

"I'm not unhappy with you, Marianne."

"You're sure? I thought—"

He pulled her down beside him. "You know what?" he said quietly. "You think too damn much."

"Oh." That was true, she acknowledged. But that was how she had survived after losing Mama and Papa, by thinking. Using her brain. She had put her wits to use and come to work for Mrs. Schneiderman.

"Lance, do I really think too much?"

"Sometimes, yeah."

She sighed. "I—I don't know how to be any other way," she admitted in an uneven voice.

Lance didn't speak. After a moment he leaned over and pressed his lips against her forehead. And then he moved lower and found her mouth.

He kissed her until he thought he would explode, but when he felt tears on her cheeks he lifted his head and wrapped both arms around her. Turning on to his side, he pulled her toward him until her bottom was tucked into his groin.

This wasn't seduction, exactly, but it was getting closer. He tightened his arms around her, and after a long while her breathing evened out.

For the next hour he lay thinking about partnerships and marriage and Marianne. There had to be a lot more to marriage than just seducing a woman. Especially if the woman was Marianne.

And because the woman he'd married *was* Marianne, he guessed he was in for a long ride and even more surprises.

Chapter Seventeen

After another largely sleepless night, Lance again woke from a fitful doze to find Marianne gone. She had left a pot of coffee on the stove, but her sturdy work oxfords no longer sat beside the folding screen in the corner, and he knew without looking that her clothes weren't there, either.

He listened for the tap-tap of Abe's hammer from below, but all was quiet. The clock read half past eight; why was it so quiet?

By the time he pulled on his jeans and a shirt, an irregular thumping sound below told him something unusual was happening down in the shop. The question was, what?

What he found when he reached the shop floor made him scratch his head. Marianne was bent over a sawhorse with a hammer in one hand and a short nail in the other, which she was positioning on top of a scrap of lumber.

"Marianne, what in blazes are you doing?"

She jerked upright and gave him a grin. "I'm practicing how to pound nails into this piece of wood. Abe said to pretend it's the sole of a riding boot."

The old man popped up at her elbow. "Don't know as them delicate little hands of yours are gonna be much good at boot-making, Miss Marianne. Why don'tcha stop and make us a pot of coffee?"

The hammer clunked down on to the piece of wood, and Marianne straightened, her mouth unsmiling and her eyes like two shards of green granite. "I will have you know, Abe Garland, that these 'delicate little hands' have scrubbed more floors and beat more carpets than you have walked on in your entire life!"

Abe backed away, and Sammy, working in the far corner on a piece of cowhide stretched across a table, looked up with an expression like a startled deer caught in the sights of a rifle. But Marianne wasn't finished.

"I own this business. I will not be relegated to house-maid duties," she pronounced in careful, clipped tones. "Don't any of you ever, *ever* ask me to make coffee again! Is that clear?"

Abe thrust both hands in the air. "Yes, ma'am, Miss Marianne, that's plenty clear."

She swept her gaze from Abe to Lance to Sammy and back to Abe. "We will *all* share coffee-making duties." She punctuated each syllable with short, chopping motions of her hand.

Whew! When she was mad, Marianne was hell on a fast horse. Lance had seen her this angry only once before, and that was when one of the boarders, who claimed to be an actress, wanted to practice a scene from a play and had insisted Marianne play the part of the wicked witch. The woman left the boardinghouse soon after.

While Abe and Sammy goggled at her, Lance retreated to Abe's tiny room, filled the coffeepot and set it on the small potbellied stove. Before he left he scanned the stack of dime novels in the corner and sighed gloomily. With Marianne so out of sorts, he figured it was going to be another long, lonely night planning the next step in his Seduce Marianne campaign.

When he returned, he found Abe and Sammy sweeping up leather scraps and sawdust around the shop with unusual vigor. Marianne propped her hands on her hips and confronted him.

"Don't you want to see what my 'delicate little hands' have accomplished?"

He hesitated, trying to catch Abe's eye, but the older man was industriously dumping his dustpan into the trash bin and avoided his gaze. She grabbed the scrap of lumber and thrust it under his nose. "Look! See all those nails?"

Lance looked. Sure enough, a double row of perfectly pounded ten-penny nails studded its length. He shook his head in disbelief.

"You hammered in all those nails?"

"I most certainly did! Aren't they beautiful?"

Behind her, Abe nodded and rolled his eyes. Lance wondered how long it had taken him to teach her how to handle a hammer. Tonight he'd check her thumb and forefinger for black-and-blue marks.

"Marianne, I never stop being surprised by you."

To his amusement she lit up like a kid at Christmas. "Did you ever think I could learn to hammer nails like that?"

"Nope. Not in a month of Mrs. Schneiderman Sundays." He meant it. He really was surprised.

"I can pound in tacks, too," she said proudly. "Tacks are lots easier than those big nails."

He bit back a chortle. "I'm doubly impressed."

"And," she added with a wicked twinkle in her eyes, "I can even make passable coffee! When it's my turn to make the coffee, I will do so."

Sammy and Abe dissolved in laughter, and then the front door flew open and their male guffaws in the shop were cut short as Eugenia Ridley bustled in. An over-feathered hat bobbed precariously on her graying head.

"I hear you're sponsoring a horse race on Fourth of July," she announced in an imperious voice.

Lance stepped forward. "Good morning, Mrs. Ridley," he said, his voice silky. "Beautiful morning, isn't it?"

She ignored him. "Well, are you or aren't you?" the woman demanded.

Marianne moved toward her. "Why, yes," she said in her most refined voice. "We are sponsoring a horse race, Mrs. Ridley. Do you ride?"

"Ride?" she snapped. "Of course I ride. This is Oregon, dearie. Everyone out here rides."

Unperturbed, Marianne smiled at her. "And do you own a horse? I understand many women out here in the West own their own mounts."

The woman's eyes narrowed. "I most certainly do own a horse," she retorted. "As a matter of fact, I own *two* horses."

"Oh, how interesting. Perhaps you have heard there will be a ladies competition? Will you be entering?"

The woman took a step backward. "Oh, well, I—I haven't ridden in some time."

"What a pity," Marianne said. "Then some other lady will win first prize. Young Annamarie Panovsky, perhaps. Or maybe Rosie Greywolf, Sammy's mother."

Eugenia Ridley's mouth opened and then clicked shut. "Really!" she said between clenched teeth. "Rosie Greywolf is fifty if she's a day. Besides, she's an Indian. I doubt if she is qualified. Indian women are not good horseback riders."

Sammy uttered something that was choked off when Abe poked his elbow in his ribs. Marianne turned a bland face on the woman before her. "I am so sorry you will not be entering. Young Miss Panovsky is a city girl, from New York City, I understand. And of course Rosie Greywolf is…"

She let her sentence trail off and waited, still smiling.

Mrs. Ridley's generous bosom swelled up into a broad shelf of red-and-yellow printed calico. "On second thought, I believe I will enter the women's race. My husband has been suggesting I get out of the house more now that our oldest daughter has married and moved to Gillette Springs."

"Excellent!" Lance said with feigned enthusiasm. "Just sign this form if you would, please. You can bring your entry fee over any time that suits you. Five dollars," he added.

Mrs. Ridley accepted the pen he offered and scrawled her name across the paper. Then she twitched her skirts into place and sailed toward the exit. "Rosie Greywolf, indeed," she sniffed. She banged the door so hard Marianne jumped.

The four of them stood staring at each other until Abe coughed loudly. "Lance, mebbe you better add some hooch to that coffee yer brewin'."

Chapter Eighteen

The Wednesday edition of the *Lake County Lark* carried not only the advertisement for Collingwood Boots Marianne and Lance had devised but an extra-long feature-length story about the upcoming Fourth of July horse race, written by editor Cole Sanders. Lance spread the front page out on the cutting table in the shop, and he and Marianne pored over every word.

"Marianne, just listen to this," he said as they bent over the paper. "'The horse-racing competition sponsored by Collingwood Boots promises to be the highlight of the July Fourth celebration. A junior boys competition and a women's race will be included in the festivities, with prizes donated by Collingwood Boots. So far, seventy-five riders have signed up to compete.'"

Seventy-five riders, Marianne thought, calculating anew the entry fees that would accrue to the business. "Why, that's almost four hundred dollars! That should buy enough cowhide to keep Abe busy for some time."

And, she thought with a spurt of enthusiasm, it would also pay for at least one advertisement in a Brooks and Cassidy dime novel.

The very next morning Eugenia Ridley was back. For a moment Marianne wondered if the woman had changed her mind about riding in the horse race, but that thought evaporated within the first three minutes of her visit. Mrs. Ridley twitched her skirt and leaned toward her in a conspiratorial manner.

"Yesterday when I visited your establishment I noticed something disturbing," Eugenia intoned direfully.

"Oh? What was that?"

"You should be more careful, dearie. Perhaps you hadn't noticed, but there was an Indian boy skulking around your shop."

"Skulking! Excuse me, Mrs. Ridley, but Sammy Greywolf is certainly not 'skulking.' Sammy is employed here at Collingwood Boots."

The woman's thin eyebrows went up. "Really?"

"Yes, really," Marianne replied sharply.

"Well, I never! I never would have thought— You do know he is an…? Oh, dear, there is simply no way to sugarcoat this. The boy is a savage!"

Marianne stared at her, feeling her hands close into hard fists.

"And—" Mrs. Ridley took a step closer "—that old man in the back? My gracious sakes, he is a *black* man."

"Yes," Marianne said, her voice tight, "he is."

"Dearie, you know as well as I do that until a few years ago his people were slaves, shiftless and uneducated. You shouldn't trust him."

Marianne had to work to keep her voice calm. "On the contrary, Mrs. Ridley. Abraham Garland has been the foreman here at Collingwood Boots for twenty years. As for being shiftless, if it were not for Mr. Garland's hard work, Collingwood Boots would have gone bankrupt years ago. And," she added with a bite in her tone, "Abe is not uneducated. Mr. Garland owns more books than my husband and I do between us."

Eugenia Ridley worked her rather prominent jaw back and forth but said nothing.

"Did you wish to withdraw from the July Fourth competition?" Marianne asked in her sweetest tone.

The woman drew herself up to her full height, which Marianne judged could be no more than five feet. "Certainly not," she exclaimed. "Why would I do that?"

"Mrs. Ridley, I hate to mention it, but your entry fee of five dollars has not been paid yet. I thought perhaps you had changed your mind."

"Nonsense!" the woman snapped. "I never change my mind. About anything."

Marianne clenched her jaw. "I can see that, Mrs. Ridley. Once your mind is made up, it most certainly remains—" she bit the inside of her cheek "—closed."

She expected the woman to flounce out of the shop in a huff, but instead she extracted five crumpled dollar bills from her reticule, grasped Marianne's hand and slapped them into her palm.

"I expect that I will win first prize in your ladies competition, dearie. And I will expect the pair of boots to fit my foot exactly." She lifted her skirt and waggled her black leather shoe.

Marianne bit back the words that danced on the tip of her tongue. Instead, she looked into the unblinking, hostile eyes of the Ridley woman and made an instant decision.

That afternoon Sammy set out to scout the course he would be laying out for the race. Both he and Lance were gone all afternoon, and by suppertime Marianne had worked up not only an appetite but a healthy dose of apprehension about her decision.

Chapter Nineteen

That evening, while she squished her fingers through the bowl of ground beef and chopped onion she was mixing up for her meat loaf, Marianne thought about what she had agonized over all day. Peeling potatoes and scraping carrots was not helping her to stay calm, and by the time she'd cobbled together an apple crisp for dessert she had worked up a full-blown case of nerves.

She wanted Lance to approve of her. She wanted him to keep on liking her. In fact, she was surprised at how much his regard mattered. It made her feel something she had never expected as the result of this marriage…valued. Not just tolerated, or obeyed, but valued. It made her feel that she truly *mattered* to him.

But this morning Eugenia Ridley had visited, and every other sentence out of the officious woman's mouth made Marianne cringe. The woman disapproved of Indians. She didn't trust Negroes. Somehow Marianne had thought people in the West would be free of that sort of prejudice.

When she and Lance had arrived in Smoke River the townspeople had been friendly and accepting. Now she was beginning to see something else; under the surface perhaps things weren't so different from the undercurrents of prejudice she had experienced back in St. Louis. Even though Mrs. Schneiderman had come from Germany when she was a young woman, she'd steadfastly refused to rent a room to anyone with a foreign-sounding name like Cohen or Wachowsky or Bloomberg. And the schoolteacher who taught at the private girls academy had been denied lodging just because her last name was Lipinsky.

She couldn't deny Eugenia Ridley's right to enter a horse race that was open to everyone. But she also couldn't pretend to like the woman. And for some reason she couldn't explain she didn't trust her. The uneasy feeling nagged at her.

She pressed her meat loaf into the baking pan and set it in the oven, then began mixing up the topping for her apple crisp and tried to keep her mind on what she was doing. The closer suppertime came, when Lance would climb up the stairs for their evening meal, the more nervous she grew.

When he finally appeared, dead tired after a long day of laboring under Abe's critical eye, she put her dilemma out of her mind and concentrated on feeding him. Everything went well until dessert, when she finally confessed her plan.

Lance stabbed his spoon into his bowl of apple crisp and stared at his wife. "You're going to *what*?" he shouted.

"I have decided to enter the ladies horse race on July Fourth."

"Have you gone crazy?"

Marianne slowly laid aside her fork and turned mossy green eyes on him. "No, I have not 'gone crazy,' as you put it. This is something I need to do."

"Why? You don't ride. You don't even own a horse!"

Calmly she spooned out a second helping of dessert for him and rose to refill their coffee cups. "I do ride," she said. "Though I admit I haven't been on a horse since I was ten years old." Her voice shook just the tiniest bit.

"Then why are you thinking of doing it now?"

She sidestepped his question. "Sammy said I could ride one of his mother's horses."

"You haven't answered my question," he pursued. "Why on earth do you want to enter this horse race?"

She looked everywhere but at him, at her coffee cup, at the pan of apple crisp, even the cream pitcher. "Well, I want to do it because…because Eugenia Ridley is so worked up about Rosie Greywolf's being an Indian that I am afraid she will cheat."

"Cheat? How could she cheat?"

"Oh, there are lots of ways. She could put a cocklebur under Rosie's saddle. She could feed Rosie's horse cough syrup to make it drowsy. She could slice through Rosie's reins so they would break during the race. She could… Oh, I don't know. I just know Eugenia Ridley can't be trusted."

Lance gulped down a swallow of coffee. "I don't even want to ask how you would know about shenanigans like feeding a horse cough syrup."

Unexpectedly she grinned at him across the supper table. "I listened to a lot of talk around Mrs. Schneiderman's dining table. You would be surprised at some of the things I learned."

Lance stared at her. *God help me, I don't know this woman sitting across from me at all!* Sure, he slept next to her every night, and he'd kissed her until he ached so bad he couldn't bear it, but did he actually *know* her? Know what went on inside her head? What she felt?

Good Lord, did all men feel their wives were total strangers to them?

Marianne was looking at him like a sleek cat who'd just finished a saucer of cream, and that made him wary. "Let me get this straight. You're going to ride in the horse race because you don't trust Eugenia Ridley."

"Yes."

He resisted the impulse to roll his eyes to the ceiling. "Marianne, just stop and think a minute. Even if Mrs. Ridley does do something unfair, what could you do about it?"

"Oh, Lance, I don't know. I just know that I don't trust the woman, and I have to do *something*. I can't let her think that nobody is watching what she does."

"I don't like it. Marianne, I don't want you to do this. You haven't ridden for years. It's dangerous."

"Lance, I'm not going to try to *win* the race. I just want to ride on the course along with the others, along with Annamarie Panovsky and Rosie Greywolf and Eugenia Ridley and the other women who enter. Carl Ness's wife, for instance."

"Huh?"

Marianne sent him a smile that made him uneasy and subtly changed the subject. "Did you know that Carl Ness's wife, Linda-Lou, was a fine horsewoman when she was young?"

"How young?"

"When she was sixteen."

"Yeah? How old is Linda-Lou now?"

Marianne shrugged. "Forty-something, I think."

Lance groaned. "Please don't do this, Marianne. Please."

"Why not?"

"Because you could get hurt." He set his shoulders. "Marianne, I forbid you to ride in that race."

That stopped her. Or at least it slowed her down for a minute or two. She pressed her lips together and said nothing for a long time. Then she exhaled a deep sigh and straightened her spine in that way he remembered from the years at Mrs. Schneiderman's, and suddenly he tensed.

"Lance, we have a partnership of equals. We do not have a marriage in which a husband can forbid his wife to do something."

"Maybe that's what we should have," he replied. "Didn't we promise to love, honor and obey?"

"We promised to love, honor and keep each other in

sickness and in health. We did not promise to 'obey,' if you remember."

He snorted. "Well, that was damned shortsighted of Reverend Pollock."

She flashed him an annoyingly sweet smile. "I think it was quite farsighted, if you ask me."

"Marianne…"

She picked up her spoon and swirled it around and around in her bowl of apple crisp. "I will need a pair of riding boots," she said slowly. "Tomorrow I'm going to ask Abe to measure my foot."

Chapter Twenty

Abe jerked away from the iron boot last he was hunched over and pinned her with disbelieving brown eyes. "You're gonna do what? Miss Marianne, ya wanna run that by me again?"

"I am going to enter the ladies' race on the Fourth of July."

He slapped his hand down on the leather sole he was stitching. "No, ya ain't, girl. Horse-racin' is dangerous out here if ya don't know what ya doin'."

She went on as if she hadn't heard him. "And I will need a pair of riding boots."

"No, ya don't." He shoved the boot last to one side.

"I most certainly do, Abe."

He shook his head. "Maybe I shoulda asked if Lance approves of this harebrained plan you come up with. Does he?"

"Well, no, he doesn't."

"But yer gonna do it anyways," Abe muttered. "It's writ all over yer face. I shoulda knowed a woman pretty as you ain't got a lick of sense."

Marianne reached over and patted the gnarled hand resting on the half-finished boot. "You know that's not true, Abe. I have very good sense." *Usually.*

He surveyed her with shrewd brown eyes. "Been kind of a short marriage, hasn't it?"

Marianne felt her cheeks grow warm. "Our marriage isn't over," she protested. "It's just, well, undergoing some, um, growing pains."

"Miss Marianne, I been married before. And if there's one thing I know for sure it's this—a marriage that's got 'growin' pains' is a marriage that's about to bust wide open."

Marianne shook her head. "Abe, didn't you and your wife ever disagree on something?"

He thought for a minute. "Well, I had plenty of disagreements with wife number two," he said slowly. "And me an' wife number four fought like wet cats."

"And what happened?"

His face changed. "Well, now, me and wife number two argued 'bout most everything. Her name was Clarabelle, and she was real fussy. She didn't like her bacon too crisp or her dresses too loose or her husband too spine-stiff. She didn't like a whole lotta things, and after a while I decided I didn't like her not likin' so many things, an' I called it quits."

"You mean you gave up," Marianne accused.

Abe's graying eyebrows pulled into a frown, but he didn't answer. "Now, wife number four, name of Lacey, she just up an' left."

"Because of a disagreement?"

"Guess so. Never did know 'xactly what tumbled her out the door. One mornin' I jest woke up and she was gone. Didn't leave me a note nor nuthin'."

"What was your disagreement about? It must have been about something important."

"Near as I kin remember, it was whether brown sugar or white sugar tasted better in a cup of tea."

Marianne laughed. "Abe, no woman leaves a man over a cup of tea. There must have been something else going on in your marriage that she wasn't happy with."

"Huh! Most often a feller don't have a gnat's idea what's goin' on in his marriage."

"I think Lance might," Marianne said quickly. Her face must be scarlet by now, she thought. She was remembering Lance's kisses and how much she looked forward to night-time when they lay close in their cobbled-together bed. "I think Lance understands many things about his marriage," she repeated.

Abe went on as if he hadn't heard her. "Now, wife number one, she didn't like a lot of things, either, but I usually jest gave in. That's why we stayed married as long as we did."

Marianne thought guiltily about Lance's disapproval of her decision to enter the ladies' race. About his actually *forbidding* her to enter. Was she wrong to want to do something Lance didn't want her to do? Did being married mean that a wife could do only those things her husband allowed?

Abe was looking at her with a strange expression on his lined face, half sympathy and half worry. "Miss Marianne, I'd be honored if you'd come back to my little room and let me make you a cup of strong coffee. You look like you need some shorin' up. And," he added in a low voice, "some good advice, straight from the shoulder."

She followed him to his tiny quarters at the back of the shop and watched him fill the speckleware pot with water and dump in a handful of ground coffee beans. His place was neat as a pin, she noted. She'd bet Eugenia Ridley's kitchen wasn't half as tidy.

"Set yerself down a spell, Miss Marianne, an' get ready to listen to the smart things ol' Abe's gonna tell you 'bout bein' married." He gestured at a blanket-draped wooden apple box. She perched uneasily on top and watched Abe lift two coffee mugs off the nails in the wall.

"You ain't been married but a month, Miss Marianne."

"A month and four days, to be exact," she said.

"An' already you're rockin' the boat. Now, is that 'cuz you got yer man so tied up in love knots he cain't tell whether he's comin' or goin'?"

"No," she answered quickly. "I don't believe Lance is tied up in…knots. He's just flexing his male muscles by telling me what I can and can't do because…well, because no doubt that is how his parents raised him."

"An' how's that?" Abe inquired.

"Oh, you know. A man is supposed to provide for his wife, and in return a good wife is supposed to obey her husband."

"Lemme ask ya this, Miss Marianne. Ain't you tied up in just a teeny tiny love knot yourself?"

Marianne opened her mouth to reply, then thought better of it. Instead, she bit her lip and focused her gaze on the coffeepot. Yes, she supposed she was just a teeny-tiny bit in love with Lance. "What difference would that make, Abe?"

"Makes a whole passel of difference! You wanna do things that please him, don'tcha?"

"Yes, I do."

"Well, then? Seems to me what ya need to do is obvious."

"Abe, I am used to being independent, making my own decisions. All those years I spent at the boardinghouse, from the time I was thirteen years old and on my own, taught me that I, and I alone, am responsible for my life."

Abe snorted. "Well, ya ain't thirteen years old now, my girl. You're all growed up and married, and that means you have diff'rent responsibilities. Like I said, what ya need to do, or in this case *not* do, is obvious."

But it was *not* obvious, she thought. Did caring for a man mean that a woman didn't have a mind of her own? That a woman didn't have her own ideas about things? To say nothing about her own preferences about things and people and events in life?

Abe laid a work-worn hand on her shoulder. "I kin see yer brain is rasslin' around inside that head of yours. Is it producin' any sensible thoughts?"

Marianne sighed. "Abe, here is the problem in a nutshell. I think my thoughts *are* sensible. I think any woman, even a married woman, has to make up her own mind about things and do what she thinks is right."

Abe groaned. "I knowed you was stubborn the minute I set eyes on ya that first day you came to the shop. Miss Marianne, ya ain't dumb, jest stubborn. So I want you to set still and listen to what I'm gonna tell ya. Agreed?"

She nodded.

"Peace between a man and a woman is a beauteous thing," he began. "But it ain't always easy to get to. You followin' me?"

"Yes, I'm following you," she murmured.

He grabbed a pot holder and lifted the coffeepot off the stove, poured out two mugs and handed one to her. "Well, then, ya gotta ask yourself this here simple question. What's more important, getting' yer own way or havin' peace between you an' Lance?"

She wrapped both hands around the coffee mug. "Abe, it isn't really about 'getting my own way.' It's about thinking for myself. Deciding what is important *for me.* Can you understand that?"

"Nope," Abe shot. "An' I wager Lance don't understand it, either."

Marianne took a sip of her coffee and wondered what to say. She took another sip, and then another, and then suddenly she knew. "Abe, the truth is, any person, male or female, even a married woman, needs to do what she thinks is right."

"You're sure about that, are ya?"

Marianne stared at him. "Yes, I am. The more I think

about it, the more sure I am. I have the right to think for myself and to make decisions for myself."

Abe looked skeptical. "But don't fergit that now you're a wife. And when there's two in the saddle, they gotta work together. A wife don't make decisions jest fer herself, does she?"

"But does 'working together' mean that a husband and wife have to think the same way about everything? Agree on everything?"

Abe frowned and slurped coffee in through his teeth. "Well heck, Miss Marianne, now ya done asked me a question I cain't rightly answer."

Marianne tried to smile at him. "It's like going to war, in a way. You march out to make sure something happens, or that something *doesn't* happen, but either way you're standing up for what you believe and what you think is right. Do you see?"

"Nope. Well, maybe. But think on this, Miss Marianne. There's a heap of difference between thinkin' fer yerself an' actin' on something. 'Specially if yer partner don't want you to do whatever it is. It's the same in a business partnership. You an' Lance own Collingwood Boots together. You're partners, right?"

Marianne nodded.

"Well, ya wouldn't go off an' make a business decision about Collingwood Boots without gettin' his approval, wouldja?"

She hesitated. "No, I wouldn't."

"Well, ain't a marriage the same kind of a partnership?"

Tears welled up in her eyes.

Abe reached over and awkwardly patted her shoulder. "Aw, now, honey-girl. Ain't no need to dissolve in a puddle of unhappiness."

But there *was* a reason for the puddle, she admitted. She never, never should have blackmailed Lance into marrying her. She was a terrible wife, and the awful thing was that she didn't know how to do any better. She knew Lance wanted more from her. He wanted a real marriage, not a marriage of convenience, but she didn't know the first thing about what a "real" marriage entailed.

And if a "real" marriage meant always obeying your husband... She swiped tears off her cheeks.

"Gosh, Miss Marianne, I didn't mean to get you all upset-like."

"Oh, Abe, I am a failure as a wife."

"No, ya ain't, honey-girl. No, ya ain't."

"Yes, I am. I feel so...so inadequate. Before Lance and I even met I was an over-the-hill spinster. On the shelf, other women said. He could have married someone much better than me—I won't ever be enough for him."

"Now that's plumb crazy talk, Miss Marianne." He reached into his pocket and pulled out a big white handkerchief. "You're a right pretty woman, and it sure seems to me you're plenty 'enough' for any man. He couldn't do no better 'n you." He pressed the handkerchief into her hand.

She mopped at her eyes. "Even if I could learn to be the kind of wife Lance really wants, is the price a woman has to pay for a happy marriage simply obeying her husband regardless of how she feels?"

He snatched the handkerchief back and blew his nose. "I dunno, honey-girl. But I do know one thing. You sure do ask the damnedest questions!"

Chapter Twenty-One

The next day Lance worked all day bent over a table cutting out boot patterns from a sheet of prime cowhide under Abe's supervision. By six o'clock his back muscles ached and he was hungry and dead tired. Marianne had made herself scarce since morning, retreating upstairs to their quarters after sharing a cup of coffee with Abe. She had looked red-eyed and distressed, and that was so unlike her Lance wondered what was wrong.

As evening came on, Abe set his hammer aside and laid a hand on his shoulder. "Quittin' time, Lance. Ya got nuthin' left on that cuttin' table but leather scraps."

Lance plunked down his shears and began to massage the thumb on his cutting hand. "Never thought carving out pieces of cowhide could be so tiring. Worse than building a fence any day."

Abe chuckled. "Yeah, makin' boots is a lot harder'n folks realize. Ranchers know. That's why they're willin' to pay top price for a fine pair."

"Sure makes a man hungry," Lance muttered.

Abe sent him an odd look. "Maybe Miss Marianne's cookin' up somethin' delectable for yore supper. She hasn't poked her head out all day."

"She looked upset this morning, Abe. Any idea what's bothering her?"

Abe busied himself gathering up scraps of cowhide. "Where's Sammy?" he inquired in a low voice.

"Off delivering sacks of chicken feed for Abraham Stockett. He's been gone a couple of hours. You didn't notice?"

"Been busy," the older man said shortly.

"Abe, have you got any idea what Marianne is upset about?" It was the second time he'd asked that question, but maybe Abe hadn't heard him the first time.

"Yeah, kinda...sorta," Abe said. "It's about you forbiddin' her to ride in the horse race on July Fourth. You know, expectin' her to obey you just 'cuz you're her husband."

Lance stared at him. "You really think that's what got her so het up? She hasn't been riding since she was a kid, Abe. I don't want her to get hurt."

"Mebbe. I don' wanna be tellin' ya what to do, Lance. But it might be somethin' to think on, givin' her an order like you was in the army."

"Okay, I will think on it. I promise."

Abe grinned. "Another thing ya don't wanna do, son, is be late for supper."

Lance cleaned his cutting shears and put them away, then tramped up to the apartment. His shoulders ached. His temples throbbed. And with Marianne upset about something, his spirits were dragging.

The sight of Marianne bustling about the tiny kitchen in a ruffly red gingham apron lightened his mood. Partly it was the delectable smells coming from the oven; partly it was just watching her tend to the pots and pans with that determined look she got in her green eyes when she was concentrating on something.

He was a lucky man, he acknowledged. Lucky to have married a woman he admired. One he genuinely liked. Every time he looked at her, he got all sorts of quivery feelings inside.

She gave him a tentative smile. "You look tired, Lance."

"Yeah. Cut out about a thousand leather pieces today. Abe wanted them done just so, and it's not as easy as it first appears."

Marianne nodded. "A whole day with Abe looking over your shoulder cracking a whip must be worse than a whole day at Mrs. Schneiderman's with me cracking *my* whip."

"Not true," he said. He took a step toward the kitchen table where she was laying out the plates. "You're a lot prettier than Abe."

She laughed, and then her cheeks turned the most delectable shade of pink. Suddenly he wasn't near as tired as when he'd walked in. In fact, he felt a definite warmth flooding through his aching body, rejuvenating it in the most exciting way.

But he could sure sense the tension in her; he felt like he was walking on eggshells. Something was seriously bothering her, and he hoped to God it wasn't him.

"Sit down, Lance. Supper is ready." She dished up a bowl of savory-smelling stew and plopped two big, fluffy dumplings on top. He sat down and leaned forward to breathe in the delicious aroma.

"Lordy, that smells good!" He looked up and their eyes met. "You're a really good cook, Marianne. That means a lot to a hungry husband."

She looked startled, then a little flustered, and then a slight smile turned up the corners of her mouth. "Eat, Lance. Before it gets cold." She served a bowl of stew for herself and settled on to the chair across from him.

They ate in silence. Lance gobbled the dumplings first, then spooned carrots and potatoes and chunks of tender beef into his mouth until his spoon scraped the bottom of the bowl.

Marianne barely touched her supper. He watched her toy with her spoon, idly turning over chunks of onion but not putting anything into her mouth. She glanced at his empty bowl and without a word she rose and ladled out another serving for him, added two more dumplings, and set the coffeepot on the stove.

Lance studied the glistening dumplings before him and racked his brain for something to say. "Marianne," he said at last, "you're not eating any supper. Is…is something wrong?"

"N-no. Well, yes, Lance. I'm worried about the Fourth of July race."

"What about it?"

She didn't answer for a long minute, just trailed her spoon around and around in her bowl of stew. "I'm worried about, um, about the riders. The women riders."

"You still worrying about whatshername, Eugenia Ridley, huh?"

"Yes."

"Anything else on your mind?"

After a pause she nodded her head, and he waited, his nerves jumping, until he thought he'd crawl out of his skin. "Yeah? What else?"

"Oh…" She turned her spoon over and over in her hand. "About what to do about Eugenia Ridley."

He clanked his spoon down on the table and leaned forward. "Marianne, you can't ride in that race. You haven't ridden for years, and it isn't that easy to get used to sitting on a horse in a hurry."

"I know that."

He elbowed his bowl of stew to one side and reached to capture her hand. "Doesn't anything ever scare you, Marianne?" She squeezed his fingers compulsively and bent her head, and all at once he realized she was close to tears.

"Yes," she said in a shaky voice. "When I am cold and hungry I get frightened. I've been that way ever since I was young."

It tore him up inside to see her cry. In all the years he'd known her he'd seen Marianne cry only once, when a little orange kitten she'd adopted had been killed by the neighbor's dog. That morning she sank down on the back porch step and mopped away at her tears for a good half hour.

"I'll tell you what scares me," he said slowly. "It scares me that you want to ride in that horse race. And—" he looked away from her "—it scares me when I think you might get hurt."

"You know what I've always hated?" she said suddenly.

"Besides me forbidding you to enter that race?" he said with a tired smile.

"Yes, besides that. Actually it has nothing to do with you, or that horse race, either. When I was a girl, after my mother and father died, I grew to hate wearing hand-me-downs. Underclothes, especially. I think that's why I always want to have pretty, frilly undergarments. Even before I purchase aprons and sensible work skirts, I buy lacy underwear. I bet you've never noticed that."

Oh, he'd noticed, all right. Every night when she undressed and draped her garments on top of the folding screen he could scarcely take his eyes off her camisole and those lace-edged drawers. He'd have to be a statue to not notice.

"Look, Marianne. I'll wash up the dishes tonight. Why don't you crawl into bed and...um...maybe read one of Abe's novels?"

"I made a peach cobbler for dessert. Don't you want any?"

"Sure, but I can dish it up myself. You take it easy."

She gave him a searching look, then stood up, slid the bubbling pan of cobbler out of the oven and set it on the stove top. She sent him a quick look and plunged an over-sized serving spoon into the center.

"Smells good," he murmured. "Sure you don't want any?"

She shook her head. "I'm not hungry."

He found he had no more appetite, either, even for Marianne's peach cobbler, so he cleared the dishes off the small kitchen table and poured the bucket of heated water into the sink. While he washed and dried the cups and bowls, Marianne disappeared behind the folding screen in the corner.

He heard her shoes clunk on to the floor, and he tried not to watch as once again her garments appeared over the top of the screen. First came her blue work skirt, then a white petticoat, followed by her camisole. By the time her lacy drawers appeared, Lance was so aroused he had to grit his teeth.

Methodically he wiped the dishes and stowed the clean silverware in the cutlery drawer, then snatched up the novel he'd borrowed from Abe's library. *Rustler's Revenge*. He moved the kerosene lamp to the night table, stripped off his clothes and crawled into bed.

But instead of cracking open his novel, he found himself waiting for Marianne to emerge from behind the screen.

Chapter Twenty-Two

Before she stepped out from behind the folding screen, Marianne heaved a long, tired sigh. A lamp burned beside the bed, and Lance was propped up against a stack of pillows, an open book in his hands, something with a red cover featuring a masked rider and some cows. She hesitated, then padded across the floor, slipped under the quilt and curled up on her side, facing away from him. Closing her eyes, she tried to talk herself into falling asleep.

No luck. She was excruciatingly aware of him. She could hear his slow breathing, smell the piney scent of soap on his skin and feel the warmth of his body next to hers. She even fancied she could hear the soft, steady thump of his beating heart.

She couldn't confess how alone and uncertain and just plain scared she was that she was going about this marriage all wrong. She lay without moving, willing herself not to roll toward him and seek solace in his arms.

She heard the rustle of paper as he turned a page. Was he really reading? Or was he watching her?

Another page flipped over, and she bit her lip. She had done nothing all day but worry and cook and think about Lance. Was he thinking about *her*? How could he focus on that silly cowboy story when she was feeling so undone inside?

Oh, be reasonable. I barely spoke to him all day. Why should he feel anything but indifferent toward me now?

She hunched herself into an even tighter ball and struggled to hold back tears. *What on earth is wrong with me? I feel like crying because...because I don't know what to do.*

She hated not feeling in control. Ever since she had found herself alone in the world she had tried to control the uncertainties in her life. Lance was the biggest uncertainty she had ever encountered. Now, God help her, they had quarreled, and she didn't know what to do.

Lance studied Marianne's inert form beside him until he couldn't stand it one more minute. He snapped his book shut, puffed out the lantern and edged closer to her. She didn't so much as twitch, so he carefully curled his body around hers and settled his arm across her waist. After a long minute she did something that surprised the hell out of him. She snuggled her bottom into his groin.

She felt soft and warm, and if he bent his neck he could smell the lemony scent of her hair. He smiled into the dark and kept on smiling, even when his body began to react to her closeness.

God, he wanted her so much he ached.

"Marianne," he whispered.

"Yes?" Her voice sounded drowsy.

He tightened his arm across her waist. "Nothing. Just... Marianne."

Chapter Twenty-Three

The following week Marianne looked up from the counter and smiled as Ivan Panovsky opened the door of Collingwood Boots and escorted his sister, Annamarie, inside.

"Good morning! Have you come to place an order?"

"Ah, no, Missus," the tall, dark-haired man replied. "I bring my sister Anna to pay entry fee for horse race."

"Oh?" Her smile deepened. "For the ladies' race, is that right?"

"Is right," Ivan affirmed.

"And will you be entering the men's race?"

A laugh burst out of Annamarie. "Ivan? Oh, no, Mrs. Burnside! Ivan has hated horses ever since one stepped on his foot back in New York."

"But my Anna," the young man said, "she likes to ride. She can now enter race?"

"She most certainly can, Mr. Panovsky."

"What is cost, please?"

"Five dollars." Mentally she tallied up the entry fees collected thus far. Over three hundred and seventy-five dollars now, enough for one full-page advertisement or two smaller ones with the biggest publisher of dime novels in the country.

"Are you an experienced rider, Miss Panovsky?" Marianne asked as she filled out the entry form.

"Oh, yes, ma'am. At least I think I am. The sisters who

taught horsemanship at the orphanage in New York said
I was a natural. Whatever that means," she added with a
soft laugh.

"Is not natural," Ivan interjected. "Kicking heels in side
of animal is not pleasant for horse."

"Ivan," the young woman intoned. "Please."

The young man sighed. "Is not natural, but my Anna,
she want to be like Western girl, so she wish to race."

Marianne caught the girl's pleading look and nodded.
"Very well. Sign here, please." She pointed to the signature
space, and when the girl scrawled her name, Marianne sent
her another smile. "The race course will be laid out soon,
Annamarie. Perhaps you would like to inspect it?"

"Oh, no, I—"

"We will inspect," her brother interrupted. "Is more safe
to inspect before riding."

Marianne bit her lip. Sammy would be marking off the
final route shortly. Maybe she should inspect the course,
as well.

When Ivan and his sister left the shop, Marianne took
herself off for a long walk to sort out her thoughts. She
marched down one side of the main street and up the other,
weighing the pros and cons of disobeying her husband. She
hadn't actually signed up for the race yet; she wanted to be
absolutely sure about what she was doing.

When she returned to the shop she found Sammy's
mother, Rosie Greywolf, pacing up and down outside. The
sinewy Indian woman stopped short at the sight of her.

"Hello, Missus. You know me?"

"Yes, you're Sammy's mother. You work at the restaurant."

The woman's tanned face dipped in a short nod. "I hear
about horse race."

They moved on into the shop. "Yes, on Fourth of July.
Sammy is laying out the course for it."

"I want to ride in race. Okay?"

Marianne blinked. "Of course it's okay, Rosie. I already believed you were going to. Sammy said you taught him to ride when he was young."

The woman grinned. "I teach good," she asserted. "Horse good, skill good. I teach."

Marianne studied the Indian woman. "Rosie, I—"

"You ride in race, Missus?"

She opened her mouth to reply, then snapped it shut. "I'm not sure. It has been many years since I have ridden a horse."

"No problem," Rosie said. "I teach."

Marianne blinked. "What?"

"I teach, like Sammy. You have horse?"

"Well, no, I don't."

"No problem, Missus. You ride one of my horses. Very gentle."

"Oh, but I... I have to think about it."

"You could do," Rosie insisted. She held Marianne's gaze. "Husband not know," she murmured.

"Oh. Oh, but—"

The woman's dark eyebrows rose and fell. "You want husband to know?"

"Oh, Rosie, I'm not sure I—"

"Rosie is sure." Her eyes twinkled. "Rosie see many things."

Marianne leaned toward her. "I tell you what, Rosie. I will pay your entry fee if you let me ride one of your horses."

"Deal," Rosie said. She thrust one hand forward, firmly clasped Marianne's fingers and pumped her arm up and down. "First lesson tomorrow morning, Missus. Before sunup."

For the rest of the day, Marianne drifted in a fog of indecisiveness. Whatever was she thinking, talking with

Rosie Greywolf about riding lessons? She hadn't been this apprehensive about anything since the day she walked up Mrs. Schneiderman's front steps and asked for a job.

Now she was facing another crossroads, and another decision. Was she really going to defy Lance and ride in this horse race?

Chapter Twenty-Four

"Abe, you have any idea what's eating Marianne?"

Abe sent Lance a wry look across the cutting table he was bent over. "Son, I stopped tryin' to figger out a female before you was born."

Lance met the older man's gaze and frowned at the expression he saw on his face. He'd bet his last two-bit piece Abe knew more than he was telling. But how was he going to worm it out of him?

"Know what I think?" he ventured.

"Nope," Abe said.

"I think Marianne's hiding something from me."

"You do, huh?" Abe said, his voice bland. "Hidin' what?"

"Hell, if I knew that I wouldn't have to ask, would I?"

"Nope, ya wouldn't, and that's a fact."

"I just can't figure out what a sensible, straightforward woman like Marianne would be hiding."

"Mebbe you figger she's in love with somebody else," Abe said with a sly grin.

Lance fumbled the pair of leather shears, which flipped out of his hand and sailed on to the floor. "Huh?"

Abe scooped up the shears and tried not to laugh.

Lance stared at him. "Abe, c'mon. What do you know that I don't?"

"Nuthin'. It'd take a smarter feller than me to figger out Miss Marianne."

"Yeah," Lance said, his tone disbelieving. Abe knew something, he was sure of it. But the man was closemouthed as a clam.

"Listen," the older man said. "We got pretty near eighty riders signed up for the horse race now."

Lance recognized a red herring when he heard one, but he figured he'd play along. "Oh, yeah?"

Abe slapped his leather shears down on the cutting table. "Yep. Old 'uns. Young 'uns. Even ladies."

"Ladies," Lance echoed. "Any ladies we know?"

"Yep. Real sweet little gal, Annamarie Panovsky, come in with her brother and paid her five bucks yesterday mornin'. And then Sammy's ma, Rosie Greywolf, signed up. And that nosy busybody Eugenia Ridley, the one who allus wants to know everythin' 'bout everybody, she's signed up, too."

Lance snapped the blades of his leather shears open and closed four times. Abe hadn't succeeded in distracting him as much as he thought. He still figured the canny old man knew more about Marianne than he was telling.

"You notice anything different about Marianne lately, Abe?"

Abe studied the boot last he was bent over. "Well, yesterday she done borryed one of my new dime novels. *Cowboy's Lady*, it was. Kinda flowery title, iff'n ya ask me."

Lance said nothing. Marianne had packed a few books in her trunk when they'd come out to Oregon, a Bible, an etiquette book, *Oliver Twist* by Charles Dickens, a volume of crochet patterns, and lots of cookbooks. *Cowboy's Lady* wasn't typical of his wife's reading preferences. But he had to admit yet again that Marianne was still very much an unknown quantity.

"That strike you as odd, Abe? Her reading a dime novel?"

"Cain't say, son. All women have secrets that a man, even a clever one like you, ain't never gonna guess."

Lance gritted his teeth. Oh, hell. He was never going to figure out what went on in Marianne's head. *I might as well give up and just concentrate on what happens between us in bed at night.*

That idea made him feel better. Just thinking about lying next to Marianne in the dark made him hot all over. He guessed he was smiling because Abe sent him a sharp look.

"Somethin' funny, Lance?"

"Not exactly. I was just working out a plan for tonight." Thinking about that kept him on edge for the rest of the day.

Late that afternoon, Lance found himself seated at the kitchen table, poring over Marianne's well-thumbed copy of *Mrs. Beeton's Household Receipts*. His wife had gone off to the telegraph office and then to visit dressmaker Verena Forester with young Annamarie Panovsky, and Lance planned to surprise her with supper when she returned.

He should have considered his plan more carefully, he realized, because the truth was he didn't even know how to boil an egg! After staring at the pages of recipes and instructions for an hour, he set off to the mercantile for help.

Carl Ness took pity on him. "Baked beans and coleslaw," he suggested. But then the mercantile owner said the beans should be soaked overnight, and that stopped the baked beans idea.

Abe was more help. "Why don'tcha make my Poverty Pie? It's real simple, just bacon, tinned tomatoes and sweet corn, and some grated cheese on top. And ya don't need no recipe."

No recipe, huh? That made him heave a sigh of relief. He climbed the stairs back up to the apartment, slipped Marianne's ruffly red-checked apron over his neck and tied it in back. Then he opened the cooler, found the slab of bacon and carved off four thick slices, laid them in one of Marianne's medium-sized skillets and chunked up the fire in the stove. While the bacon sizzled he pried open the tinned tomatoes and studied them. Should he pour off the juice or not? What about the corn? While he thought it over, he grated a couple of cups of cheese and forked over the bacon.

Marianne would sure be surprised, he thought with a smile. And pleased. But it wasn't the surprise he was really after. What he wanted was to keep her from getting tired before, well, before coming to bed. He figured he'd cook supper for her and hope.

When the bacon was crispy he lifted it out and laid it on a plate to cool, poured the juice off the tinned tomatoes and the corn and grated the rest of the cheese. Then he came face to face with the empty pie pan.

Poverty Pie needed a piecrust, surely? Well, how hard could that be? He looked it up in the recipe book and exhaled with relief. Just flour and butter and enough water to make it all stick together. Simple as…pie.

He mixed it up, patted it into a big lump, and searched for Marianne's rolling pin. He hadn't a clue where she kept it, and after a fruitless ten minutes, he substituted the whiskey bottle she kept on the top shelf of the china cabinet. He flattened the sticky blob of dough with his fist and then, using the sloshing bottle, he spread it out into a sloppy circle.

But when he went to lay it in the pie pan, the mess kept sticking to the counter. Finally he gave up, scooped it up in both hands and plopped it into the tin, then smooshed it out to the edges and up the sides with his thumbs. It looked pretty awful, but the filling would cover it all up, and Marianne would never know.

He laid the bacon slices on top of the crust, then dumped in the tomatoes and the corn. Last he sprinkled the grated cheese over the top. His pie was ready to bake; the oven was hot. What could go wrong?

* * *

Four blocks away, Marianne stood outside the dressmaker's shop with Annamarie Panovsky. "Come on, Mrs. Burnside," the girl urged. "We're here now, so let's see what Miss Forester can suggest."

Annamarie had talked her into coming, pleading that her brother was no help in feminine matters and she needed a woman's advice. Reluctantly, she now followed the girl into the tidy shop.

Verena spun away from a tower of fabric bolts and frowned. "Ladies, what can I do for you today?"

Annamarie grinned at the woman. "I need one of those funny skirts you can ride horseback in."

"A split skirt, you mean?"

"Exactly."

Verena's eyebrows pulled together. "What about you, Miz Burnside?"

"Me? Oh, I don't need a thing, thank you, Verena."

"Really?" the dressmaker muttered. "In that case you're the only woman in town who doesn't need something. It's the middle of the summer and every female in the county wants a new something-or-other."

"Well, I don't need a thing, truly."

"Are you maybe entering the Fourth of July ladies' race?"

She didn't answer for so long Verena's frown deepened. "Well?" the woman snapped. "If you're riding, you're probably going to want a split riding skirt, like Annamarie here."

Annamarie saved her. "Miss Marianne, could you suggest an appropriate fabric?"

"Denim," Verena announced. "Sturdy as possible."

"What color?" Annamarie inquired with a sidelong look at Marianne.

"Blue," the dressmaker pronounced. "It's called *blue* denim for a reason."

"Oh, of course." Annamarie sent the dressmaker a melting smile. "Could you measure me for a split skirt, please?"

Verena grabbed her tape measure.

"And measure Mrs. Burnside, too," Annamarie added. "Just in case she wants to go horseback riding."

Marianne blinked. "Annamarie, I have to confess I haven't been on a horse since I was your age."

"Really? But Mr. Garland at the boot shop said—" She broke off when Marianne glared at her.

"Come now, ladies," Verena interjected. "I haven't got all day." She slapped out her measuring tape and Annamarie stepped forward and raised both arms.

"It'll be ready on Friday," the dressmaker announced as she measured the girl's waist. Then she sent an expectant look at Marianne, but when she said nothing, Verena rolled up her tape measure and retreated behind the pattern counter.

Outside, Marianne took Annamarie's arm. "Just what did Mr. Garland tell you?" she demanded.

"Only that you're new to Oregon and you used to ride years ago and that you might ride again someday."

"Someday," Marianne echoed. "Maybe. And that is a very big 'maybe.'"

"If you say so, Mrs. Burnside," Annamarie said with an innocent smile. "Maybe. But if you do, you will need a riding skirt."

Chapter Twenty-Five

While his Poverty Pie baked, Lance consulted Mrs. Beeton's book of recipes. He needed a dessert to go with the pie. He riffled through several pages. Stewed peaches? Nah. Fruit compote? Nah. What about apple crisp?

Perfect.

By the time he'd peeled and sliced up the apples and mixed up a topping of brown sugar and flour and butter, his Poverty Pie looked done. He slid it out of the oven, and just as he was shoving in the baking dish full of apple crisp he heard Marianne's footsteps on the stairs.

The door opened and she stepped inside and stopped dead. "Oh, my goodness, what smells so good?"

"Supper," he said proudly.

"Oh, Lance." Her mouth went all trembly. "Oh…" Her voice broke. "Not since I was eleven y-years old has anyone m-made supper for me. How did you—?"

"I found one of your cookbooks and, I uh, studied it a bit."

Marianne stared at the man she had married barely six weeks ago. Were all men this surprising when you got to know them? "I never dreamed you c-could cook."

"I can't, not really. But I can read. And Abe helped."

She studied him. He was wearing her red gingham apron, and he looked so wonderfully out of place she wanted to laugh and cry all at the same time. "Lance, you really are the most—" she searched for a word "—unexpected man."

"Is that good or bad?" he asked.

She just smiled. "Unexpected is…unexpected."

He rolled his eyes. "Oh, boy, wait 'til you see what I made for supper, Marianne. *That* will be unexpected. It's something called 'Poverty Pie'."

Her eyes widened. "W-what?"

"Are you hungry?"

"Well, yes, I am, but—"

Lance grinned. "Then wash up and get ready!"

She went to the sink, washed her hands, and settled into her chair at the table. Lance set his creation down before her, and she eyed the dish without speaking. It smelled good, and the cheese had melted nicely.

"I sure hope it tastes all right," he said. He sat down across from her, picked up a butcher knife and cut a big slice. "Jumpin' jennies, it cuts just like a real pie!"

That made Marianne laugh out loud.

Halfway through her serving of Poverty Pie, she began to sniff the air. "Is something in the oven?"

"Yep," he said proudly. "Apple crisp."

She stared at him. "How on earth did you figure out how to bake an apple crisp?"

"Mrs. Beeton," he said. "There's a recipe in her cookbook."

"Lance," she said with a tired smile, "if I had known you could cook all those years I was slaving in Mrs. Schneiderman's kitchen, you could have helped me."

"Oh, heck, no, Marianne. I don't know a thing about kitchen stuff," he confessed. "I just took a deep breath, and, like they say about the proverbial fool, I rushed in."

She laid down her fork. "I am impressed. Actually, Lance, I am amazed. Your Poverty Pie tastes very good."

"Beginner's luck, I guess." He knew he was turning red, but he couldn't help it.

She was silent, so he rose and strode to the oven, pulled

out a bubbling pan of crumb-topped apple crisp and set it on the stove top.

"Marianne?"

"Hmm?"

"Marianne, I… Oh, I don't know. I can't think straight around you sometimes. Do you want some coffee?"

When she nodded he busied himself dishing up the crisp, poured her a cup of coffee and passed her the cream pitcher. She doused her apple crisp with the cream and picked up her spoon.

Lance was watching her so closely her hand began to shake. She tasted the apple crisp and sent him a grin. "This is delicious! Really it is."

He thought his heart would float right out of his chest. More than her approval of his apple crisp was his elation at making her smile at him.

She finished her dessert without saying anything else, then sat sipping her coffee while Lance wondered why he couldn't taste anything.

"Lance?"

"Yeah?"

"There's something I've been meaning to ask you?"

His heart spiraled right back into his chest. "Yeah? What about?"

"It's about the advertisement I wired to Brooks and Cassidy this afternoon."

"What about it?"

"Well, what if the three hundred dollars we spent on that advertisement brings in so many orders we can't keep up with production?"

That thought had occurred to him, too. "Then we'll all have to work like demons."

"Abe is the expert boot-maker, Lance. You and Sammy and I are just apprentices. I wonder if we're really ready to increase production to such an extent. Maybe I should have listened to Abe when he warned me about becoming overwhelmed with orders."

"Marianne, let's not borrow trouble. Let's just keep on with what we're doing, and—"

"Pray a lot," she said dryly.

He laughed out loud, and after a few seconds she joined in. "Do you think we were crazy to take on this business?" he asked.

"Yes," she said quickly. "This whole thing is a huge gamble."

Lance hesitated. "I bet you think getting married was a gamble, too, huh?"

"Well…"

"Are you sorry?" he asked.

She waited a long time, toying with her spoon and turning pink. "Do you mean am I sorry I married a man who can make me laugh, to say nothing about a man who can make Poverty Pie and apple crisp?"

He choked on a swallow of coffee. "Marianne, do I really make you laugh?"

"Sometimes," she answered.

He could tell nothing, absolutely nothing, from the slight smile on her face. "You know, never in a million years am I gonna figure you out."

She looked at him over the rim of her coffee cup, and the blush on her cheeks turned deep rose. "You don't have to figure me out, Lance. All you have to do is put up with me."

Marianne watched in disbelief as Lance nodded, but she noticed he was biting his lip. She must be extremely hard to put up with. She was a tired, short-tempered spinster who had woefully little experience with men. Who had a lamentable lack of knowledge about being married to a man. She also, she realized suddenly, lacked a good deal of knowledge about the man she had married.

And that was *her* fault. Other women, younger women

with more sophistication, with more feminine arts and skills, would know how to draw a man out, get him to... what? Well, share his deepest thoughts with her, for a start.

She risked a good long look at Lance. Underneath his handsome appearance and his kindly manner, who was he, really?

She watched him clear away the dishes from the table and dunk them in hot soapy water. She didn't know what to do with herself while he splashed around at the sink, so she undressed behind the folding screen, donned her nightgown, and slipped under the quilt on her side of the double cot.

She opened *Cowboy's Lady* and tried to concentrate on Duke and Genevieve and their silly antics until her eyelids began to droop. Lance was humming "Clementine." When his voice cracked on a high note she tried hard not to laugh. After a while she felt him crawl in next to her and puff out the kerosene lamp.

"You awake?" he whispered.

"No," she murmured.

"Liar," he said softly. He reached out, pulled her across to his side of the bed and wrapped his arms around her. She sighed and tucked her head into the hollow between his neck and his shoulder. He smelled of bacon and apples.

She had certainly married an unusual man. A good man. A surprising man. She had been fortunate in choosing Lance Burnside.

But.

Abe was right about their partnership in Collingwood Boots. She wouldn't think of making a business decision without Lance's approval, but Collingwood Boots was not a marriage. Forbidding her to ride in the Fourth of July horse race, expecting her to obey him just because he was her husband...that was something she could not accept.

Did other women obey their husbands unquestioningly?

Perhaps. But something inside her rebelled at being judged less important just because she was a wife. She felt all tied up inside. But when Lance began pressing his lips against the back of her neck she stopped thinking. A shiver of pleasure rippled through her.

"Do you like that?" he murmured. His breath ruffled the hair at her nape and sent a jolt of sensation all the way to the pit of her stomach.

She closed her eyes. When Lance touched her like that it made her feel all shaky inside. "I— Yes, I do like it. Ever since we were married I have been quite surprised by how much I like it. You," she amended. It was…frightening somehow.

He tightened his arms around her. "You know something, Marianne?"

She smiled, even though she was half asleep. "What?" she said, her voice drowsy.

"In a lot of ways I never thought this would work out, marrying you and coming out West. Did you?"

"Yes," she murmured. "I thought it would work out."

"Yeah? How come?"

"Because…because of something my mother said when I was very young."

"Yeah?" He kissed her behind one ear. "Tell me."

She sighed at the memory. "My mother was from Poland," she said. "She didn't speak good English, which is probably why she insisted that I go to school. But in the evenings, Mama taught me to cook, and I always remembered what she told me one night."

"Yeah? What was it?"

"'Kissin' don't last,' Mama said. 'Cookery do.' That's why I thought that marrying you would work out, Lance." She stifled a yawn. "Because I can cook."

He gave a low laugh. "Huh. I'm kinda hoping the kissin' will last, too."

"Maybe it will," she murmured. "And now that you can cook, too, I think we might have an even better chance."

"That's not exactly what I wanted to hear," he muttered.

Marianne said nothing. Lance waited for her to say something more, and when she didn't he lifted his head off the pillow so he could see her face.

Hell and damn, she was sound asleep. Again!

Chapter Twenty-Six

Lance woke to a shaft of sunlight warming his face. He opened his lids and studied the light pouring in through the blue-curtained window, then studied the curtains themselves. Not only could Marianne cook, he thought irrationally, she could also sew. She could probably do a dozen other things he knew nothing about. Sing, maybe? Dance a Virginia reel? Yesterday Abe told him rancher Peter Jensen was holding a barn dance on Saturday night. Everybody in Smoke River was invited. Maybe he'd get a chance to see if Marianne could dance as well as she could cook.

"Marianne, when you were growing up in St. Louis did you go to dances?"

No answer.

"Marianne?" He rolled over and patted the space next to him.

Empty.

He sat up. "What the—?" Had she gone downstairs to work in the shop before breakfast? He swung his legs on to the floor. She was sure taking this apprentice thing seriously. Well, so was he, he admitted. Neither of them wanted Collingwood Boots to fail.

He pulled on his jeans and a plaid shirt, splashed water on his face and ran one hand through his tousled hair. But when he tramped downstairs to the shop expecting to find her, Abe just shrugged.

"Dunno where Miss Marianne went," the older man said. "Afore I was even outta bed I heard the shop door close, and when I scooted over to peek out the window, her tail feathers was just disappearin' around the corner. I figgered you two had words this mornin' an' she went out to walk off her mad."

Lance stared at him. "Words? Heck, no. When I woke up this morning she was gone. Last night we…um…well, I cooked supper like you said, and she seemed real friendly."

The older man sent him a sharp look. "You sure?"

"I thought so, Abe. But I'm learning that with Marianne you can never tell. Then later we, uh…well, there's no need to go into later, I guess."

Abe nodded and a smile crossed his face. "Glad to hear that," he said. "Mebbe she just wanted to go off somewhere alone and do some thinkin'."

Lance sucked in a breath. *Thinking about what?* Thinking about Poverty Pie and apple crisp? About Collingwood Boots? About…kissing? Was he making any progress at all on his Seducing Marianne project?

He shrugged and tramped back upstairs to figure out how to fry eggs.

Marianne circled around the block and peeked into the livery stable. It was so early the sun wasn't up yet, and the predawn stillness gave her a moment to collect herself. Was she absolutely sure she wanted to do this?

No, she wasn't.

She took a deep breath and stepped in through the livery door. The interior was dim and quiet and smelled of hay and horses and manure.

"Rosie?"

The Indian woman appeared at her elbow. "You come, see horses." She led the way to a stall and pointed to a sleek gray mare with a white blaze on her forehead. "That one mine. Good horse." A grin split her handsome face. "Very fast."

Marianne followed the older woman to the next stall where a shiny chestnut-colored mare whickered gently. "That one Sammy's," Rosie said. In the same stall was a smaller bay mare with soft black eyes.

"You ride this one, okay? All saddled and ready for you."

Marianne nodded. "Okay."

The woman led the animal out and laid the reins in Marianne's hand. "Talk to horse," she instructed. "Name is Black Dancer." She then opened the stall gate and began saddling her gray mare.

Marianne and Black Dancer looked at each other. Hesitantly she reached out one hand and patted the animal's neck.

"H-hello, Dancer."

"Tomorrow you bring apple," Rosie advised. "Make friends." She motioned Marianne over to the mounting block and opened the double-wide stable door.

Marianne bunched up her blue denim work skirt, stepped into the stirrup, and swung herself up into the saddle.

"Petticoat no good," Rosie observed. "Scare horse. Next time wear trousers." Then she and the mare led the way outside and around the back of the building on to a well-worn path bordering a stand of sugar maple trees.

Marianne followed the mare for ten minutes, gradually remembering how to use the reins, sit tall, and move with the animal. After another ten minutes, Rosie looked back at her and grinned. "Go slow one more mile, then run."

The next thing she knew both horses were cantering along the wooded path, and after an initial wave of fear, Marianne began to enjoy herself. She remembered riding as a girl; she had forgotten how much she liked it.

They rode for half an hour, and then Rosie drew rein. "No more today," she called. "Will be sore."

On the way back to the stable Marianne pressed Dancer into a trot until Rosie called a halt in front of the livery stable.

"Come tomorrow early. No petticoat." She began unsaddling the horses and Marianne smiled her thanks. She had enjoyed the outing. What she didn't enjoy, she thought with a gulp, was deceiving Lance.

She left a grinning Rosie at the stable, hurried back to the shop and raced upstairs. When she opened the apartment door, Lance was standing at the stove, frying bacon.

"You're back," he said, his voice quiet.

She opened her mouth to deliver the explanation she'd rehearsed. "I went horseback riding with Rosie Greywolf."

"Oh."

That part was true. But she purposely didn't tell him why.

The silence stretched until she thought her nerves would snap. He turned back to the stove. "Want some breakfast?"

His voice sounded odd.

"Yes, I would. Thank you, Lance."

He didn't answer.

On Saturday, they worked all morning cutting and stitching cowhide until their hands ached, and Abe finally ordered a break. They gobbled cheese and bacon sandwiches and guzzled the rest of the coffee Abe had made that morning, and went right back to work.

All afternoon they followed Abe's directions for their next task, tacking hardened leather soles to the uppers, until Sammy drove up in his wagon. "Charlie at the station house says your bed's arrived."

"Just in time," Lance murmured under his breath.

"You want me to deliver it this afternoon?"

Abe snorted. "'Course we want it delivered! You think I like sleepin' on my floor?"

"To say nothing about sleeping on two cots with a dip in the middle," Lance said under his breath.

"Yeah," Abe said. "That cain't be too comfy, neither."

Late in the day Marianne sat down with the account book and began adding up columns of figures. Then she wrote out more advertising copy for the Wednesday edition of the *Lark*. But she couldn't stop thinking about their new bed.

Abe stopped at the small table she was using as a desk and set a mug of coffee at her elbow. "You're workin' too hard, Miss Marianne. Oughtta save some energy fer tonight, don'tcha think?"

She twiddled the pencil between her thumb and forefinger. "Is Sammy here with the bed?"

"Yep. Ya don't look too excited 'bout it, though."

"I guess I'm a little nervous about tonight."

"Naw, it's not that, Miss Marianne. I meant you should save some energy for the big wingding at Jensen's barn tonight."

"What wingding?"

"Didn't Lance tell you? Jensens are holding a barn dance, like they do every summer."

"Oh. I guess I forgot all about the dance."

Abe's heavy eyebrows went up. "Fergot about it, huh? Ain't like a woman to fergit about a dance. Care to tell me what was on yer mind instead?"

"No, I would not." She bent her head to check a column of figures, and suddenly Abe peered out the front window and let out a whoop. "Just lookit that! Sammy's out front in his wagon with yer new bed!"

Both Lance and Abe barreled outside and wrestled the shipping crate out of the wagon, knocked the wooden slats free and dragged the bed frame and the mattress up the stairs. Sammy brought up the rear with a cardboard box labeled Pillows.

Marianne struggled to keep her mind on the last column of expenses, but the thumps and bumps from upstairs sent her thoughts zinging around in her brain like drunken butterflies. Their new bed was narrower than the double-cot arrangement they'd been using. And narrower meant… She closed her eyes. Narrower meant that she and Lance would be even closer together at night.

Suddenly she was too warm. She opened her eyes to watch Abe and Lance wrestle Abe's narrow cot back down to his room and load the old cot from the apartment into Sammy's wagon, and then the boy rattled off down the street. Why hadn't they remembered to keep the old cot, as they'd thought they would do, to give them that extra space in bed?

Very well, Marianne counseled herself. She would simply continue adding up the columns of figures, and then she would go upstairs and dress for the barn dance. *And I will not spare one single thought about that new double bed.*

Lance and Abe worked steadily in the shop until late afternoon, and she sipped her now cold coffee and tried to concentrate. Finally she gave up and climbed the stairs to finish making the potato salad she would be taking out to the Jensens' and get dressed for the dance.

She couldn't stop looking at the bed. Tonight would be the first time she and Lance had slept together in a real bed. She tucked in the sheets and fluffed the pillows and tried not to think about it.

At dusk, Lance came upstairs, changed his shirt and then sat down at the kitchen table. He stared first at the new bed, then at her, and then at the new bed and smiled.

She paced around and around the small kitchen and finally settled into a chair where she sat watching him watch her. It made her nervous. And curious. What was he thinking? Was it about tonight? About lying closer to her in their new bed?

Which, she acknowledged with a catch in her breath, was what *she* was thinking about.

She studied the ceramic bowl of potato salad and tried not to let her gaze stray to the far corner of the room. Under the blue-flowered quilt the new bed looked just the same as the double cot arrangement they had been sleeping on, but she couldn't stop thinking about what was *under* the quilt, not two cots divided down the middle but a real double bed, with nothing to prevent two people from lying really, really close to each other.

Lance's voice startled her. "Marianne, what's the matter? Your expression looks…funny." He settled across the table from her.

She jerked to attention. "Oh? Funny, how?"

"Kinda worried about something."

"I—I was thinking about Collingwood Beds—I mean Boots," she amended instantly.

"Yeah?" he said with a grin. "What about it?"

"I've been going over the accounts. Even with the fees from the horse races, we are losing money overall. I guess I'm a little bit scared that we can't make this business work. If we can't, my dream of owning my own business will burst like a soap bubble."

"It's more important than just your dream, Marianne. If we don't make it work we're going to go hungry. Abe, too," he added.

She said nothing in response to that, and Lance peered at her across the table. Weeks ago Marianne had told him about her fears for the shop, he remembered. It wasn't like her to repeat herself, so he guessed she had something else on her mind. Something she didn't want to tell him about. Maybe something like sneaking off this morning to ride horseback with Rosie Greywolf.

But he knew she was riding with Rosie, so what in God's name was making her frown like that?

Chapter Twenty-Seven

Sammy Greywolf loaded his mother and Lance into the wagon for the drive out to Jensens' ranch, and then the three of them sat waiting in front of the shop for Marianne. She kept them waiting another ten minutes, and when she emerged, Abe was with her, dressed in a clean checked shirt and denim overalls. He climbed up beside Rosie on the driver's bench, and Lance settled Marianne in the wagon bed, propped against his bent knees.

She wore that same pretty yellow dress he remembered from their wedding day, and she looked so beautiful his throat got tight. How was it possible he had been married to Marianne all these weeks and he hadn't ravished her yet?

Because, he reminded himself, a man didn't just ravish a woman he valued, and he valued Marianne. True, he had nights when his resolve wavered, when he felt like tossing his slow Seduce Marianne campaign out the window and speeding things up. After all, he was only human. But he wanted Marianne for more than just a roll in the hay; he wanted her for the long haul so he was prepared to be patient.

He couldn't have asked for a more perfect summer night. The heat of the early July day had faded into a soft warmth, and it was so peaceful even the evening sparrows were silent. The wagon wheels crunched over a patch of dry leaves, and Sammy leaned over to say something to his mother. Lance heard her quiet laugh.

Rosie Greywolf was the handsomest Indian woman he had ever seen. She didn't say much, Marianne had confided, but when she did speak, it paid one to listen. Which was why, he supposed, his wife had returned from the mercantile one afternoon with a pair of boy's jeans and a red plaid cotton shirt. "For horseback riding," she had said. Lance had hid his surprise and went on reading *The Montana Renegade*. He couldn't help wondering how his wife's predawn riding lessons were going; she had confided how much she wanted to fit in out here in the West, and he knew most women on the frontier rode horseback.

The wagon turned into Jensen's lane and rolled to a stop in front of a large red barn. Music rolled out the open double doors, and with a dart of apprehension Lance acknowledged he had never danced with Marianne. They were sure doing things in reverse. First the proposal on the back steps of Mrs. Schneiderman's boardinghouse and then the wedding and *then* the courtship. It was all backwards. For other couples, the courtship part came first. Life with Marianne would always be surprising. It sure kept things interesting, and he didn't want a wife who wasn't interesting.

Rosie had brought a platter of what she called "sand cookies." Abe sneaked one and grinned in approval before Rosie batted his hand away, then they both climbed down from the bench and waited for Sammy to park the wagon.

Lance handed Marianne's potato salad to Abe, who sniffed at it appreciatively. Then he vaulted out of the wagon, held his arms out for his wife, and swung her to the ground.

"I'm a little nervous," she confessed.

"It can't be any worse than our wedding reception, meeting all those new people," he offered.

"Or getting married in the first place," she said. "I was nervous then, too."

Lance chuckled and took her elbow. "You weren't the only one. I'd never been so scared in my life."

She looked up at him. "Really? Someday will you tell me more about how you felt that day?"

"Uh, sure."

They moved through the barn door into the interior, and Marianne gasped. "Just look at all these people!"

Behind them, Abe chortled. "Ever'body in the county comes to these here dances so they kin whirl around with each other and let off some steam." He set Marianne's potato salad on the long wooden table already crowded with salads and covered dishes and an assortment of pies and cakes and marched off toward an arrangement of three wide planks laid over a pair of sawhorses which served as a bar.

Music poured over the crowd, two guitars, a banjo, a violin played by Sheriff Rivera, and a washtub bass strummed by none other than mercantile owner Carl Ness.

"I think they're playing a two-step," Lance said.

Marianne looked at him in disbelief. "I think it's a waltz."

"Dance with me anyway. We'll compromise." He took her arm and turned her toward him.

"Oh. I... I..."

"It's a dance, Marianne," he said with a smile. "We're supposed to dance."

"Shouldn't we first find our hosts?"

He sighed. "You were taught too many good manners when you were growin' up," he murmured. "I wasn't." He swung her into his arms and moved out on to the dance floor.

Those were the last words they exchanged for a long time. Lance might not have been taught a lot of society manners, Marianne noted, but somewhere along the way he had certainly learned to dance! She couldn't help wondering where. He guided the two of them around and around the huge barn with ease, and gradually his assurance calmed her jittery nerves.

They were playing a schottische. He surprised her by not only knowing the steps but adding some turning-under-his-arm flourishes. He certainly knew what he was doing on a dance floor. Lance Burnside was turning out to be a most unusual man. She scanned the other couples swirling around them with varying levels of expertise and counted herself fortunate. Not only could Lance cook, he could dance, and he was by far the best-looking man in the room. Of course none of those things were important, she reminded herself. Of greater significance was a man's integrity.

With a stab of guilt she recalled how she had blackmailed Lance into marrying her with that outdated Wanted poster. She wondered if he was even the slightest bit sorry. She wasn't.

"I can almost hear your brain whirring," he said near her ear.

She glanced up with a look of amusement in her green eyes. "Oh? What am I thinking?"

"You're thinking you don't know how you got to this point, and you're wondering where we go from here."

He said it with such certainty she almost missed a step. "I was not!"

"Liar," he whispered. "I bet you're also thinking about our new bed."

She missed another step. "What?"

He grinned at her. "Well, aren't you? I know I am."

She came to a complete stop. "I am certainly not thinking about our new... Certainly not," she lied.

Lance laughed. His eyes darkened to a midnight blue when he was amused. Odd that she hadn't noticed that before, but of course, when he had been amused in the past, she hadn't been this close to him.

Or maybe she was just noticing more about him tonight.

Or maybe she *was* in fact thinking about their new bed. About lying close to him tonight and…and…

She bobbled another step. Lance's arm tightened across her back, pulling her closer, and she closed her eyes. He smelled of leather and pine soap. He folded her hand under his chin and began to hum along with the music. "Oh, my darling…oh, my darling Clementine." Her breasts brushed the front of his blue shirt, and he stopped humming.

All at once she was short of breath. Light-headed. Hungry.

And confused. Oh, Lord, what was happening to her?

Nothing, said a reasonable voice inside her head. *Just the normal feelings a woman has for a man when she*—she sucked in a shaky breath—*desires him.*

"Something wrong?" he asked. "You're breathing funny."

"Am I?" She worked to keep her voice steady. "My mind may have been wandering."

"Yeah? Was it wandering any place interesting?" he murmured.

Suddenly she wished she was a cold, hard marble statue whose mind *couldn't* wander. As it was, she felt decidedly *not* made of cold, hard marble but flesh and blood. Warm flesh and even warmer blood.

"Did you ever in a million years think we could be this happy together?" he whispered. "Like we are now?"

All at once she felt like crying. And then just as suddenly she wanted to stop dancing and press her mouth to his.

Lance felt her stop moving, and when she gazed up at him, her eyes looked shiny. She tried to smile, but her lips were trembling. What the—?

"Marianne?"

"Don't talk, Lance. Please."

"Do you want to sit down and rest? I could bring you some lemonade and—"

There was that funny smile again. She smoothed her fingers over the front of his shirt, and he caught her hand and held it against his chest. Again she tried to smile at him, and this time she succeeded.

"No, I don't want any lemonade, Lance. I am perfectly happy right here, dancing with you."

His pulse skittered into an irregular rhythm and then sped up. He couldn't wait for this damn dance to end so he could be alone with her. He wished there was something he could do to speed things up because he could hardly wait to get back to their apartment and try out that new bed.

Chapter Twenty-Eight

By the time Rosie, Abe, Lance and Marianne got back to the shop and climbed down from Sammy's wagon, the moon was floating high over the maple trees and the barn owl that lived above the livery stable was making *tu-whooing* sounds. Lance walked a sleepy Marianne up the stairs into their apartment, where she immediately slipped off her shoes and stepped behind the folding screen. He wished she hadn't; he wouldn't mind watching her take off her clothes instead of her hiding behind that screen.

After twenty minutes of total silence he began to worry. It was sure taking her an extra-long time to undress tonight. Seemed kinda funny that she was still so shy after weeks of marriage.

Face it, Burnside. You know nothing about women or about being married. And you know even less about Marianne.

For some reason that made him chuckle.

"What's funny?" she asked from behind the screen.

"You. Me. Everything, I guess. Life is hard to figure out sometimes," he admitted.

"It's a little like one of Abe's dime novels, isn't it?" she said. "Just when you think you know what's going to happen next, it doesn't."

"Abe's novels are unrealistic," Lance said. "Real life isn't like that."

She stepped out from behind the screen in her long white nightgown, but instead of getting into bed, she floated aimlessly about the room. Her gown was just sheer enough for him to see the outline of her body in the lamplight, and that made the last of his patience dissolve.

She stopped to look out the window over the kitchen sink. He knew she couldn't see anything; it was pitch-black outside. So why was she—?

All at once it dawned on him. Marianne was purposely delaying coming to bed. But that made no sense. She'd slept next to him every night since their wedding, so why was she being so skittish tonight?

Because tonight we have a real bed for the first time. And she knows that I want a real marriage.

He tossed back the quilt and strode across the room toward her. "Marianne…"

"Yes, I know," she said quickly. "I'm… I'm coming."

He moved behind her and cupped his hands around her shoulders. "Not very damn fast," he whispered. He turned her into his arms and laid his cheek against her hair. It smelled of violets. When she said nothing, he bent and scooped her up in his arms. She sighed and nestled her face against his neck, and he moved toward the bed.

"You know what?" he murmured.

"Oh, yes," she said with a soft laugh, "I think I do know what."

"No, you don't." He laid her down on top of the quilt and bent to blow out the kerosene lamp. "You couldn't possibly guess what I'm thinking."

"Tell me," she whispered.

"Nope."

"No?" She sounded so surprised he chuckled.

"Nope," he repeated. "I'm gonna show you." He leaned over and kissed her. To his surprise, she reached her arms around his neck, and when he lifted his mouth from hers she kissed him back.

His senses ignited. When she kissed him again, a choking sense of humility flooded him. It warred with his physical desire for her, but in a flash of clarity he resolved he would ask nothing of her that she did not freely want to give.

She continued to surprise him, encouraging him to touch her by moving suggestively and occasionally murmuring, "Yes, I like that," when he did. He tried not to rush things, but God knew he wanted her. He ached to smooth his hands over every inch of her body, caress her breasts and run his tongue over her nipples. He wanted to make her his.

"Lance?"

"Mmm?"

"Kiss me other places, too," she breathed.

He concealed his surprise and drew her nightgown over her knees, then kept going, pushing it higher, past her waist. Finally she sat up and shrugged it off over her head. Then she slid back down and reached one hand to his chest. He caught her palm against his bare skin and bent to press his mouth to her breast.

Her quick inhalation told him she liked that, too, and he licked first one nipple and then moved to the other until her breathing told him she was ready for more.

Very slowly he slid his hand to her waist and then on down across her belly to the soft curls between her thighs. She sighed, and he could tell she was smiling, so he moved lower and slipped one finger inside her.

"Oh," she breathed. "Oh, yes."

She was wet and hot, and he fought to go slow, but when she moaned and opened her thighs, he changed his mind. From her response he guessed she didn't *want* him to go slow, and that halted his breath.

"Don't stop," she whispered.

"You sure? I know you've never—"

She reached up and touched his lips with one finger. "I'm sure," she murmured.

He hesitated, swallowed hard and rolled on top of her.

Taking Marianne was the biggest surprise of all. She was responsive and spirited in ways he would never have dreamed possible. At the end she cried out and clung to him, and he lost himself inside her.

Afterward they lay side by side, breathing heavily, while Lance tried to float back down to earth. Finally she rose up on one elbow and leaned over him.

"Lance," she breathed. "Why did we wait so long? Being married is wonderful!"

Chapter Twenty-Nine

When he awoke, Marianne was gone. The space where her body had lain was still faintly warm, and the sheets were faintly scented with violets.

"Marianne?"

No answer. He flung back the quilt and swung his bare feet to the floor. Damn it was cold! But a warm kernel of pleasure still glowed inside him, and he caught his breath. He padded to the stove, stirred the banked coals to life and added some wood.

She had left slices of raw bacon in the iron skillet, and a bowl of eggs sat on the counter. Looked like she was planning to make breakfast, but maybe he'd beat her to it. He moved the skillet over the flames, stepped behind the screen to splash water on his face and pulled on his jeans.

It wasn't exactly clear who had conquered who last night, he mused. A man would probably say that he was the victor, having taken his wife for the first time, but this morning he felt so poleaxed he felt like *he* was the conquered party.

The bacon began to sizzle. He moved the coffeepot over the heat, snagged two mugs from the hooks in the china cabinet and stared at the bowl of eggs. Marianne was… somewhere. Maybe out riding with Rosie Greywolf.

But, he realized, today was July Fourth. The day of the horse races. He figured Rosie wouldn't be riding this morning; she'd want to save her horse for the women's race this afternoon.

The eggs sat in the bowl, looking back at him. He could have them fried or scrambled, but he had to admit he didn't know how to fry or scramble them. Well, he reasoned, he could at least get them out of the shells.

He reached for Mrs. Beeton's recipe book. *Let's see, eggs...eggs...*

"Fried eggs," it read. "Break eggs into a skillet…"

He scanned down the page. "Scrambled eggs. Break eggs into a bowl…" He groaned. Cookbooks were written for people who already knew how to cook!

He picked up one of the eggs and cracked it against the edge of the bowl. Too hard, he realized when it oozed sticky yellow yolk all over his hand. The next eggshell didn't crack at all, and when he tapped it just a bit harder, runny egg stuff slopped on to the counter.

He began to perspire. So much for making breakfast this morning. This egg business was harder than cutting out pieces of cowhide.

He was pretty sure he had succeeded in satisfying Marianne last night, but he sure wasn't succeeding at breakfast; he couldn't cook eggs worth a damn.

When Marianne arrived at the livery stable she found Rosie waiting. But she was not saddling up the horses. Instead, she insisted the two of them should walk the racecourse Sammy had laid out the previous day. "On foot, see everything," the woman said. "Think like horse."

So the two of them tramped along the wide path where Sammy had marked the route. It ran behind the stable, past the train station and over the wide, dandelion-studded meadow and through the woods, then back along the river and up the hill to the church and around the big oak tree.

Then it doubled back on itself to the finish line at the edge of town.

The sun was just turning the sky peach-colored when they returned to the stable. "Eat little," Rosie advised. "Otherwise, get belly jiggles."

Marianne nodded, fed Dancer a ripe red apple and a handful of oats and walked back to the shop. She already had "belly jiggles." Just the thought of tearing along the racecourse with lots of other horses gave her the shakes. Part of her apprehension was just plain fear; part of it was knowing she was deliberately ignoring Lance's objection to her riding in this race. Knowing she was deliberately deceiving Lance about riding in the race.

She'd thought a lot about it these past weeks. She felt caught between her wish to be a good wife and her fear that Eugenia Ridley was up to no good and needed watching during the ladies' race. The more she wrestled with her dilemma, the more uncertain she got. Lance might never forgive her for defying him. And after their glorious night together last night she knew it mattered a great deal to her if she displeased him.

But she knew she couldn't have it both ways. As much as she needed to please Lance, she needed even more to do what she felt was right.

She returned to the apartment to find Lance bent over one of her cookbooks. When she came in he glanced up and his frown evaporated. "Thank God you're back! I finally figured out how to crack an eggshell, but I made a real mess doing it."

Sure enough, the kitchen counter was awash in egg yolks which were now dripping on to the floor, and frizzled bacon slices lay in the skillet, swimming in congealing bacon grease. Lance looked so abject she took pity on him. Together they mopped off the counter and cleaned the floor, and then she gave Lance a quick lesson on how to scramble eggs.

"You mean that's all there is to it? Just add some milk and pour them into the skillet?"

Marianne grinned. "That's all."

"What if I want to fry an egg instead of scramble it?"

"Why don't I show you that tomorrow morning? Today is the Fourth, and Collingwood Boots is sponsoring the horse races, remember? Abe and Sammy will need help."

Lance watched her run a fork through the eggs in the pan until they began to look scrambled. She kept looking up at him and smiling, and once she put down the fork and stretched up on her toes to brush her lips over his cheek. That made him so happy he felt he could fly.

"You, um, wouldn't want to go back to bed before the races start, would you?"

Her cheeks turned the most enticing shade of rose. "I—I don't think there is time."

He was disappointed, but he guessed it didn't really matter; there was always tonight. Maybe they'd skip the fireworks down by the river when it got dark and come home early.

The rest of the morning he spent in a daze. After breakfast he found Abe and volunteered his services, but even when Abe assigned him the simplest job of the day, firing off the starting gun before each race, Lance found himself grinning at the older man like an idiot.

Abe sent him a puzzled look. "Ya don't mind jest standin' there with my revolver?"

"Nope. Don't mind at all."

The older man shook his head and marched off to find Sammy. Lance went out for a walk until the first race. He didn't really feel like walking. He felt like dancing a jig, but he figured the townspeople would think he'd gone crazy.

When he returned to the shop, it was almost time for the

ladies' race, and Abe and Sammy were heading out to their stations on the race course. Abe handed him the revolver.

"Careful, son. It's loaded."

"Where's Marianne? Upstairs?"

Abe's face shuttered. "Like I said, you be careful with that gun."

All at once he began to feel uneasy. "I thought Marianne and I would watch the races together," Lance said.

Abe laid a hand on his forearm. "Ya better get on out to the startin' line, son. I'm goin' out to the meadow where the course veers off toward the river. Sammy's stationed out at that big oak tree by the church."

Lance nodded. "Yeah, but where's Mar—?"

"'Member what I said 'bout that revolver," Abe interrupted. "Go on, now, Lance. Better get out there."

Abe slammed the shop door behind him, and with a shrug, Lance followed the older man outside and strode behind the stable to the starting line.

The women riders were already lining up, checking their saddles and nervously patting their horses. Young Annamarie Panovsky grinned and waved at him. Her older brother, Ivan, stood beside her caramel-colored mare, his eyebrows lowered in an apprehensive frown. Lance knew Ivan was nervous about his sister's riding in the horse race.

Next to the girl, Sammy's mother, Rosie Greywolf, sat on a handsome gray gelding, looking calm and controlled as she always did. On the other side of her was Eugenia Ridley, her face tight with disapproval. Then Linda-Lou Ness, the mercantile owner's wife, walked her horse up to the starting line, and the gathered riders moved closer to make room. Linda-Lou sat her shiny bay mare with the assurance of a seasoned rider.

Lance stepped forward to start the race, carefully pointing the revolver at the ground. Just as he approached the starting position he heard another horse approach and turned to see a black mare walk into position next to Eugenia Ridley. Sitting stiffly erect in the saddle was—

Good God, it was Marianne! He blinked to be sure he wasn't imagining it. She was wearing a split riding skirt and a boy's shirt, and she had a look on her face he'd never seen before. She looked nothing like the Marianne he knew. Or thought he knew. *What in God's name was she doing on that horse?*

And then he realized she had been deceiving him all this time about riding in the race.

Chapter Thirty

Keeping her head down to focus on every step, Marianne walked Dancer up to the other four lady contestants who had arranged themselves at the starting line. Annamarie Panovsky's brother, Ivan, boosted the girl into the saddle and stood talking to her. Probably still trying to talk her out of riding, from what Annamarie had previously confided.

Next to her light brown horse sat a perfectly immobile Linda-Lou Ness, looking so unruffled she might have been setting out for a quilting bee instead of lining up for a horse race. Rosie Greywolf's gelding was just moving aside to make room for Eugenia Ridley, mounted on a large white horse with a dark blaze on its forehead. Mrs. Ridley apparently said something to Rosie, because the woman shot her a surprised look and edged her gelding away. Marianne deliberately inserted Dancer between Rosie and Mrs. Ridley.

All the horses were jittery, tossing their heads and sidestepping, except for Linda-Lou Ness's handsome bay, which stood quietly at the starting line and didn't flick an eyelash.

Ivan Panovsky's face was a mask of concern, but Annamarie bestowed a wide smile on each competitor in turn. Not all the ladies smiled back. Linda-Lou preserved her stately, stone-faced aspect, and Eugenia Ridley was so intent on scowling at Rosie Greywolf she didn't even look up. But nothing dimmed young Annamarie's sunny expression.

Something about the expression on Eugenia Ridley's face sent a chill up Marianne's spine, and she made sure there was sufficient space between Dancer and Rosie on one side and Mrs. Ridley's white mare on the other. The older woman clutched a braided rawhide riding whip in one hand. Linda-Lou Ness also carried a whip, but she kept it securely tucked under one arm.

Marianne kept her head down, purposely not looking at Lance. She knew he must be staring at her, and she didn't want to see the accusation in his eyes. She was doing something terrible, she knew that. It was a betrayal. Her heart began to thud against her ribs, and she found it hard to breathe.

Then she sensed the mounted riders beside her go still and understood that the race was about to start. *Oh, God, she was terrified!*

"On your marks…"

Lance's voice.

"Get set…"

The gunshot exploded, and the horses on both sides of her dashed away. She dug her heels into Dancer's flank and jolted forward. Dimly she heard voices as the throng of townspeople gathered along the way began to cheer.

The noise of pounding hooves rolled over her, and for a moment she wanted to close her eyes and blot everything out. But she knew she couldn't. She had to keep her attention on what she was trying to do.

The riders streaked away from the starting line and thundered past the train station, where the course made a gentle turn into a grassy meadow dotted with wildflowers. Here they spread out, some galloping two abreast across the green vegetation, their hooves tearing up the grass and flinging bits of earth into the air. A clod struck her cheek, and Marianne shut her eyes.

When she opened them the horses were halfway across

the meadow, approaching the woods where the trail narrowed. The wind snapped strands of hair into her face, and when she looked down, the grass was a fuzzy green blur. She fell in behind Linda-Lou's bay and risked a peek ahead. Three riders were jockeying to be the first to enter the woods, Rosie on her gray gelding, Annamarie Panovsky, and Eugena Ridley. Marianne guessed that the minute they were out of the woods Linda-Lou would try to move forward. Marianne resolved to stick to Eugenia Ridley like a cocklebur. She put her head down and fought to keep up with Linda-Lou.

Tree trunks flashed by, then tangles of shrubby undergrowth. The stretch through the woods seemed to last forever, and when they emerged, Marianne was gasping for air, but she managed to stay on Linda-Lou's tail. All at once she realized the woman's strategy; she planned to hang back until the course widened out, and then she could make her move to take the lead.

Dust stung into Marianne's eyes. The route veered toward the river, and she wanted desperately to see which horse was in the lead, but everything in front of her was a gray blur. She gritted her teeth and continued to dog the flashing heels of Linda-Lou's bay mare.

Suddenly the air cleared, and she could see the meadow ahead and hear tumbling water. The horses were strung out single file, but she couldn't tell which rider was ahead. She narrowed her eyes against the sun, and once more clouds of dust obscured her view of the leaders. She prayed one of them was Rosie Greywolf.

The route along the river was long enough that many yards developed between the riders. Marianne strained to see ahead as the path curved where the river widened, and she swung out to the left and saw Linda-Lou move forward and overtake one of the riders.

But which rider was it? Annamarie's mount churned

ahead of her, and Marianne could see the girl bending low over her horse's neck. She wasn't giving up! *Good for her.*

Far ahead a three-way battle raged for the lead. Linda-Lou was pressing ahead toward Rosie's gray gelding and the white mare ridden by Eugenia Ridley. The riders started up the long hill, pounding toward the oak tree next to the church, and Marianne's chest began to ache. She fought to keep going. At least she could see the leaders more clearly now, and that told her she must be gaining on them.

She and Annamarie were dead last, and then all at once the girl's mount shot forward. Marianne watched her overtake Linda-Lou, and then all three of the front runners swung wide around the oak tree and headed back toward her. Here was where the course doubled back and the two paths ran parallel but in opposite directions. As the horses galloped toward her, she realized the riders would be almost face-to-face as they passed each other.

Rosie Greywolf was in the lead! She was followed closely by Eugenia Ridley, and then came Annamarie. Marianne glimpsed Rosie's face as she thundered toward her, her head down, her eyes intent on the course. Behind her, Eugenia Ridley was lashing her white mare to get more speed. Annamarie's tan mount was so close as it passed by that Marianne could have reached out and touched its hindquarters.

Inexplicably, Linda-Lou's bay faltered and fell back. Marianne overtook her and raced onward toward the oak tree. Ahead of her, the two leaders, Rosie and Eugenia Ridley, were jockeying for position. Both riders swung around the turn near the oak tree, their mounts neck and neck, fighting for the lead. Annamarie was behind and slightly to the left of Rosie's gray.

Suddenly Eugenia raised her whip, and in an instant Marianne saw what the woman was about to do. With a cry, she veered off the course, heading straight toward the

oncoming riders. Rosie raised her head and motioned her
out of the way, but just as the Indian woman leaned forward in the saddle, Eugenia bent and slashed at the gray
gelding's front legs. Rosie's horse faltered.

Eugenia pulled up even with Rosie's mount and lifted
her whip again.

Without conscious thought Marianne rode straight for
Eugenia's white mare, and at the last second, she put her
head down and drove Dancer between the two lead riders.
She would never forget the fury and hatred on Eugenia Ridley's face.

With a cry, Rosie veered off-course to get out of the way,
and Eugenia's white mare thundered past, taking the lead.
Just as she passed Marianne, the woman raised her whip
and slashed it across Dancer's face and the horse plunged
sideways.

Half a head behind both women came Annamarie. She
slipped between Rosie's faltering gray and Eugenia's horse
and streaked forward toward the finish line.

Marianne fought to stay in the saddle as Dancer twisted
under her. The last thing she remembered was a puffy cloud
in the patch of blue sky overhead and then blackness.

Abe reached her first. And then Rosie, who circled back
around instead of finishing the race.

"Get the doc!" Abe yelled. Rosie pivoted and raced off
toward town.

Lance watched Annamarie streak across the finish line
on her sleek tan mare, but instead of reining to a stop she
turned her horse in a tight circle and headed back on to the
course. Then Linda-Lou Ness galloped up. "Get help!" she
screamed. She, too, raced off the way she had come.

Lance stared after the woman, and then he started to run.

By the time he arrived, a circle of people surrounded
the figure on the ground, and with a sickening jolt he rec-

ognized Marianne's red plaid shirt. Just as he approached, Rosie rode up with Doc Dougherty.

"Don't move her!" the doctor yelled as he slipped off the horse. He knelt over the still form on the ground, and someone—Annamarie, he guessed—began to cry.

Abe stepped into his path. "Don't look, son. Doc's takin' care of her."

He shoved the older man out of his way. "Marianne!"

The doctor looked up. "She can't hear you, Lance. Stand clear and let me do my job."

He stared down at the still form on the ground. Her face was dead white, and a trickle of blood ran across one cheek. He started to kneel beside her, but Abe caught his shoulder.

"She ain't dead, Lance. Best give Doc some room."

His legs went weak. "What happened?"

"Not exactly sure," Abe said.

Suddenly Annamarie gave a cry and flung herself into her brother's arms. "I saw it all," she sobbed. "That lady, Mrs. Ridley, tried to whip the Indian lady's horse. Marianne ro-rode right between then to try to s-stop her."

"Ya mean goin' in the opposite direction?" Abe queried.

"Y-yes," the girl choked.

Sammy ran up. Rosie met him with an order. "Get wagon and blanket," she commanded. "Make stretcher." She slipped off her horse and handed him the reins; in the next instant Sammy was in the saddle and racing toward town.

Marianne's face looked sick-white, but Lance could see her chest rise and fall, so he knew she was breathing. But she didn't open her eyes.

Minutes passed while Doc Dougherty worked over her and Lance sweated. Then Sammy clattered up in the wagon and tossed down a blanket. The doctor motioned Lance down beside his wife. "Talk to her," he ordered. He began folding the blanket in thirds.

Lance picked up Marianne's limp hand and leaned over

her. "Marianne, wake up. Open your eyes, honey, and look at me."

No response.

"Keep talking to her," the doctor urged. He began feeling along her legs, then pressed his hands along the length of each arm. When he touched her shoulder, she moaned.

"Marianne," Lance entreated, his voice unsteady. "Can you hear me? Please, honey, wake up."

"Sammy," Abe ordered. "Go get the mattress from my cot at the shop."

The boy nodded, and the wagon rattled off.

"Good thinking," the doctor said.

Lance brought his mouth close to Marianne's ear and began to talk. He didn't know what he said, just kept calling her name and urging her to open her eyes. When Sammy returned with the mattress, Doc carefully rolled her on to the folded blanket and then he and Lance lifted her on to the mattress in the wagon bed. Lance and the doctor climbed up beside her, and Abe joined Sammy on the driver's bench.

"Take it slow, son," the doctor cautioned. "Don't want to jostle her too much."

It seemed like hours before they reached the Smoke River hospital, and still Marianne hadn't opened her eyes. Lance began to suspect there was more wrong with her than the doctor was admitting.

"Doc?"

"Concussion," the physician answered. "Her collar bone's bruised, and she's got three broken ribs. I also suspect her sternum might be cracked." He sent Lance a quick look. "Try not to worry."

Lance snorted. "Are you kidding?"

"No, I am not kidding. Keep talking to her but don't touch her. She's banged up pretty bad."

Chapter Thirty-One

She was swimming under water, but it hurt. Was she dead? No, she reasoned. She hurt too much. It wouldn't hurt if she were dead, would it? Death was supposed to be painless.

Everything hurt. She could hear Lance's voice, but it sounded far, far away. How strange. He must be near, because she could smell his pine soap, but his voice was coming from somewhere way off.

He was saying things. Sweet things, like how much he loved her. He'd never said that before, that he loved her. Maybe she was dead after all.

"Marianne, open your eyes," he said. His voice sounded funny. Quavery. "Wake up and look at me. Please, honey. *Please.*"

He kept on talking, but his voice was odd. Kind of clogged-up.

Then there was another voice, and someone was feeling her shoulders and her chest. It hurt.

Lance was back, saying her name. She liked it when he said her name. She liked it when he touched and when… There was something else she liked, but she couldn't remember what it was. Something nice.

She felt awareness slipping away, and Lance's voice in her ear grew fainter and fainter until she couldn't hear it anymore. A hand was gripping hers. A strong, hard hand.

She decided she would hold on to that hand as tight as she could and let herself fall into a quiet place.

Lance sat by Marianne's bedside at the hospital until he could no longer hold his head up. Very carefully he stretched out beside her, moving slowly and deliberately to avoid jostling her. He closed his eyes, but sleep wouldn't come. Instead, he lay beside her still form and tried not to think.

Abe had come, and Rosie Greywolf and Sammy. Abe said they had postponed the other races until tomorrow, and he'd had some strong words with Eugenia Ridley, but the town fireworks display would go off as planned. Later, through the window of the hospital room, Lance watched the bursts of color light up the sky.

Every hour or so Doc Dougherty stepped into the room, listened to Marianne's chest with his stethoscope and peered under her closed eyelids. He didn't say anything, just pressed Lance's shoulder as he passed.

Toward morning he fell asleep, and when sunlight flooded in through the window he opened his eyes to find Marianne looking at him.

"Lance," she said in a drowsy voice. The next words out of her mouth left him wondering about the state of her mind.

"Is the horse hurt?"

"What?" He struggled to grasp her question. "You mean the horse you were riding? The mare is fine, Marianne. It's *you* who is not fine."

"Oh. I wondered why it hurts when I take a breath."

"Doc says you have three cracked ribs and a bruised collarbone."

"Did Annamarie win the race?"

"She did. Linda-Lou Ness came in second, and old Mrs.

Ridley came in last. Folks said she looked madder than a wet bobcat."

"Good," Marianne murmured. "She deserved to lose. I saw her attack Rosie Greywolf's horse with a whip. I tried to stop her, but… I couldn't reach them in time."

"You're lucky to be alive," Lance growled. Now he saw clearly what Marianne had been up to these past few days, not just riding with Rosie Greywolf for pleasure but getting herself ready to race. She had defied him, had risked her life without telling him. White-hot anger flooded his brain. He loved Marianne. *But right now he wanted to kill her himself!*

"Lance?"

"What?" he grated.

"Are—are you angry with me?"

"Yes," he said shortly. "I sure as hell am angry with you."

"What are you going to do?" she asked.

He groaned. "To be honest, Marianne, I don't know."

The following day Lance tore himself away from Marianne's bedside at the hospital long enough to search out Eugenia Ridley and say some things he swore he'd never say to any woman and then joined Abe for the postponed horse races. He fired the starting gun for each race, then returned to the hospital later and reported the results to Marianne.

"Sammy Greywolf won the boys' race," he told her. "Came in three full lengths ahead of his closest challenger, Teddy MacAllister. The men's race was a real nail-biter. Sheriff Hawk Rivera battled it out with Judge Jericho Silver, and at the last minute the judge won by no more than a nose. The townspeople along the route cheered themselves hoarse."

Marianne noticed those were almost the only words that passed Lance's lips. He sat beside her for hours without saying anything else, and he was obviously preoccupied. He stared out the window in her hospital room, and when Doc Dougherty said she could go home, Lance didn't even smile. His expression remained frozen, and that sent a tremor of unease through her. She could feel him withdrawing from her, and that hurt more than her cracked ribs and achy collarbone.

When they walked through the door of the shop, Abe greeted them with a big smile. "Don't guess you feel much like doin' anything 'cept readin' those dime novels of mine, Miss Marianne. I'll bring up a new excitin' one this afternoon."

"Thank you, Abe. The doctor says I can't do anything at all for another week, not even get out of bed. So I'll need a lot of reading material."

Lance said nothing.

"Not sposed to get outta bed, huh? Ya mean yer man here is gonna do the cookin'? Guess I should give him more recipes like my Poverty Pie."

"I guess so," she said, her voice subdued.

Very slowly Lance took her elbow and helped her up the stairs into their apartment. The first thing she noticed was Abe's narrow cot sitting across the room from their new double bed. The message was obvious. Lance would not be sharing her bed at night.

A choking sense of disappointment flooded through her. She remembered the last time they had slept together, the night before the race, when they had made love. How glorious, how beautiful it had been!

He helped her out of her clothes, and as soon as he deposited her on the blue quilt and tucked it around her, he headed back down to the shop. "Got three new pairs of boots to help Abe with," he explained.

She watched the door close behind him and blinked back

tears. Not for one minute did she believe Abe needed help making just three pairs of boots.

For the rest of the afternoon she slept on and off, but when she heard Lance's step on the stairs, she struggled to sit upright against the stack of pillows.

"Abe sent you a new book," he said. *"The Outlaw and the Angel."* He laid the slim volume beside her.

But he said nothing else for the next hour, just sat at the kitchen table staring out the window. Then he started to thumb through the pages of Mrs. Beeton's recipe book, and she heard him huff out a long sigh.

"Macaroni and cheese," he muttered.

"One of my favorite dishes," she ventured.

He nodded. "Do we have any macaroni?"

"In a big jar in the pantry."

"What about...uh—" he peered at the recipe book "—green peas?"

"Yes. I'll help you shell them."

He sent her a blank look. "Shell them?"

She laughed, and instantly wished she hadn't. Laughing hurt worse than breathing. "You have to get the peas out of the pods to cook them," she explained.

"Oh. Maybe we should have carrots instead."

She laughed again, and then groaned. "Lance, please don't say anything funny. It hurts to laugh."

"Sorry. Didn't mean to be funny. Let's see, now..." He turned over a page. "How do I cook carrots?"

She stuffed down another urge to laugh. "It depends. You can slice them up and boil them. Or grate them. Or—"

"Could I bake them?"

"Well, yes, I suppose so."

He ran his forefinger halfway down the page. "Carrots... uh...uh... I can't pronounce it."

"Carrots *au gratin*," Marianne said. "That means they are baked in a cream sauce with breadcrumbs on top."

"Cream sauce? What's that?"

"Well, you cook some flour and butter in a saucepan and then you stir in—"

"Too complicated," he interrupted.

He looked so frustrated she wanted to get out of bed and help him, but when she tried to move her chest hurt so much she gave up the idea. "Lance, macaroni and cheese is a bit complicated."

He looked up, a frustrated expression in his eyes. "Complicated? How complicated?"

"Well, you have to make a béchamel sauce and—"

"Right," he sighed. "Too complicated."

"Lance, why don't we have scrambled eggs for supper tonight?"

He looked so relieved she couldn't help the giggle that bubbled up. That hurt almost as much as laughing.

Lance scrambled six eggs and made some toast for supper that night. The next night he made hard-boiled eggs and toast, and on Wednesday he made egg salad sandwiches. The next day he managed a potato salad, and after that he'd exhausted his repertoire.

But he could still make toast, so on Thursday they had cheese toast. After that it was bacon sandwiches. Then French toast. Then, with Marianne's guidance, he mastered pancakes, and just when he felt he was getting the hang of being in the kitchen, Marianne decided she had healed enough.

The next morning she very slowly and carefully got out of bed, managed to pull on a skirt and button a shirtwaist, and began to move around the apartment.

"You have struggled heroically to feed me and take care of me," she announced. "And I have been in bed quite long enough."

Lance frowned. Yeah, he was relieved to no longer be splitting his time between taking care of Marianne and working for Abe, but he had mixed feelings about something. He hated to admit it, but it would be even more of a relief not to be around her at all. She was noticing how short-spoken he was, and while she no longer commented on the long silences that hung in the air, he knew she was aware of his withdrawal from her. It still smarted that she had purposely deceived him about riding in that horse race.

Deceiving one's husband might be a small matter in some marriages, but it didn't feel small to him. He no longer knew who Marianne was, his wife or a woman who just did exactly what she wanted and kept secrets. He could no longer trust her.

"Marriage is a mis'ry," Abe said one afternoon. "A man promises to love and honor and all them things, and then his woman ignores all that and does whatever the hell she wants. Cuts up yer heart in little pieces." He set a mug of coffee at Lance's elbow. "Drink up, son. It's half whiskey."

"Thanks, Abe." He studied the older man's lined face. "You think things will be different with Marianne and me when she gets better?"

"Dunno."

"What should I do, Abe? You got any ideas?"

"Nope. If'n I knew 'bout these here mysteries of married life I'd be a rich man, not slavin' away at Collingwood Boots." He smacked his hammer on to a tack harder than necessary.

Lance set his leather shears down and swallowed a big gulp of the whiskey-laced coffee. His heart felt like it was being pummeled into a quivering lump of something he couldn't begin to describe. He'd lost his appetite, and that was saying something since Marianne was now strong enough to take over the cooking. He couldn't think straight, and he didn't want to talk about it, even with Abe. The old man kept poking at him with questions, but Lance didn't have any answers. Maybe he'd *never* have any answers.

Sammy, though, was another matter. The morning after his victory in the boy's race, Sammy had taken one look at Lance's face and started to pepper him with questions. "You mad at Miss Marianne? How come you never smile anymore? Are you leaving Smoke River?"

Lance had said nothing.

"Man, I'm never gonna get married," the boy had muttered. "Must be pure hell."

After a while, Sammy clammed up. Ever since then, the boy had worked quietly at his side at the cutting table and rarely said a word beyond "Hand me the hammer."

Except for Abe's constant whistling, these days Collingwood Boots was a mighty quiet shop.

Then one morning everything changed. Lance gulped his coffee, and the closer he got to the bottom of the mug, the clearer it was to him that he couldn't go on like this. He had to do something.

He gazed out the front window of Collingwood Boots and started to make a plan.

Chapter Thirty-Two

Marianne snapped open the latest dime novel Abe had loaned her and let out a cry. "Lance! Lance, guess what?"

He raised his head from the cot where he'd been sleeping. "What?"

"Look!" She turned the book toward him.

He sat up straight and squinted across the room. "What is it?"

She bent toward him, then sucked in her breath. It still hurt to move in certain ways. "Our advertisement," she explained. "For Collingwood Boots. It's right here in the middle of this book."

Lance climbed off the cot and padded across the room to where she sat propped up in the double bed. "Yeah? Show me."

She turned the page toward him and pointed. "I didn't expect it to appear so soon."

"Abe says they publish so many new books every month they must have presses running day and night."

She tapped the book cover. "We should have hundreds of orders pouring in."

"You think so?"

"Oh, yes, of course. Orders are sure to come in, and just in time, too. Our bank account is almost empty after buying materials and paying for advertising, and the three pairs of boots you and Abe are making won't bring in any money because they're the prizes we donated for the horse races. We need orders. Lots and lots of orders."

"And when all these orders come pouring in, you figure just you and me and Abe and Sammy can handle them all?"

She bit her lip. "We will have to."

"Let's hope they don't all come in next week, Marianne. You're not ready to go back to work in the shop yet."

But orders did not pour in. A week went by, then two, and Collingwood Boots received not one single order. Every day Marianne walked to the mercantile, which served as the post office, praying she would find their small wooden mail slot overflowing with orders for boots.

And day after day she found nothing. No orders. In fact, no mail at all.

At the shop Abe had long since finished the riding boots Annamarie Panovsky had won, then a pair for Sammy and finally a pair of hand-tooled cordovan leather boots for Judge Jericho Silver, who had won the men's race.

And then they waited for more orders. Funds in the bank account dwindled until Lance had to open an account at the mercantile just to pay for coffee and flour and sugar. Abe seemed to live on air, Marianne thought. She never saw him unload even a small sack of tomatoes, so what was he eating?

"I thought I felt low when I fell off that horse," she confessed to Lance over a frugal supper of scalloped potatoes and applesauce. "Now we're watching our business fail, and I can't imagine feeling any worse than that."

He listened in a silence that stretched until her nerves began to hum. Finally she laid her fork aside and reached across the table for his hand.

"Lance, what are we going to do?"

He squeezed her fingers. "The first thing we do is not

panic. Then I think we should publish more advertisements in more dime novels. And after that we pray like hell."

She laughed, and then immediately clutched at her chest. "Ouch! It still hurts to laugh."

"You don't want me to make you laugh?"

She nodded.

"You want me to be serious."

It wasn't a question, but she nodded anyway.

"Okay, Marianne," he stated. "Here's something serious. First, we like living in Smoke River. Second, we are both intelligent, and neither one of us is afraid of hard work. And third, if we have to, we'll find something else to do in this town. No matter what happens with Collingwood Boots, *we* are going to be all right."

"What about Abe? What is he going to do?"

"Abe is a canny old guy, and he's a survivor. Abe will be all right, too. Does that make you feel any better?"

She sighed. "No, not really. I keep thinking about our wedding vows, and the 'for better or worse' part."

"Yeah, I remember. What about it?"

"This must be the 'worse' part, don't you think?"

He shrugged. "Maybe. But I'm not giving up, Marianne."

She stared at him. "You're not? Why not? Why would any sane man put up with a failing business and a wife who—"

"Deceives him?"

She closed her eyes. "Well, yes."

He reached over and touched his forefinger to her cheek. "Damned if I know. Guess I must like scalloped potatoes."

Marianne choked back a burst of laughter. "Oh, Lance, please don't say anything funny. It hurts too much. Please!"

"Sorry, honey. Guess I didn't realize I was so amusing."

Honey? He still thinks of me as 'honey'? After deceiving him the way I did?

Tears stung her eyes. "Oh, Lance, I am so s-sorry for

lying to you. What I did has s-spoiled everything between us, hasn't it?"

He stood up and very gently put his arms around her. He didn't say a word, but he didn't need to. She breathed in his scent, part wood smoke and part sweat with a whiff of pine soap, and suddenly she felt much better.

"Are we friends again?" she asked shyly.

"Nope." He bent his head and tipped her face up to his. "Not friends," he murmured. "Maybe lovers. *Maybe*."

He kissed her, very gently, and rested his forehead against hers. "But not tonight," he breathed.

Chapter Thirty-Three

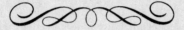

Marianne had been back in the shop for only one hour when the already shaky stability of Collingwood Boots was further threatened. It started when Eugenia Ridley paid a visit.

The woman bustled through the front door and swished her considerable bulk up to the table where Marianne sat poring over the account books.

"Well, dearie," the woman said in a grating tone, "I see you're still here."

Marianne leveled an icy gaze on the woman. "Yes, we are still here, Mrs. Ridley," she said evenly. "What do you want?"

The woman leaned over conspiratorially. "You can do this town and yourself a favor."

"Oh? What favor would that be?"

"Get rid of that Indian boy I've seen skulking around your shop."

Very deliberately Marianne laid her pen down on the table, drew in a steadying breath and looked directly into the woman's narrowed eyes. "Mrs. Ridley, who Collingwood Boots employs is the business of no one but Collingwood Boots. Do I make myself clear?"

Mrs. Ridley drew herself up until the buttons that marched down her bosom threatened to pop off. "You don't understand. Indians are untrustworthy. They're lazy. And no one in Smoke River wants anything to do with them."

"On the contrary, Mrs. Ridley, I understand perfectly. You just don't like Indians. I am afraid Collingwood Boots does not share your prejudice."

"I'm not prejudiced!" the woman shot back. "It's a fact. Just ask anybody in town."

Marianne clenched her fist under the table. "I have heard not one single thing from anyone in Smoke River that supports your feeling. And even if I did, Collingwood Boots would not alter the employment of a valued employee." She stood up. "I bid you good morning, Mrs. Ridley."

She resisted the impulse to add "and do not come back." A good businesswoman could not afford to insult anyone, even someone as reprehensible as Eugenia Ridley. But she was glad, glad, *glad* she had thwarted this woman's vicious attack on Rosie Greywolf during the race. She never wanted to lay eyes on Eugenia Ridley again.

Without dropping her gaze Marianne waited until the woman pulled her shawl around her ample shoulders and swept out the shop door. Then she sank back on to her chair and dropped her head in her hands.

Someone slid a mug of coffee on to the table in front of her. "Brung ya some coffee, Miss Marianne," Abe said. "Consider it yer reward fer not killin' that old biddy."

"I don't suppose you added any whiskey?" she asked, her voice hopeful.

He barked out a laugh. "I sure thought about it, but then I figgered you'd want to stay sober fer tonight."

"Oh? Why tonight?"

A crimson flush turned Abe's dark cheeks even darker. "No partic'lar reason," he said lightly.

"I don't believe you," she said. "What about tonight?"

His eyebrows rose. "Well, jes' that Mister Lance is…

well...he's... Aw, I cain't tell ya, Miss Marianne. Pretend I never said nuthin'."

Her curiosity swept away the bitter taste Eugenia Ridley's visit had left in her mouth, but Abe moved away without explaining. For the rest of the morning she tried to concentrate on the columns of figures before her and stop wondering about what was happening tonight.

Late in the afternoon, Abe reappeared and slipped another one of his dime novels under her elbow. *Rusty of the Rio Grande*. He gave her shoulder a pat. "Why don'tcha call it a day, Miss Marianne? Them numbers'll add up jest the same tomorrow."

"That's just the problem, Abe," she said with a sigh. "The numbers *don't* add up. Unless we get some orders, we're going to go bankrupt."

He pursed his lips. "That so? Collingwood's been down before, honey-girl. Old Mistuh Collingwood, he allus pulled us outta the hole."

Marianne snapped the account book shut. "But old Mister Collingwood isn't here now, Abe."

He patted the closed volume. "Miss Marianne, it ain't 'rithmetic that's important."

"This is a business, Abe. If arithmetic isn't important, what *is* important?"

"What's important is grit. You got it. Lance got it. I got it. Even Sammy's got it. Jest gotta keep goin' no matter what."

Marianne tipped her head down so he wouldn't see the tears flooding her eyes. How could he possibly believe they could survive with no work coming in? When they couldn't even afford to buy food? She was more worried about Abe than about Lance and herself; she and Lance were young and strong. Abe was an old man.

She gritted her teeth to suppress a sob. "I—I'm going upstairs to cook supper now."

"You do that, Miss Marianne. Me, I'm takin' supper with Sammy and his ma tonight. That Rosie, she can cobble up a meal outta dribs and drabs like nobody I ever seen."

Marianne sent him a wobbly smile, stood up and started to drag herself up to the apartment. Halfway up the stairs she heard a thump and Lance's voice shouting a profanity. My heavens, she had never heard such a word come out of his mouth!

Then she shook her head. Why should she be surprised? Lance was as frustrated and depressed as she was. But when she opened the door, he was standing in the middle of the kitchen with a big grin on his face.

"What was that noise?" she asked.

"I was…uh…folding up something, and I dropped it."

She recognized a hand-in-the-cookie-jar expression when she saw it. "Folding up what?"

He didn't answer. Instead, he turned away and lifted two plates from the china cabinet. "I made supper for you. Baked potatoes and…"

She sniffed the air appreciatively. "And what? Something smells wonderful."

"And, um, cheese. Melted."

"Is that the last of our potatoes?"

"Almost. We still have some cheese, though. Abe's been getting some from Mrs. Hinckley. Seems her cow gave more milk than she expected last fall, so she made lots of cheese. And I think she's got a soft spot for Abe."

Marianne bit her lip. "What were you folding up?"

"The cot. Now that your cracked ribs are almost healed I figured we didn't need it any longer."

She caught her breath. *Does that mean he's forgiven me for lying to him?* She tried to catch his eye, but he had turned away.

Lance scrabbled in the cutlery drawer. Marianne's

cracked ribs were one reason why he'd folded up the cot. He didn't want to tell her the other reason. Not yet, anyway.

He watched her put one of Abe's new dime novels on the night table beside the bed and tried not to smile. With any luck she'd never get to read it.

But he'd have to go slow, not so much because of her cracked ribs, but because of their cracked relationship. Relationships, he was learning, were much harder to heal than bones.

While he busied himself setting out the plates and forks for supper, Marianne puttered aimlessly about the apartment. He noted that she sent an extra-long look at their double bed, and for the hundredth time in their marriage he wondered what she was thinking. He wondered even more what she was feeling about their relationship. About their marriage. About *him*.

He lifted the potatoes out of the oven, split them open and grated the small block of cheese over each half. It was a pretty sparse supper, but he had a surprise hidden in the pantry. He'd slaved over it all afternoon, and he sure hoped she liked it.

She didn't say much during their meager supper, just listlessly poked forkfuls of cheese-topped baked potato past her lips. But something about the tentative expression in her eyes made him wonder. It gave him a sliver of hope, but he took pains not to let it show.

When he had finished all of his baked potato and half of hers, he sprang his surprise. "Marianne, I… I made something extra for supper tonight."

She looked up, a question in her green eyes. "What is it?"

"I hid it in the pantry." He pushed his chair back and stood up. "I made some coffee, too. Thought you might want some after…" He didn't finish the thought, just opened the pantry door, ducked inside and fumbled with the match he'd hidden in his shirt pocket.

When he emerged with his creation on a china platter, her eyes widened and the expression on her face was worth the hours of frustration he'd spent all afternoon.

"A cake!" she breathed. "And…a candle!"

He set it on the table. "Happy birthday, Marianne."

"Birthday! Oh. *Oh.* I'd forgotten all about my birthday!" Her eyes filled with tears which slid slowly down her pale cheeks.

"Yeah, I thought maybe you'd forgotten about it. But I recalled last year when you thought nobody remembered about your birthday and how surprised you were when Mrs. Schneiderman baked you a cake."

"Oh, Lance." She clasped her hand over her mouth, and the tears trickled over her fingers.

"It's an applesauce cake," he said. "I did everything Mrs. Beeton said in her book, but—"

The sound of breaking glass stopped him mid-sentence. Marianne jerked upright. "What was that?"

"Don't know. Sounded like a window breaking." He moved to the door, swung it open and peered down into the shop.

Shards of glass shone in the faint light. He was halfway down the stairs before he figured out what the noise was. Someone had heaved a brick through the front window.

Marianne came to stand beside him.

"Why on earth would anyone—?"

"Because whoever it was wanted to break the window," he said shortly. "Someone must have a beef of some kind with Collingwood Boots."

"But who—?" She broke off with a cry. "I know who. Eugenia Ridley. How *could* she?"

"And on your birthday, too," he murmured. He put his arm around her. With a choked sob she turned toward him, and he pressed her head into his shoulder. "Let's have some applesauce cake," he said. "And afterward we can…"

"Go to bed," she whispered.

He opened his mouth to reply, then closed his eyes and held his breath. It wasn't at all what he expected Marianne to say.

Chapter Thirty-Four

Andit wasn't what Lance expected later, after she had devoured two pieces of his applesauce cake and wept into her coffee. Later, when she was undressing behind the folding screen in the corner, he could hear her sniffling, and his spirits sank. He wanted to hold her close and assure her that he still cared for her. Even if he was still angry with her, Marianne still mattered.

He wanted to make love to her, but he guessed it wasn't going to be tonight.

She said she liked the cake he'd baked. And she was touched that he remembered her birthday. Even if she was unstrung tonight, he hoped to God she cared about him the way he cared about her.

Why was she crying? Because that witch Mrs. Ridley had thrown a brick through the shop window? Or was it because they had no orders for boots and they were running out of money?

He watched her garments appear over the top of the screen, then heard water splashing into the ceramic bowl and the catch in her breathing as she wept. It tore him up inside, made his chest hurt and his eyes sting.

When she finally stepped out from behind the screen her eyes were red and swollen and her lips were trembling. A knife sliced into his gut. He leaned over and puffed out the lamp and lifted the quilt so she could slide into bed.

She edged close to him and reached for his hand under the covers. "Lance, I want to say something to you."

His belly dropped down to his toes. "Yeah?"

She delayed so long he knew it was going to be bad. In silence he lay waiting for the ax to fall and chop his heart into little pieces.

But that wasn't what happened. She simply held on to his hand and said nothing. If any other woman was upset with her husband she would unleash a stream of harsh words or scream or even pound her fists against his chest. But Marianne, his Marianne, wasn't like other women. She wasn't like other wives, and he now knew that she never would be. Marianne was...Marianne.

"Lance, that first morning when I sneaked out to go riding with Rosie I felt just awful. And then when I deliberately didn't tell you about riding in the women's race I felt even worse."

"Yeah," he said cautiously. He knew what was coming. He didn't want to hear it.

"But then something happened, and I turned some kind of corner. About us," she added. "About being married to you."

He said nothing. The truth was he didn't trust his voice.

She brought her hand to rest on his thrumming heart. "I think that our marriage is a real marriage," she said in a watery voice. "I know it's not always going to be happy, but..."

Lance gritted his teeth.

"I made a terrible mistake by not telling you what I intended to do, but I have learned something. I learned that it matters. Our relationship matters. *You* matter."

He rolled toward her. "Marianne..."

She laid one finger across his lips. "I am not finished."

Oh, God, here it comes. He tensed, waiting for the blow.

"This has been a really dreadful time. Everything was awful. I hurt our marriage, and I hurt you. And what did you do?" She swiped tears away with her fingers. "You baked me a birthday cake."

"And folded up the cot," he reminded.

She brushed her lips against his cheek. "I am so glad you—" Her voice broke, but she went on. "F-found Mrs. Beeton's recipe book."

"Yeah? How come?"

"I think that should be obvious," she said softly. She shifted her body closer to his and tucked her head under his chin. After a long while he realized she had fallen asleep. God in heaven, his Marianne was asleep in his arms!

Very slowly, he reached out and touched her hair.

Marianne woke to bright sunlight streaming in the window and Lance sound asleep beside her, one arm stretched out on the pillow and the other draped across her waist. It was lovely to wake up this way, enveloped in his warmth. If she wasn't feeling a twinge from her still sore ribs every time she moved or took a deep breath, she would wake him with kisses and…more. Much more.

She rose, dressed carefully in her denim work skirt and blue striped shirtwaist and stirred up the coals in the stove. Then she filled the speckleware coffeepot, added a handful of ground beans and set it to boil.

In the pantry she found three eggs and half a loaf of bread. She would have to bake today, and that meant a trip to the mercantile to buy flour and coffee beans and whatever else Mr. Ness would let her put on their overdue account. If they didn't get some work orders soon, they would use up all their credit. And if that happened, they would be without food.

That thought was so paralyzing she brushed it out of her mind and whipped up the eggs with the last few tablespoons of milk. Then she cut four thick slices of bread and laid them on the oven rack to toast. By the time she poured the eggs into the iron skillet, Lance was awake.

She knew he was watching her. She could feel his gaze so keenly it was difficult to concentrate on scrambling the eggs.

They ate slowly, without talking. She felt close to him this morning, maybe because she had confessed her feelings the night before. Or maybe because she had slept all night in his arms.

How surprising relationships were! Just when she thought she knew who Lance was, she discovered something new. Last night she learned he could be angry and not lash out at her, and that she could hurt him. He had revealed a vulnerability she had never seen before. That knowledge sent a shiver up her spine. Knowing you could hurt someone made a person cautious.

"I'm going to help Abe chop wood this morning," he suddenly announced. "His wood box is low, and so is ours."

"I am going to visit Rosie Greywolf," Marianne announced. Lance raised his eyebrows, but she took a deep breath and continued. "I feel more and more uneasy about Eugenia Ridley. If she could throw a brick through our shop window, who knows what she might do to Rosie's place?"

When she went down to the shop, Abe looked up from his broom and tipped his head toward the pile of broken glass on the floor. "I see you got a taste of Indian fever last night, Miss Marianne."

"Indian fever?"

"Nuthin' new to me. It's 'xactly like Negro fever, and I seen plenty of that in my time."

"Here? In Smoke River?"

"Naw, not here. But when somebody like that Miz Ridley gets her dander up, you kin bet yer boots sooner or later she'll be rilin' up others."

"Oh, Abe, surely not."

"People are funny, Miss Marianne. Somethin' comes along an' scares 'em, and they start lookin' fer a scapegoat."

"Scapegoat? You mean us? Collingwood Boots?"

"Folks don't like to be scared. They need somethin' they can point to an' say 'it's *their* fault'."

"Yes, it was the same back in St. Louis."

"It's jes' human nature for people to slide outta takin' responsibility fer their mistakes or failures or whatever ain't to their liking at the moment. So they look fer somethin' besides theirself to blame. It's 'cuz they're scared, like I said."

"But why would Mrs. Ridley be scared?"

"Aw, who knows. She's a female, fer one thing." He pushed the glass shards into a pile, leaned his broom against the wall and reached for the dustpan. "She's losin' control over that man of hers, Oliver Ridley. Works at the sawmill, and a sorrier lookin' gent I never seen."

"Abe, is Oliver Ridley ill?"

Abe scooped up bits of glass. "Naw, he ain't sick. Just lazy. Started as a tree-skinner and never advanced none in all the years he's been at the mill. The other fellers can saw up seven or eight big logs in the time it takes ol' Oliver to roll one itty-bitty one on to the green chain."

"I'm going to visit Sammy's mother this morning," she announced.

Abe shook his head. "Rosie won't be home, Miss Marianne. She'll be at the restaurant, washin' dishes like she always does. Good worker, that Rosie."

"Sammy is a good worker, too."

"Oh, sure, Sammy works real hard. Jes' wish I had somethin' fer him to work *on*."

Marianne turned away. She fervently wished the same, but a business didn't survive on wishes. She waved goodbye to Abe and started off for the Smoke River restaurant. When she arrived she walked around to the back kitchen door to find Rosie.

She was bent over a huge double sink, scrubbing away on a tower of dirty plates. "No time for talk," she said. "Too busy."

Marianne picked up a dish towel and lifted a wet platter from the hot rinse water. "This isn't a social call, Rosie. It's a fact-finding visit."

The woman's eyes flicked up. "Find fact about what?"

"About your life here in Smoke River."

"Nothing to tell, Missy. Husband die. I bring baby son to town, get job."

"I understand you sent Sammy to school. He has grown into a fine young man, Rosie."

"Not man yet," she insisted. "Still a boy."

Marianne slid the dry platter into the rack of china and picked up a plate. "Nevertheless, Sammy drives the delivery wagon for Mr. Ness at the mercantile, and he is working as an apprentice at Collingwood Boots. You must be very proud of him."

Rosie splashed a stack of dirty plates into the sudsy wash water. "Sammy is good son. He work hard, like I do. Together we buy house near town. Very proud day when we move from tent."

"Rosie, has anyone in town ever made trouble for you?"

"Lots of trouble when first move to house," she said. "Someone try to burn down, but stable man smell smoke and help put out flames."

"Did anything happen after that?"

"One boy at schoolhouse start fight when Sammy was little. Sammy punch him hard. No trouble since."

"Did anyone ever object to your having a job here at the restaurant?"

Rosie looked puzzled. "Why you ask?"

"Because of what happened during the horse race. When Mrs. Ridley purposely interfered with your horse."

Rosie barked out a laugh. "More than interfere. I think she try to hurt me."

"Yes," Marianne said slowly. "I think so, too."

Another stack of china splashed into the soapy water. "When I first come to restaurant to work, was big noise in dining room. Somebody not like me washing dishes. But—" her grin spread wide "—I wash anyway. I could maybe spit on plates, but I didn't."

Marianne laughed out loud, then caught her breath as a shard of pain laced into her chest. She liked Sammy's mother. The woman had real grit.

"You drink dandelion and comfrey tea for hurt in bones," Rosie advised. "I bring dried leaves to shop."

"Thank you, Rosie."

"Is there other reason you ask about trouble?"

Marianne bit her lip. "Yes. I'm afraid someone in town doesn't think Sammy should work at Collingwood Boots. And last night someone tossed a brick through our front window."

Rosie methodically slid four cups into the rinse water. "Sammy know what he wants. He will fight."

Marianne plucked out a teacup and dried it. "We will fight, too."

A smile flitted across Rosie's features, but she merely nodded and went back to scrubbing an egg-encrusted plate.

On her way out, Marianne stopped in the dining room for a cup of coffee and some information. "Rita, are there many people in town who object to an Indian family in Smoke River?"

The waitress smoothed her apron over her stomach. "Not so's you'd notice. But folks like that tend to lie low and not say much. I heard what happened at the horse race, Miss Marianne. How you got hurt."

"I think Mrs. Ridley wanted to injure Rosie more than me," Marianne said quietly.

Rita nodded. "Lots of folks were real upset a few years back when Uncle Charlie moved to town 'cuz he was Chinese. One night 'is niece Leah MacAllister, she's half-Chinese, gave 'em all what-for at a town meeting that nobody'll ever forget."

"Have you ever overheard any dinner-table talk about Rosie Greywolf and Sammy not being welcome in town?"

"Not for more'n a dozen years," the waitress said. "Most folks don't pay them any mind. Say, honey, you want some fresh peach pie?"

Peach pie! Her mouth watered at the thought, but she couldn't afford it. She shook her head. Maybe Mr. Ness would let her have some overripe peaches from the display in front of the mercantile. She could bake a pie for dessert tonight.

Ness's mercantile was jam-packed. Townspeople clogged the aisles buying brooms and boys' shirts and hoes and everything from ripe tomatoes to strawberries. The peaches on display were so ripe they were mushy.

"My, you are busy today, Mr. Ness."

"We're always busy on Saturday when people come into town to pick up their mail in the back room. Guess you're here to pick up yours, too."

Marianne blinked. "Mail? Collingwood Boots hasn't gotten any mail for the past few weeks."

Mr. Ness's pale eyebrows went up. "Huh? That's not right, Miz Marianne. Collingwood Boots gets more mail than anybody in town! Your mail slot is stuffed plumb full every day."

"But I check our mail every single day and the slot is always empty."

"Can't be," he insisted.

"It most certainly *can* be!"

The mercantile owner stepped away from the counter.

"Come with me, Miz Marianne. Just yesterday I shoved five letters in your mail slot. Are you sayin' you never found them?"

Marianne folded her arms across her waist. "That is exactly what I am saying."

"Well, now, that's real strange."

A sudden suspicion glimmered in Marianne's brain. "Mr. Ness, could someone else have taken our mail?"

"Well, um, yeah, they could, all right. But that'd be illegal, ma'am. Takin' somebody else's mail is a crime."

Marianne leaned toward the mercantile owner and spoke quietly. "Have you noticed anyone besides me who comes in to pick up their mail every day as I do?"

He scratched his chin. "Now that you mention it, there has been someone. All these years she's never been in to check her mail more'n once a week. Fact is, she never got much mail before, but a few weeks ago she started comin' in every day. Usually around suppertime."

"Eugenia Ridley," she murmured.

The mercantile owner nodded.

"Mr. Ness, thank you very much for telling me this. I will be back at suppertime."

Chapter Thirty-Five

"Lance, I have a surprise for you."

Lance looked up from the kitchen table. "Peach pie, right? I've been smelling it for the last hour."

"Well, yes. Eventually."

He frowned. "Huh?"

"I… I have to go to the mercantile for something."

"Now?"

"Yes. Before supper."

"You want me to go instead?"

"No," she said quickly. "This is something I need to do alone. And I need you to watch what's in the oven. Keep my pie from burning."

Lance studied his wife. "What's the surprise, Marianne?"

She sent him that sweet smile that always melted his insides. "You'll have to wait and see."

"Marianne…?"

"I will be back in an hour. Or less."

Lance stared at her. She was keeping something from him. Another secret. The back of his neck began to itch. *Well, two can play at this game.*

"Marianne, you know what we're going to do tonight?" She spun toward him. "What?"

"Tonight," he repeated. "In bed."

"I cannot imagine." But her cheeks were getting all pink. "What are we going to do?"

He took her shoulders and deliberately turned her toward the door. "Guess you'll have to wait and see."

She gave him a look he had to interpret as Very Interested, and in the next instant stepped out the door. He smiled to himself. Let her wonder. In the meantime, he corralled his eagerness for her return and bent to peek at the pie in the oven.

Marianne marched over to the mercantile at such a fast pace that when the bell over the door chimed she found she was short of breath. She gave Carl Ness a brief look and then moved quickly toward the bank of mail slots at the back of the store where Carl distributed the mail every day. She stationed herself in the fabric aisle and settled down behind the bolts of denim and flannel piled on the shelves to watch.

She didn't have long to wait. The bell over the door rang once more, and she heard Mr. Ness greet his customer.

She waited.

An agonizing minute passed while she desperately tried to calm her racing heart, and then a figure moved toward the back of the mercantile and the bank of mail slots. Marianne held her breath, counted to sixty and moved forward to observe the person.

She watched Eugenia Ridley run her forefinger along the third tier of wooden slots. She paused on the fourth slot from the left, the one belonging to Collingwood Boots, and her plump hand flicked out to gather up a small pile of letters.

Marianne stepped forward. "Mrs. Ridley."

The woman jerked, and the mail spilled on to the floor. "Oh! You startled me."

"I intended to," Marianne said. She leaned over and scooped up the envelopes. "These are addressed to Collingwood Boots," she said, her voice hard. "Not to you."

"Oh, well, it's simply an oversight, dearie. I accidentally reached into the wrong mail slot."

Marianne just looked at her. "No, you did not, Mrs. Ridley. I hope you are aware that stealing mail is a crime."

"Well!" the woman huffed. "I am certainly not stealing—"

"Yes, you are," Marianne said quietly. "And if all those letters addressed to Collingwood Boots are not delivered to the shop within an hour, I will notify Sheriff Rivera that you are committing mail theft."

The color drained from the woman's face. "You wouldn't dare!"

"Try me," Marianne said calmly.

"I'll say… I'll say it was just a misunderstanding."

"And I will prove that it wasn't."

Carl Ness appeared at her elbow. "And I will be here to back up Miz Burnside."

"Oh. Well. I—I will return home and see if I have accidentally taken any of your mail."

Marianne said nothing. Carl Ness took Mrs. Ridley by the elbow and walked her to the front door. When the woman had disappeared, Marianne's legs turned to jelly.

"Thank you, Mr. Ness."

"You did the right thing, Miz Burnside. And you did it real direct and quiet-like. Good for you."

"Let's hope it will be good for Collingwood Boots," she said. "We are just a breath away from going broke."

The proprietor stepped away and returned in a moment to press a bag of fresh apricots into her hand. "Go on home, Miss Marianne. In an hour I predict you and your husband are gonna be opening a whole lot of mail."

Marianne was so relieved she practically floated out the door and down the street to the shop. Lance met her at the top of the stairs.

"The pie's done," he announced. "So, what's the surprise?"

She threw her arms around him. "I'll tell you in an hour.

In the meantime…" She kissed him, laughed happily at his puzzled expression and kissed him again.

They dawdled over supper while Marianne struggled to keep a most unladylike grin off her face and Lance worked to keep his impatience under control. After slices of peach pie and coffee, he carefully settled her on his lap and buried his nose in her hair.

"Where's my surprise?" he murmured.

"It's coming." She kissed his cheek and wound her arms around his neck, then kissed his other cheek.

A minute later they heard the shop door open downstairs and Abe's surprised voice. In the next minute his footsteps pounded up the stairs, and Lance opened the door to find him setting a large cardboard carton of letters on the landing.

Marianne came to stand beside him. "Lance, just look! Who would ever dream that Christmas could come in August?"

"Is this the surprise?" he asked, staring down at the carton of mail.

She nodded. "Do you want to open them now?" she whispered.

"Let's open just one," he countered. "In bed."

Ten minutes later he drew off her nightgown, and while she read aloud the contents of one letter, he pressed his lips in places she had never dreamed of. Very soon, she confided, she would be able to move without pain from her still tender ribs.

He lifted the sheet of paper out of her hand and puffed out the lamp. "That," he said with a sigh, "will be a surprise worth waiting for."

Every single letter Marianne and Lance and Abe and Sammy opened the next morning contained at least one order for a pair of Collingwood Boots, along with a bank draft.

"Jumpin' Jiminy, Miss Marianne, we can't begin to fill all these orders! I never seen so many people wantin' boots all at once. Ridin' boots. Fancy dress boots with hand toolin'. Ladies boots, even little kids boots. You'd think a thousand folks been goin' barefoot all summer!"

"Maybe wearing boots is becoming fashionable," Marianne said with a laugh.

"Mebbe." His tone sounded doubtful.

Lance looked up from the pile of envelopes in his lap. "Fashionable or not, how the heck are we gonna make this many pairs of boots?"

"We could work double shifts?" Marianne suggested.

Sammy spoke up for the first time. "Golly, Abe's the only person here who really knows how to make boots. I'm still learning the trade, and so is Lance and you, Miss Marianne."

Abe nodded and scratched his chin. "Yep, there's only the four of us. We'll have to work like the devils from hell are nippin' at our heels."

"Do you think we can do it?" Marianne asked.

"Sure," Abe said. "I got three good apprentices, ain't I?"

Lance ran his hand through his hair. "And we're learnin' the boot-making business as fast as we can."

"And praying," Marianne murmured under her breath.

They started on the long list of orders the very next morning. Marianne cut and trimmed pieces of cowhide until her hands ached, and then Sammy took over the cutting while she practiced her skill with the tack hammer. Abe and Lance worked together over the boot lasts until past midnight every night. Then they slept three hours and started in again.

Sammy started curling up in one corner of the shop to sleep between shifts. It seemed to Marianne that Abe never slept. He cut out leather pieces and nailed on boot soles and labored over his embossing dies and made pot after pot of coffee and never seemed to tire. He swore he slept some each night, but even though he had his cot back, she was not convinced. He was always in the shop working, instructing, advising and encouraging.

Making boots was exhausting, Marianne realized. They all worked day and night, and little by little they learned. She was also discovering that making very fine boots took time.

"That's why Collingwood Boots are known from Texas to New York," Abe reminded her. "'Cause they's the finest boots that ever got pulled on to a human foot."

They filled nine orders for Texas Rangers. Ladies in Arizona wanted fancy riding boots to show off in a parade for some mayor's birthday. So many orders poured in Marianne began to wonder if the four of them could survive at the pace they were working.

"We can never keep this up," she groaned to Lance one night after supper. "Success is like opening Pandora's box. What we have set in motion is more than we can handle."

She was undressing behind the screen, but Lance was so exhausted he couldn't keep his eyes open. Instead he lay in bed listening to her voice and thanked God for the few hours they stole each night to be together. But they were both so weary after a day of boot-making they fell asleep as soon as their heads touched the pillows.

Marianne had come close to fainting that evening, and Abe had sent them both off to rest tonight. But he was still working down in the shop.

"We wanted to own our own business, Lance," she said after two cups of strong tea. "But this feels dreadful. We never see each other. We grab sandwiches at odd hours and we never sit down for a meal together. We hardly ever talk because we're so tired."

She crept into bed beside him. "We cannot survive this pace."

He opened his eyes. "We can try," he whispered. "God knows we're both so tired we can't see straight, but we've got to keep going."

"I can't," she said in a shaky voice. "Never in my entire life did I think I would ever say those words, but..." She choked back a sob.

He rolled to face her. "For better or worse, remember?"

She tried to smile at him. "I thought we'd already been through 'worse.'"

"Yeah, me, too. Guess there's more, huh?"

"Lance, is this what a marriage really *is*? Just one calamity after another?"

He tucked her head under his chin. "I think this is what *life* is, Marianne." He pressed his lips to her forehead. "Go to sleep. We're both too tired to make love, so I guess it'll have to wait some more."

"Until when?" she asked in a sleepy voice.

"I don't know. We have thirty more orders to fill before the end of next month."

She groaned. "I bet Mrs. Schneiderman would laugh if she could see us now. It feels like we left a peaceful pasture in St. Louis and walked right into the lion's den in Smoke River."

He was quiet for so long she thought he'd fallen asleep. "Yeah," he said at last. "But we're in the lion's den *together*. I bet if Mrs. Schneiderman could see us now she'd be jealous."

Chapter Thirty-Six

The next morning Abe and Sammy went off to the railway station to pick up a shipment of cowhide, and Lance found himself alone in the shop. He was hunched over a pair of fancy riding boots, applying oil to the uppers and buffing it to a shine, when the door opened and a young woman stepped in. She was wearing a fancy-looking red print dress with lots of ruffles, and she sent Lance a dazzling smile.

"Oh, yoah just the man Ah want to see!" Her blond curls bobbed with every word.

"You need something, Miss...?"

"Moreland. Fanny Moreland." She offered a hand dripping with rings. "Miss," she emphasized.

He wiped his sticky fingers on a towel and awkwardly shook her fluttery ones, then found he couldn't escape her grip. "Uh, you wanted something?" he reminded her.

"Why, yes." She gave his hand an extra squeeze. "Mah birthday is next week, and a gentleman admirer wants to give me a pair of riding boots. Fancy ones. You know, with lots of designs in the leather."

"Ma'am, I'm afraid we're backed up with orders into next month, so..."

She sent him a dimpled smile and playfully wound one long blond curl around her forefinger. "Ah will be so disappointed if Ah can't have them for a whole month. Y'all wouldn't want to disappoint me, would you?"

Lance straightened to his full height. "Sorry, Miss Moreland. I don't have much choice. We've got so many orders coming—"

She laid her hand on his arm. "Really?" She drew the word out. "Re-ahl-ly."

"Really," he said dryly. He moved away from her. "Best I can do is measure your foot."

"Why, goodness me, that would be so awfully nice of you. Lance, isn't it?"

"Burnside," he supplied. "I'll get some paper and a pencil to trace your foot." He opened the top drawer of Marianne's desk, and when he turned back, Miss Moreland had hiked up her skirt and was unlacing her high-heeled pump.

"No need to take your shoe off, Miss Moreland. You can just step on this paper, and I'll draw an outline of your foot."

She looked up with a slow smile. "But mah new boots will have to fit evah so close. Ah'll just slip this ol' pump off and…"

Before he could stop her, the black leather oxford dropped to the floor. He knelt before her and slid the heavy sheet of paper forward. "Put your foot down here."

"Oh, surely you want mah *bare* foot!" She steadied herself with one hand on his shoulder and hitched her red skirt over her knees.

"No," he said quickly. "Leave your stocking on."

Her skirt fluttered down, but she kept her hand on his shoulder. Lance gritted his teeth, positioned her foot on the paper and hastily sketched the outline.

"Don't y'all want to trace mah other foot?"

"No need," he said tersely. "One foot's the same size as the other." Maybe it was and maybe it wasn't, but he didn't really care.

"Really?" *Re-ahl-ly?*

He stood up. "I'll keep your measurement in our files,

Miss Moreland. We'll get around to your boots as soon as we can."

She made no move to put her shoe back on. "Lance, Ah do hope y'all will be callin' on me soon. With my new boots," she added.

"They will be delivered by our driver, Miss Moreland. Just as soon as they're ready." He moved past her, swung the shop door open and waited for her to leave. She shot him a look and bent to slip her shoe back on.

"'Bye now, Lance," she murmured as she swished past him. "Y'all won't make me wait too long, Ah hope?"

"Just as long as it takes, Miss Moreland." He shut the door after her and blew out a long breath.

Marianne had just stepped out onto the apartment landing when she glimpsed Lance down on his knees before a young blonde woman who stood with her hand on his shoulder. Fanny Moreland, she remembered. They had been introduced months ago at the wedding reception. She ducked back inside the apartment.

Miss Moreland certainly seemed friendly this morning! She shook the image of Fanny's hand possessively gripping Lance's shoulder, waited until she heard the shop door close and walked down the stairs. Lance gave her a wordless nod, then went back to oiling a pair of dark leather boots.

Marianne picked up the account book from her desk. For the first time in over a month, Collingwood Boots was operating in the black. Ever since she had retrieved their missing mail, orders and payments, some in bank drafts and some in cash, had poured in. When Abe and Sammy returned, she tallied up the finances and took a big leather deposit bag over to the Smoke River bank.

On the way back to the shop she stopped in at the restaurant for coffee and a slice of peach pie. She had just picked up her fork when Rita dropped a cannonball in her lap.

"Seems your husband's caught the eye of Fanny More-land," the waitress said.

"Oh?"

"Yep. Might need to keep a real close eye on him. And her," Rita added.

"Oh. I don't think Miss Moreland is interested in us."

Rita snorted. "Isn't *you* she's interested in, Miss Mari-anne. It's Mr. Lance."

Marianne's cup clanked on to her saucer. "What? Oh, I don't think…" Then the image of Lance kneeling before the young blonde woman and her hand resting on her hus-band's shoulder floated into her mind.

"The whole town knows Fanny Moreland's a real shame-less flirt," Rita intoned. "'Specially when it comes to other women's husbands."

"I see," Marianne murmured. Well, she did and she didn't. Since the riding accident when three of her ribs had been broken, she and Lance had not been intimate. They had resumed sleeping in the same bed just two weeks ago, but she still couldn't move in certain ways without pain, and Lance had not pressed her.

But it has been weeks since we… Surely he wouldn't have lost interest in her? She'd heard that men's physical needs were more urgent than a woman's, but…but… Would that drive a man into another woman's arms? Another *flir-tatious* woman's arms?

Rita cleared her throat. "Somethin' wrong with your pie, Miss Marianne? You're not eating any."

"What? Oh, no, Rita, the pie tastes fine."

It's my marriage that isn't fine.

Back at the shop she decided to talk to Abe about it. She waited until late afternoon for a break in their work sched-ule, and when Lance left to go to the mercantile, she cor-nered Abe at the table where he was nailing on a boot heel.

He laid down his hammer and peered into Marianne's

face. "Yer lookin' all consternated, Miss Marianne. What's wrong?"

"N-nothing," she lied. She swallowed. "Oh, everything is wrong, Abe."

"Aw, now, honey-girl. Cain't be all that bad now that we're makin' boots an' rakin' in money."

She bit her lip. "Abe," she said quietly, "can I talk to you about something?"

"Why, sure. About what?"

She glanced over to where Sammy was bent over the cutting table and lowered her voice. "About Lance. And me."

"Oh? What about Lance an' you?"

She drew in a long, slow breath and dropped her voice even lower. "Abe, when a man... I mean, when it's been a long time since..."

Sammy's cutting shears halted with the blades half open.

"Yeah? A long time since what, Miss Marianne?"

"Since...um...well, you know, when a man and a woman..."

Sammy cocked his head toward them.

"Ya mean you an' Lance, huh? You haven't...?"

"Well, um, no. Remember when I fell off that horse and broke my ribs?"

"Sure do. Go on, I'm listenin'."

Sammy was listening, too, she noted.

"Well, ever since then Lance and I have not...have not..."

Sudden comprehension lit up Abe's face. "Aha! Ya mean—"

Sammy's forehead creased into a frown, and all at once she wanted to laugh. This situation was ridiculous! Here she was, confiding in an old, experienced man while a young, inexperienced one frowned in puzzlement.

"Sammy," Abe said, "why don'tcha go back to my quarters an' bring us a couple mugs of coffee?"

The boy slapped his shears on to the table and stomped off to the back room where Abe's stove and coffeepot were. The minute he was out of sight, Abe laid his gnarled hand on Marianne's shoulder and pressed her toward the front of the shop. "Now, tell me straight out what's worryin' ya."

"What's worrying me is Fanny Moreland," she blurted out.

Abe's salt-and-pepper eyebrows rose. "Aha. I heard she paid us a visit."

"Not 'us,' Abe. Lance."

He nodded. "An' you're thinkin' 'bout yer sore ribs an' Lance and you bein', well, not too rambunctious at night, and you're wonderin' if he's got his eyes all lit up elsewhere, izzat it?"

"Y-yes. I'm wondering if Fanny Moreland has lit up his eyes."

Abe patted her shoulder. "That would surprise me some, Miss Marianne."

She expelled her breath in a rush just as Sammy returned balancing a brimming mug of coffee in each hand.

"But," Abe whispered, "t'wouldn't be the first time ol' Abe's been hornswoggled."

"Oh. *Oh*."

Sammy set the coffee down on Marianne's desk. "What's 'hornswoggled' mean?"

"It means someone pullin' the wool over yer eyes so's they cain't see."

"Huh," Sammy said with a grin. "Nobody pulls the wool over *my* eyes. I see everything."

Oh, Marianne thought. *How I wish I could see everything, too.*

Chapter Thirty-Seven

Lance sat up and studied Marianne's sleeping form, curled up on the bed with her bottom snugged against his groin and her face turned away from him. Man, she sure was acting strange lately, cooking all his favorite dishes and worrying out loud about the long hours he spent working in the shop.

He liked that she worried about him. He worried about her, too. But the hardest part of the last few weeks were the nights when she came to bed smelling so good it was all he could do to keep his hands off her. When his work schedule let up a bit he'd stop by the hospital and ask Doc Dougherty how long it took broken ribs to fully heal.

It couldn't be much longer, could it? He settled back against the pillow with a sigh. He knew she was over-tired. While he put in extra hours with Abe every day, Marianne worked ten to twelve hours in the shop, and in addition she cooked, did laundry and kept their apartment clean. She was burning the candle at both ends. No matter what came up, Marianne simply rolled up her sleeves and went to work.

He knew she was pleased about the success of Colling-wood Boots. He was pleased about the growth of the business, too, but for himself there was more to it. He liked spending time in the shop. He liked learning the craft of boot-making. He liked working with crusty, exacting Abe producing boots he could be proud of. And he liked working with Sammy. The boy was turning out to be not only a fast learner but a sunny spirit and a good source of any gossip floating around town.

Funny how things worked out, he mused. He was glad he had married Marianne. In fact, even with their exhaustion at night and his wife's injuries, married life was making him happy beyond his expectations.

And, he thought with a grin, he had a secret.

At the sound of the shop door closing, Marianne glanced up from the account book. "Where is Lance off to?"

"Dunno," Abe said.

"He said he had to see about something," Sammy volunteered without looking up. He crunched his shears into a waiting length of cowhide.

Marianne twiddled her pencil between her thumb and forefinger and exchanged a look with Abe.

"See about what, Sammy?" she queried.

"He didn't say. Just said it couldn't wait."

She bit her lip. She could guess what "it" was. Fanny Moreland. She was learning more about what "for better or worse" meant in a marriage; "or worse" meant another woman.

She put her head down on her folded arms. If Mrs. Schneiderman was watching *this*, she must be shaking her head.

All her sins and shortcomings crowded into her brain with insistent, yammering voices. She had been greedy and grasping. She had selfishly coveted Uncle Matty's business with no thought about whether she was equipped to run it. Now they were struggling to catch up with all their existing orders and stay ahead of the new ones that poured in. If they couldn't meet their production obligations, word would spread and their reputation would plummet. And it would all be her fault for taking this on in the first place.

She bit her lip and raised her head to meet Abe's steady gaze. The biggest sin of all was trapping Lance into marrying her. It was a sin not only of greed but of pride, of believing she could please a man like Lance, could attract and hold his interest when pretty, accomplished women like Fanny Moreland were around. She acknowledged she had deceived Lance about riding in the race, and now she was not only injured but bone-tired and short-tempered and exhausted every night. Lance must be even more displeased with her.

A more clever woman would have figured out some way to please a man who was disappointed in her. A clever woman like Fanny Moreland would know what to do about the muddle she was in, even if she did have three cracked ribs.

She looked away and set her jaw. If she kept digging away at all her shortcomings she would go crazy. She got to her feet and marched over to the cutting table, where odd-shaped pieces of cowhide lay in neat piles, awaiting the mallets and awls and creasers and embossing dies that would turn them into top-quality boots.

It would take half a lifetime for a person to truly master all these skills. What she was good at was cooking and sewing and beating carpets and scattering feed for the chickens. What she was proficient at was running a boardinghouse!

She longed for a big house to care for, not a tiny apartment she could dust in ten minutes. All her adult life she'd wanted her own house, a house like Mrs. Schneiderman's, with a front parlor and a piano and watered silk drapes on the windows.

But it was too late for that.

She was forgetting the most important lesson she had learned in her life: *Happiness is wanting what you get.*

With sudden clarity she knew what she wanted. What would make her happy was exactly what she had, Lance Burnside. Not a big house. In fact, not a house at all. Just Lance.

Lance stood for a long time studying the pretty blue house with the graceful maple tree shading the front yard. It sat next to Rooney and Sarah's boardinghouse, and the sign on the white picket fence said it was for sale. There was now enough money in their bank account to buy it; actually he could pay for it twice over.

Would Marianne like it? Would it make her happy to have her own house? He knew he should ask her, but something held him back. The truth was he wanted to surprise her. He wanted to see her laugh again, wake up eager for the day to start, not with aching shoulders from hammering boot heels and a headache from too many hours hunched over the account books. Marianne was wearing herself out.

He turned away and headed to Ness's mercantile for the coffee beans and cornmeal they needed.

The minute he stepped through the door he wished he had walked on past. Fanny Moreland launched herself down the garden tool aisle and cornered him between rakes and brooms.

"Why, mah goodness me, Lance." She curled her fingers over his arm. "Seein' y'all is such a great pleasure!"

"Miss Moreland."

"Oh, surely y'all could call me Fanny? After all, Ah'm now a customer of yours, aren't I?"

Over her head, Lance spotted Carl Ness rolling his eyes. "Collingwood Boots has many customers, Miss Moreland. We maintain a businesslike relationship with all of them."

Carl Ness nodded decisively.

"Of course you do," Fanny purred. "Ah find that truly admirable."

"In that case, Miss Moreland—" he plucked her hand from his arm "—you won't mind if I purchase some coffee beans for my wife."

Carl grinned. "Right this way, Lance." He gestured toward the next aisle.

"And a sack of cornmeal," he murmured as he passed the mercantile owner.

Fanny twitched her green silk skirt in place and stepped after him. "Ah'm evah so fond of the coffee the Smoke River hotel serves." She sent Lance a significant look.

"Are you?" he said absently.

Carl thrust a bag of coffee beans into his hands. "Miss Marianne likes this brand," he said. "Arbuckle's."

"Why, isn't that a coincidence," Fanny sang. "That's just the brand they serve at the hotel."

Carl plopped the coffee on the counter and added a ten-pound sack of cornmeal. "You want Sammy to deliver this?"

"Nope. Sammy's busy at the shop. I'll carry the coffee and pick up the cornmeal tomorrow morning."

He bid Miss Moreland a terse goodbye and left the mercantile. He was about to turn the corner on to Maple Street when he decided to walk past the pretty blue house again. He waved to Rooney next door, rocking away in the boardinghouse porch swing, then stopped to admire the building.

He just liked looking at it, imagining how happy it would make Marianne to have a big house like this instead of their tiny apartment over the shop. That was the first thing she'd said about her great uncle Matthew Collingwood, he remembered, that he must own the biggest house in town and how much she looked forward to moving into it.

He slowed at the front gate. The arbor that stretched overhead was overgrown with blue morning glories intertwined with tiny pink roses. He retraced his route past

Rooney, still sitting in the swing whittling on a piece of wood, and the older man motioned him up on the porch.

"Been watchin' you admire that house next door," Rooney said.

"Yeah. Sure is a handsome place."

"It's old Vernetta Stupac's place. Vernetta's eighty if she's a day, and I spose that house was built back in the day when banisters were carved real pretty and there was a fireplace in every room."

"Looks bigger than most of the houses in town, except for Doc Dougherty's mansion up on the hill," Lance said.

Rooney grinned at him. "You lookin' for a house, are ya?"

Lance opened his mouth to say *no*, then heard something else come out. "Yeah. Marianne and I are pretty crowded in that little apartment over the shop."

"Got any money?" Rooney inquired.

Lance noted the twinkle in the older man's eyes. "Well, yes, as a matter of fact."

Rooney studied him, stroking his chin with one weathered hand. "Miz Stupac's gone to live with her sister in Portland. She's lookin' to sell the house and everything in it to the right person."

Lance swallowed. "What kind of person would be the 'right person,' Rooney?"

The older man brushed wood shavings off his lap. "Somebody that's gonna stay in Smoke River permanent. You know, someone who'd keep up the house and prune the roses. Vernetta don't want just anybody in her house."

"You have any idea what she might sell it for?"

"Sure do, son. You can have the whole kit and caboodle for four hundred dollars."

Lance swallowed again. There was more than that amount in the bank. Even after paying wages for Abe and Sammy, the Collingwood account would still be flush.

Rooney was grinning at him again. "County seat's in Gillette Springs. Oughtta ride up there to pay yer money and record the deed."

Lance nodded. The prospect was tempting. After the uncertainty and heartache of the past few months he longed to surprise Marianne with something she really wanted. That's what a good husband did, wasn't it? What better way could there be to show his love for Marianne?

"You think it over, son," Rooney said with a grin.

He sure would! He nodded at the older man and headed back to the shop.

For the rest of that week, Lance thought of little else. Even when Abe shook his hand and told him he was turning into a first-class boot maker, he couldn't stop imagining Marianne's face when he told her about the blue house on Maple Street.

Would she like it? What if it wasn't what she wanted? What if it was too small or didn't have enough bedrooms? Would she like the garden? The blue morning glories winding among the roses growing over the trellis?

He set his awl down and shook his head in frustration. He'd never been able to predict what Marianne might do or what she might like. Maybe he should just give up the idea.

Oh, hell, no, he wasn't going to give up the idea. Marianne had worked hard to make Collingwood Boots a success. He wanted to give her something really special.

Chapter Thirty-Eight

When Lance completely forgot to pick up the bag of corn-meal she needed from the mercantile, went back for it and then forgot it again, Marianne began watching him. He seemed distracted. Unfocused. When she reminded him a third time about the cornmeal, he said he'd pick it up this afternoon, but even though he left the shop, he returned empty-handed once again.

That was so unlike the steady, reliable Lance she thought she knew that she began to worry in earnest. What on earth could be on his mind?

She watched him for the next few days, noting the hours he spent in the shop with Abe and Sammy, noticing that he started humming under his breath at odd hours and waking up each morning with a mysterious smile playing around his mouth. *What is going on?*

Was it Fanny Moreland?

And then late one afternoon after a marathon session of cutting leather pieces out of prime cowhide shipped from Texas, Lance volunteered to walk down to the mercantile for a tin of tea and a bag of sugar she needed. He was gone over two hours, far longer than the purchase of tea and sugar would take, and when he returned it was almost dark.

And that's when she figured it out.

He smelled…sweet. In fact, she thought, gritting her teeth, he didn't smell like tea or sugar or anything else at the mercantile; he smelled of cologne. Her stomach clenched. A *woman's* cologne!

She caught her breath as a sharp pain stabbed behind her breastbone. And this time it had nothing to do with broken ribs.

At supper that night Lance wrestled with something that had been bothering him for days. And nights. Marianne was exhausting herself working all day in the shop cutting out leather and then working half the night stitching on the supple calfskin linings. It was meticulous work, involving silk thread and curved needles, and it kept her bent over her work until Abe finally ordered her to quit.

She looked pale and drawn in the evenings, but she steadfastly refused to lie down and let him cobble up some sort of supper for the two of them. The most she would let him do was stir up some corn bread and grind the beans for coffee. Tonight he watched her lift a pot of stew from the oven and cut the corn bread he'd made into squares, and suddenly his breath caught. She looked more than just tired out; she looked worried and preoccupied.

"Marianne?"

She ladled out some stew and set a bowl in front of him, dished up some for herself and sank on to her chair with a sigh.

"Marianne, are you feeling all right?"

"Yes. Well, no. I'm just tired, I think. Not discouraged, because the shop is doing so well, just…tired. Orders are pouring in faster than we can fulfill them and our bank account is overflowing. If I had any energy I would be dancing and singing."

He released a long breath. Her dream of owning her own business was certainly coming true, largely because she wasn't afraid of hard work. Marianne was as different from frivolous, self-centered Fanny Moreland as lilies from locoweed.

Every single time he walked into the mercantile, Fanny launched herself at him. He was beginning to suspect she spent hours prowling the aisles just waiting for him to show up so she could accost him. Carl Ness had taken to warning him of her presence by cutting his gaze toward whatever aisle she was lurking in.

Two things bothered him about Fanny. First, she pounced on him the minute he walked in and persisted in sidling up too close. And second, she wore a particularly cloying over-sweet scent that made his eyes water.

But he couldn't stop visiting the mercantile; Marianne was so worn out that to save her strength he volunteered to walk over to the mercantile and get whatever supplies they needed.

Now he gazed across the supper table into his wife's tired eyes and wondered what else he could do to make her load lighter. It was a delicate matter; Marianne didn't like to accept help. She didn't like to admit defeat, either. She would work herself to death at this rate, and he was more concerned about her than the shop.

"Marianne, we need to talk."

"Oh?" she said in a weary voice. "What about?"

"Something I'm worried about."

Marianne deliberately set her spoon aside. "Worried? What are you worried about?"

She could barely meet his gaze. Oh, God, was Lance going to confess why he came home from town smelling of a woman's cologne? She clenched her hands in her lap and waited.

His eyes met hers, and she caught her breath. They were such a clear blue, the color of the sky on a summer day, and they were looking straight into hers with absolutely no hint of anything hidden in his gaze.

She had known Lance for four years before they married. She knew his work habits, his preference for chocolate cake, even his unfortunate brush with the law. She thought she knew everything about him. There was no hint of guile in his eyes. Deep inside she knew there wasn't a single dishonest bone in Lance Burnside's body.

All at once she realized something. A woman either trusted a man or she didn't. And she trusted Lance.

She ran one trembling finger around the rim of her coffee cup, and he reached across the table to take her hand. "You're looking at me funny," he said, in a quiet voice.

"Yes, I guess maybe I am."

"Some reason?"

"Yes." She couldn't help the smile that tugged at her mouth.

Lance frowned. "You gonna tell me what it is?"

Her smile broadened. She rose from her chair, walked around the table and settled herself on her startled husband's lap. "No, I'm not."

Then she bent her head and gave him a long, passionate kiss that left them both short of breath, and any thought of needing to talk was lost.

After work the following afternoon, Marianne slowly plodded up the long hill to Dr. Dougherty's home.

"Mrs. Burnside," the physician said with a smile. "What brings you here?"

Short of breath after her long walk, Marianne could only puff and follow the doctor into his office. He sat her down on his examination table, and when she could talk she explained.

"Last night my husband gave me a hug and I felt a funny pain in my chest. Surely my sore ribs should be healed by now?"

"They should be," he acknowledged. "Show me where it hurt."

She pointed at the center of her chest, and when he

gently pressed, she sucked in her breath. He whipped out his stethoscope and bent over her.

"Breathe in. Out. In again."

She complied, and after a moment he straightened. "Your ribs are healed, Mrs. Burnside. What is causing the pain might be your breastbone. I was afraid it had cracked when you fell off that horse, and it looks like I was right."

"Cracked!"

"It's a common injury resulting from a fall, especially for slim, small-boned women such as yourself. There's no cure but time."

"Could that be why I feel so tired all the time?"

"Tired?"

"Yes. Very sleepy."

"Hmm. Anything else?"

She thought a minute. "Sometimes I feel dizzy, just a little bit, but enough so I have to sit down."

The doctor had her lift away her shirtwaist, and once more he bent over her with his stethoscope. Then he had her lie flat on the examination table and applied the horn of the instrument everywhere, her neck, her back, her chest, even her abdomen. Finally he helped her to sit up, folded up the stethoscope and smiled.

"What is wrong with me?"

"Besides your cracked breastbone?" he said with a grin. "Absolutely nothing."

"But...but I feel so strange sometimes, especially in the morning."

His grin widened. "Um-hmm. That's not surprising, Mrs. Burnside. You're going to have a baby."

Marianne gasped. "A baby? That's not possible. I can't be having a baby."

"Why is that?" the doctor asked.

"Because...because my husband and I have only had...

I mean, Lance and I have had only one, um, encounter, and that was weeks ago. In early July."

"Sometimes that's all it takes."

Suddenly she felt as if she was going to faint. "Really? Isn't that...unusual for a couple to, uh, conceive that way?"

"Nope," he said with a laugh. "It's not unusual. You're just lucky."

Marianne floated out of the physician's office and down the hill in a rosy haze. A baby? *A baby!* Oh, my. *Oh, my heavens!* In the spring, Dr. Dougherty said. End of March or early April.

She could scarcely believe it. She wanted to rush home and tell Lance right away. She wanted to tell *everybody* right away!

She gazed up into the leafy branches of the maple trees arching overhead. How beautiful the world was! The soft summer air felt velvety against her skin, and it smelled delicious. Bees buzzed in the gardens she passed, flitting from rosebushes to honeysuckle vines. The sweet scent teased her nostrils.

Part of her looked forward to the challenges coming up, to making Collingwood Boots even more successful; part of her felt inexperienced and uncertain.

My lord, could it really be true? She would be bringing a child into the world! Her child. *Lance's child.*

She turned the corner and drew near the shop entrance, her heart swelling until she felt it would burst and shower her with stars. When she stepped through the door, Abe looked up, and without a word she flew to his side and smacked a kiss on his leathery cheek.

"Well, now, honey-girl, what's that for?"

"I'm just happy, Abe."

"Any partic'lar reason? Ya look all glowed-up, like a Christmas tree."

She avoided the question. She wanted to tell Lance first.

She had a big, big surprise for him. She bit her lip. Or she would have when she worked up the courage to tell him. In the meantime, Collingwood Boots had orders for twenty more pairs of boots, so she'd better give herself a good shake and concentrate on fulfilling their business obligations.

"Where is Lance?" she asked.

"Gone to Gillette Springs. Took Sammy's mare to deliver four pairs of boots to Sam Northcutt at the mercantile."

"Oh."

"Sorry to disappoint you, Miss Marianne. Lance won't be back 'til tomorrow."

"Oh," she said again. All at once she felt like crying. She must have looked odd because Abe sent her a sharp look.

"You okay, honey-girl? Ya look like the Christmas tree done collapsed."

For a moment she couldn't answer. Then she sucked in a steadying breath, squared her shoulders and tried to smile. "I left some stitching undone on a pair of boots, Abe. I'll just finish it up now."

Ignoring his puzzled frown, she moved past him to her worktable, opened the box of awls and needles and bent to snip off a length of waxed silk thread.

But she found that no matter how hard she concentrated on making small, even stitches, she couldn't stop smiling.

Chapter Thirty-Nine

Lance urged the mare to pick up the pace, but the animal seemed to have other ideas. It was too hot to insist, so he lowered his wide-brimmed hat over his eyes and resigned himself. Dust swirled over the road, and the sun was brutal. If he hadn't had a special reason for making this trip to Gillette Springs to deliver these boots, he wouldn't have volunteered to go.

But he did have a special reason. Gillette Springs was the county seat, and in the courthouse lay the deed to the blue house on the tree-lined street in Smoke River that he wanted to give Marianne.

It was a huge gamble. Maybe she wouldn't like the house. Maybe he should have consulted her before stuffing four hundred dollars in his saddlebag, along with the four pairs of boots for the mercantile owner. Maybe he… oh, what the heck.

He studied the sea of yellow wildflowers in the meadow bordering the road. When he returned tomorrow he'd stop and pick a big bouquet for Marianne.

By the time he arrived in Gillette Springs it was past suppertime. The mercantile was still open, so he delivered the boots to Sam Northcutt, collected the payment, and listened with pride when he overheard Sam talking to a customer. "These here Collingwood boots are the finest boots I've ever sold."

Grinning, Lance went off down the main street to the Emporium Hotel where he ordered steak—not as perfectly grilled as Marianne's—and fried potatoes—not as crispy as Marianne's—and finished it off with a slice of peach pie—not as sweet and flavorful as Marianne's. Suddenly he missed her so much he wanted to saddle up Sammy's mare and ride all night to get back to her.

He paid the bill and was halfway to the stables when he realized he had to visit the courthouse, and the courthouse wouldn't be open until nine o'clock tomorrow morning. A rock dropped into his belly. If he wanted to buy the blue house he'd have to stay overnight as he'd planned.

Well, hell. He breathed out a long sigh. *I guess nothing worthwhile ever comes for free.*

In the morning he walked from the hotel up the broad steps of the imposing red brick courthouse and bought the pretty blue house in Smoke River for Marianne.

Late that evening Lance rode into Smoke River with a huge bouquet of yellow wildflowers clutched in his hand and the deed to the house on Maple Street safely stowed in his vest pocket. He stood quietly in the doorway of Collingwood Boots and watched his wife add up a column of figures, take a sip from the mug of coffee Abe had just set on her desk and go right back to the account books. Singleminded as always, she didn't even look up.

His throat tightened. His Marianne wasn't working hard just for the business she'd always wanted to own. She was doing it for Abe, and for Sammy. And for him.

I guess this is what love is really all about. Giving things to each other you can't even measure.

A rush of joy flooded through his tired body. He couldn't wait to tell her about the house!

* * *

Marianne woke with a start to find Lance standing beside the bed, offering her a cup of coffee he had obviously just brewed.

"Wake up, honey. I have a big surprise for you."

"Oh?" She sat up and reached for the coffee. "I have a big surprise for you, too," she said. Suddenly she felt shy and uncertain about how to tell him about the baby.

He sat down beside her and smoothed her hair. "You'll have to get out of bed to see your surprise, Marianne. It's... outside."

"Outside? Where outside?"

He didn't answer, just gave her an enigmatic smile, so she gulped down her coffee, handed him the empty cup and tossed back the quilt. "Let's hurry!"

He laughed. "You'll cause a sensation in town wearing that nightgown."

"Oh!" She disappeared behind the folding screen and emerged moments later wearing a calico skirt and a matching shirtwaist. In her hair she stuck a few blooms from the bouquet he'd brought her yesterday, and pulled a red crocheted shawl about her shoulders.

"I'm ready, Lance. I want to see the surprise."

They waved goodbye to Abe and set off toward town. When they reached Maple Street, Lance slipped her hand into his.

They ambled along the tree-lined street until she suddenly pulled him to a stop.

"Oh, Lance, look! What a pretty house! And the garden, with all those pink roses and that blue morning glory... I've never noticed it before."

"Do you like it?"

"Oh, yes. It's just the kind of house I'd like someday."

"Want to see inside?"

She gave him a disbelieving look. "Well, yes, but surely the occupants would object?"

"It's empty," he said.

She studied the arbor over the front gate, then the wrap-around porch with roses twining through the white-painted trellis. "It's just beautiful, Lance. I wonder who owns it."

He turned her toward him. "If you kiss me, I'll tell you who owns it."

"You mean right here in public, where everyone can see us?"

"Yeah. Right here."

Her cheeks turned pink, but she stretched up on tiptoe and brushed her lips against his. "Now, tell me. There is something special about this house, and I want to know who owns it."

He traced his forefinger down her cheek. "You own it, Marianne. That's your surprise. The house belongs to you."

Marianne's head went all swirly. Oh, surely she wasn't going to faint! She grasped his arm to steady herself. "Oh, my. For a minute I thought you said… Surely you don't mean that I…that we…own this house?"

He said nothing, just stood smiling down at her.

She drew in a long, steadying breath. "Lance, w-would you like to know what *your* surprise is?"

"My surprise? I'd forgotten all about it. Is it as surprising as me buying a house?"

"Um, well, yes. In fact, it might be even more surprising."

His eyebrows went up. "Yeah? What could be more surprising than owning a house?"

She couldn't seem to stop smiling. "How about filling that blue house with a family?"

"What? Oh, sure, that'd be nice someday, but—"

"Not someday, Lance. Now. We're going to have a baby. Around March or April."

He stared at her so long she wondered if she'd forgotten to button up her shirtwaist. "A baby?" he said in a stunned voice.

She nodded.

"Did you say March?"

Again she nodded. "Or April."

And then right there on Maple Street, in front of everybody in Smoke River, Lance Burnside wrapped his arms around Marianne Collingwood and kissed her thoroughly for a very long time.

And on the very first day of April, on a day when the sky was so blue it brought tears to both Marianne and Lance's eyes, Lauralee Eleanor Burnside opened her tiny mouth and made the most beautiful sound her proud mother and father had ever heard.

* * * * *

*If you enjoyed this story
you won't want to miss these other great
Western reads by Lynna Banning*

*MISS MURRAY ON THE CATTLE TRAIL
THE HIRED MAN
BABY ON THE OREGON TRAIL
HER SHERIFF BODYGUARD*